Anne Marsh writes sexy con romances because the wor more happy ending. She sta getting laid off from her job as a technical writer – and quickly decided happily-ever-afters trumped software manuals. She lives in North Carolina with her two kids and three cats.

Also by Anne Marsh

The Code for Love

Discover more at afterglowbooks.co.uk

HOT

FOR

PREACHER

Anne Marsh

afterglow BOOKS

First Published in Great Britain 2026 by
Afterglow Books by Mills & Boon, an imprint of HarperCollins*Publishers* Ltd
1 London Bridge Street, London, SE1 9GF

www.harpercollins.co.uk

HarperCollins*Publishers*
Macken House, 39/40 Mayor Street Upper,
Dublin 1, D01 C9W8, Ireland

Hot for Preacher © 2026 Anne Marsh

ISBN: 978-0-263-42077-7

0226

Printed and Bound in the UK using 100% Renewable Electricity
at CPI Group (UK) Ltd, Croydon, CR0 4YY

For the bookworms, the page-turners and the happily hermit-hearted – may you always find yourself lost in a good story.

This is a fun, flirty romantic comedy featuring an ordained minister who most definitely has sex, a heroine who battles rheumatoid arthritis with humour and stubbornness, and a whole lot of small-town charm. That said, life isn't all meet-cutes and swoony moments – despite its very happy ending, this story also touches on parental dismissal, religion and religious authority figures, financial and housing insecurity, career anxiety, and living with a chronic illness. Please decide for yourself if these story elements will affect your emotional wellbeing.

One

Girl meets town (and preacher)

Dixie

My van dies in the middle of the smallest main street in Tennessee. Check your text messages for a second, and you'd miss the place, it's that small.

"We're so close to Nashville." *Lie.* We're hundreds of miles away. I doubt it works, but I pump the gas pedal hard. Here's to threats taking the place of routine automobile maintenance. "Don't you dare—"

Blanche's engine rattles once, the automotive equivalent of the finger, and falls silent. She's picked now to hit the pause button on the soundtrack of my life.

"Screw you, too, Universe." I coast to a stop next to a weathered sign boasting WICKHAM HOLLOW—POPULATION 403. The number *3* has been recently painted over a *2*.

My phone lights up with another text from Dear Old Dad: Still waiting on your answer, Dix. Christmas album won't record itself! Tell me you're in!

Twenty years since his one hit and he's still milking "Jingle

Bell Dash" like it's the gift that keeps on giving. Guess when you're Hank Pearl, you never let a good Christmas miracle go to waste.

I'll deal with him later. I flip the phone off with both hands, then turn the key. Nothing. Not even a click.

After three months of playing dive bars across the South, sleeping in this van, and living on gas station coffee and whatever the venues will comp, I'm finally, officially, completely screwed. And broken down—in a town so small it probably rolls up the sidewalks at sunset.

Wood smoke drifts through my busted passenger window, along with the faint scent of something that might be cow manure. *Fantastic.* I've gone from chasing country music dreams to sitting in actual cow-scented purgatory.

I climb out to assess the damage, my joints protesting like angry old ladies. The February air bites through my leather jacket, but I ignore it. Irritation chases the cold away. Plus, my whole body already feels like I've been used as a stress ball by a very enthusiastic giant.

The van looks as pathetic as I feel—listing slightly to the side, rust eating through the wheel wells, bumper held on with duct tape and spite. Home sweet home for the past two years, and now we're both stranded in Mayberry's depressing cousin.

I'm glaring at my phone while I call absolutely no one, because I have no one to call, when I hear the rumble of an approaching truck.

It's a rust bucket that's seen better decades, with a paint job that might once have been blue and a toolbox bouncing around in the bed. Through the half-open windows comes the mournful baying of what sounds like a very large, very dramatic dog.

The truck slows, then stops. Because of course it does. In a town this size, a broken-down stranger is probably the most exciting thing to happen since the cow responsible for the delightful aroma got loose.

The driver leans out his open window and tips his head at me.

Holy shit, they grow them big here.

He's enormous—easily six foot four, built like he wrestles bears for fun and wins—and his full, dark beard screams "I'm a lumberjack who chops my own firewood!" An impressive collection of deltoid and trapezius muscles are compressed in his flannel shirt. Objectively, he's hot. Subjectively, he sports the serious, proud face of a Southern Mr. Darcy. I can smell the judgment from where I stand next to my busted-down vehicle.

"Evening, ma'am," he says in a deep, male voice. Brown eyes regard (judge) me.

Ma'am. I instantly age forty years and develop an urge to tell kids to get off my lawn.

"Hail and well met," I snark back.

If he talks like a Southern gentleman from the nineteenth century, I'll do him one better and greet him like we're living in the Renaissance even if he hasn't dressed the part. His beard is not well-groomed, fashionable Henry VIII facial hair—it's thick and dark, slightly mussed as if he's run his fingers through it, and epically full. For a brief moment, I allow myself to imagine him taming its wild splendor each morning with a wooden comb.

My hairy rescuer surveys me. "Can I help?"

"Nope. I've got this. I have YouTube and a friend on the way from Nashville," I lie.

He frowns, an adorable crinkle forming between his thick eyebrows. *She refused my offer? Does not compute!*

"It's late." More frowning.

I roll my eyes. "You can tell time!"

"I don't feel comfortable leaving you here alone."

"And I don't need company."

I'm a solo act.

When the dog bays, he gives it a look. "Hush up, Huck."

"Seriously? Huck?"

At the sound of his name, the dog makes enthusiastic noises. He's on the large side for a dog (albeit proportional to his over-size owner), muscular and brindle patterned. His tongue lolls out in excitement, his nose working overtime.

"Huck is a good Southern boy who had an unfortunate encounter with some huckleberry jam when he was a pup. The name stuck." The lumberjack/truck driver delivers this information completely deadpan, radiating calm and capable. *Ugh*. "Is it okay with you if I get out of my truck?"

"And then what?" Pretty packages do not guarantee pretty presents.

His eyes crinkle up at the corners as he actually goddamn smiles. My own narrow. If I was a snake, my rattles would be sounding a warning. *Back off, dude*.

"Chains," he volunteers.

"Kinky, but no thanks."

The pink flush on his cheekbones is even more adorable than his forehead crinkle.

"I'll hook it up." We both consider this unfortunate word choice for a second. The pink on his cheeks deepens to a rosier, more embarrassed color. I think he mutters something about *a time to keep silent*, but I can't be sure and don't care. "So I can get you out of the middle of the road and over to the auto shop. Ma'am. That's it, I promise."

I eye the auto shop across the street. "Please tell me Sweet-gum Auto actually fixes cars and isn't a front for money laundering."

It seems unlikely that a one-street town can generate enough automotive repairs to sustain an auto shop, but what do I know?

"It's real. Deacon and Slate know what they're doing." He turns off his engine and climbs out, unfolding like a giant Swiss Army knife. There's zero give in the body that fills out the faded blue jeans, black flannel shirt, and no-nonsense work boots. This man can't be fussed with his clothes. "I'm Jack Carter."

"Dixie Pearl." The hand he shoves at me to shake has calluses. "And before you ask—yes, it's my real name, and no, I don't want to hear your joke about paper cups."

"Wouldn't dream of it." His eyes crinkle with amusement that makes me want to be even surlier out of principle. "I'll take a look at your engine just in case it's a quick fix."

I should tell him to go away. Stranger danger is a thing. But he has kind if judgmental eyes (damn him) and a dog with opinions, and frankly, I'm too tired and too broke to turn down help from Paul Bunyan's slightly smaller cousin.

"Knock yourself out. But fair warning—I've been running on fumes and sheer stubbornness for about two hundred miles. She may be beyond salvation."

My new friend Jack pops the hood and peers into Blanche's mechanical guts with the focused intensity of someone who actually knows what all those greasy bits are supposed to do. I try not to notice how his flannel shirt pulls across his shoulders. I have much bigger problems than attractive shoulders. Like being stranded in the middle of nowhere with seventeen dollars to my name. Dad would have a field day with this—there's nothing he loves more than being right about my "poor life choices."

"Did you change the oil recently?" Jack asks without looking up.

"Define 'recently.'"

He turns his head to give me a look that's both patient and mildly horrified.

"Look, I've been prioritizing gas over maintenance." I may sound a *touch* defensive. "Sue me for choosing forward momentum over proper vehicular care."

"Might explain a few things." He pokes around some more, straightens up to his full, mountainous height, and closes the hood. "Your fuel pump's gone. Probably been making a whining sound for the last fifty miles."

It's not a question—and he's not wrong. My stomach drops like a stone. "How long will it take to fix?"

And more importantly: Can it be done for the low, low price of seventeen dollars?

"We'll ask Deacon and Slate, but not tonight, that's for sure." His voice is annoyingly calm. I bet he'd be awesome at breaking bad news to a cancer patient. So sorry! You're terminal! "You got somewhere to stay? Or someone who can come get you?"

I look around at the handful of buildings that make up downtown Wickham Hollow. It hasn't grown any larger in the last five minutes. A bakery, a general store, and what looks like a bar. That, plus a handful of houses and a dilapidated church at the far end of the street, is it. The whole town.

"Is there a motel? Hotel? Reasonably clean bus station?"

"No motel." Jack scratches his beard thoughtfully. "Thaddeus Beauregard rents out his spare room sometimes, but he's in New Orleans for the week."

I glance down at my scuffed cowboy boots (not made for walking), then back at Jack. "Yeah, sorry to miss him. Guess it's back to Casa de Van for me."

"You sleep in there?" He sounds as if I've announced plans to winter in a cardboard box.

"It's not the Ritz, but the rent's reasonable and the commute's nonexistent. Besides, I'm tougher than I look."

"I don't doubt that." Jack nods, graciously agreeing with me. I'm sure he's secretly patting himself on the back for being absolutely right about my shitty situation. "But it's supposed to get down into the thirties tonight, and that window situation looks challenging."

He's inexplicably bothered by the cardboard duct-taped over my passenger window. "It's rustic charm."

"It's frostbite waiting to happen." Something in his voice

makes me actually look at him instead of contemplating my spectacular life choices. "My guest room's got clean sheets and working heat. You'll deal easier with the van if you're well-rested."

A slow smile crinkles the corners of his eyes, curving his mouth up behind that wild, lush beard. He looks far more approachable when he's smiling and trying to trick me into letting down my guard.

I stare him down. "You're offering me a room? We literally just met."

"Five minutes ago," he agrees solemnly.

"I could be a serial killer. *You* could be a serial killer."

It's more likely to be me.

"Could be. But I've got references if you need them." Jack nods once, like the matter's settled, and starts wrapping his chain around Blanche's front grille. "Come on. We'll tow your van over to Sweetgum and I'll take Huck here home. It won't take me two minutes to get him settled and then I'll come back and buy you dinner. Deacon will work his car magic tomorrow."

"I don't need—"

"I know you don't need anything." He cuts me off with unsurprising firmness. "But seeing as this is Wickham Hollow's first impression, I'd prefer it not be 'stranger abandons you to freeze to death in broken van.'"

I hurry to catch up with his annoyingly long strides. "And what would be a better first impression?"

Jack's smile is warm and annoyingly mysterious. "How do you feel about karaoke?"

Two

Girl versus preacher

Dixie

Southern Comforts has committed woodland critter genocide in the name of decor—enough mounted taxidermy crowds the walls of the bar to stock a natural history museum, assuming natural history museums specialize in the animals that died with their mouths open in eternal surprise. The aesthetic is "Southern stereotype had a baby with a flea market," featuring neon beer signs, license plates from every state below the Mason-Dixon line, and an alarming number of barrels. Seriously, it's like someone told the decorator that barrels were the only acceptable furniture and they took it as a personal challenge—they've been chopped into seats, hammered into tables, and have defied gravity to colonize the ceiling like wooden parasites.

"Wow." It's a lot to take in. "Way to commit to a theme."

Jack grins as he steps through the door he's insisted on holding open for me. "Deacon's not known for his subtlety."

The place is packed even for a Friday night, which in a town of 403 people probably means literally everyone who can legally drink. Someone is murdering what might be a Kenny Chesney song on a makeshift stage hammered together from wooden pallets.

"Welcome to karaoke night," Jack says proudly.

A dark-haired mountain of a man—even taller than my good friend Jack and in possession of the kind of broad shoulders that make cheap airline seats a no-go—waves enthusiastically from behind the bar. Tattoo sleeves disappear beneath his rolled-up flannel, and his full beard in no way hides the grin that transforms his otherwise intimidating presence from grizzly bear to teddy bear. "Jack! You brought a friend!"

"That's Deacon," Jack tells me. "Fair warning—he has no filter, a grumpy brother, and the social skills of a golden retriever."

We make our way to the bar, where Deacon is simultaneously pulling beers and grinning at me like I'm the most fascinating thing to happen since indoor plumbing. Or maybe since the last time a stranger wandered into this taxidermy graveyard—which, judging by the dust on the deer heads, was back when people still rented movies from Blockbuster.

Jack does the honors. "Deacon, meet Dixie. Dixie, this is Deacon."

Deacon gives me a head tip. "Drink?"

"Water. Two, please." I look around, but I don't see the evil doppelgänger brother I was promised.

When he slides the glasses over to me, I shove one in front of Jack. "A thank-you drink. I'm buying."

My stomach growls loudly enough to drown out Jack's appreciation. Reaching over the bar, he snags a laminated menu and holds it out. "The food's good if you're hungry. Dinner's on me."

"I'm fine." I'm saving my seventeen dollars for tomorrow and, no, he's not buying me dinner.

"Never drink nothing on an empty stomach, darlin'," Deacon announces, setting down a bowl of boiled peanuts. Tiny stars march across the back of his hand. "Learned that the hard way more times than I care to count."

I want to be offended, but the peanuts are salty and perfect, and my dignity makes one, last valiant stand before surrendering to basic human needs. "So you didn't actually learn, did you?"

Deacon shrugs, studying me with curious eyes. "What brings you to Wickham Hollow?"

"Just passing through," I say. "I was heading back to Nashville after a gig and my van died."

"What kind of gig?"

I gesture vaguely with a peanut. "I sing. Bars, mostly. Wherever they'll have me."

"No kidding." Deacon's eyebrows shoot up. "Well, you picked the right night to break down here. It's karaoke night, and we've got a little competition going. Winner gets dinner on the house. All-you-can-eat fries or our famous chicken and dumplings."

My empty stomach perks up with interest. "How do you pick the winner?"

"Biggest crowd reaction wins. Preacher here's been champion for three weeks running."

Preacher. That name is perfect for my new lumberjack acquaintance. He leans against the bar all casual-like, but the glint in his eye suggests he's not as modest as he appears.

"Three weeks? That's quite a streak."

Jack shrugs, but I catch that hint of smugness. "What can I say? I know my audience."

"Uh-huh." I finish my water and stand up, already feeling the familiar thrill of competition singing through my veins. "Well, I've got news for you."

"Yeah?" Jack's eyebrows rise. "What's that?"

I grin, feeling more alive than I had in weeks. "I don't lose."

The crowd whoops as the Kenny Chesney–murdering

singer finishes (thank you, sweet baby Jesus), and Deacon cups his hands around his mouth. The bellow that comes out could wake the dead three counties over—it's that deep and booming. "Alright, folks! We've got ourselves a challenge! Defending champion Jack Carter versus our lovely newcomer!"

His voice bounces off every mounted deer head and barrel in the place. The entire bar erupts in cheers and good-natured trash talk as a dozen pairs of curious eyes turn our way.

"You sure about this?" Jack is—he's already moving toward the stage. "I should warn you—I've got home-field advantage."

"And I should warn you," I yell after him, no more quiet than Deacon, "I've been singing in dive bars since I was sixteen. Remember the name Dixie Pearl!"

Jack takes the stage with surprising confidence for someone who looks like he'd be more comfortable splitting logs than entertaining drunks. He plants his booted feet, turns to the audience, and shakes his head. Smooths a hand down his beard like a thespian getting ready to say his lines.

"Y'all are out awful late. You'd better not sleep in on Sunday."

This earns him whoops and good-natured teasing. Multiple voices exhort him to PREACH. He shrugs, as if to say *what can you do?*

It's so hot.

And that's *before* the fast-paced, staccato fiddle line of "The Devil Went Down to Georgia" fills the bar.

Jack drops his polite reserve like a wet towel and sings his heart out.

Gone is the polite, firmly helpful gentleman who rescued me from vehicular disaster. In his place is a performer who owns every inch of that ridiculous pallet stage. He throws himself into the song with theatrical flair, complete with air violin solos and dramatic gestures that have the crowd singing along. He hams it up on his invisible fiddle, dancing around that stupid stage, and, man, is he *good*.

When he reaches the part about the devil's bet, he points right at me and winks.

The bastard winks.

The entire bar goes nuts, howling *the DEVIL will get your SOUUUUULLLLLL*. By the time Jack finishes with a dramatic bow, the applause is deafening.

"Beat that!" someone shouts from the back.

Don't mind if I do.

Jack hops down from the stage and saunters back over to me, not even breathing hard. "Your turn, Nashville."

I study his face—the confident smile, the challenge in his dark eyes, the way he settles back against the bar like he's already won. The poor man has no idea who he's dealing with.

"You're pretty good, Preacher—but let me show you how it's done."

I might wink, too. He started it.

After a quick pit stop to queue up my music, I jump onto the stage. The familiar feeling of being in front of an audience sweeps through me, the sense of expectation, of being *alive*. *Take that, rheumatoid arthritis. I've still got it.* My boots tap out a rhythm. Too bad I left my guitar in the van.

Resting a hand on my hip, I salute the crowd. "Preacher's a tough act to follow." This sends them into whoops. "But, ladies and gentlemen, pride goeth before a fall."

The room erupts. Deacon bounces on his toes behind the bar—every towering inch of him vibrating with excitement—waving a towel over his head like an overgrown kid at his first baseball game. "Give it to him, Dixie!" He's loud enough to rattle the mounted deer heads on the walls.

The opening chords of "Any Man of Mine" play, but I ignore the karaoke screen because, for the first time in ages, my own lyrics dance in my head and pour out of me to the borrowed tune.

"Let me tell you what a woman needs…"

The crowd roars with laughter and encouragement.

"A partner who lifts me and plants the seeds,
Of laughter, love, and loyalty, too,
With every little thing he's gotta prove it's true."

I let my voice drop low and sultry, then slowly extend one finger until I'm pointing directly at Jack. Every soul in the bar swivels to stare at him and the adorable pink flush creeping up his neck.

"Any man of mine better stand the test,
Better be my partner, giving me his best.
I need a man who knows how to roll with life,
He's gotta be a strong-huggin', joke-lovin',
Steady-as-we're-runnin' kind.
Any man of mine!"

I jump off the stage, weaving through the tables as the crowd parts to give me room. Someone wolf-whistles. Someone else starts a slow clap. This is what I live for—the electricity of live performance, the connection with an audience, the moment when a room full of strangers becomes co-conspirators in whatever magic I'm spinning.

"If you want to be a man of mine, you better step it up. Better walk that line."

When I reach Jack, I set my hand on his knee, my voice dipping low for the next verse. Jack looks equal parts amused and flustered. He raises his water in a mock toast, his lips quirking into a lopsided grin, but I'm not done with him.

"We'll shimmy, shake, and spin on through. Life's a rodeo, just me and you. So, tell me—"

YEAH, the crowd bellows, led by Deacon.

Under cover of their enthusiastic noise, I ask, "May I sit down?"

He nods, the pink in his cheeks the flamboyant color of radishes and flamingos, and I settle myself on his lap like I'm claiming my throne. The crowd absolutely loses their minds.

"Shimmy, shake, take my hand. Yeah?"

I hand him the mic with a wicked grin. "Your line, big guy."

Jack stares at the microphone like it might bite him, then looks at me, then at the expectant crowd. The pink in his cheeks has deepened to full-on red.

"Come on!" I sing. "Don't leave me hanging!"

The crowd picks up the chant: "SING! SING! SING!"

Jack rolls his eyes but can't resist. He raises his voice, deep and gravelly. "Yeah!"

The crowd explodes with laughter and applause, stomping harder than ever. I finish the song with a flourish, voice soaring through the final notes.

"Move to the beat of life we've planned.
Heel to toe, love will flow,
Till we're old and the story's told! Because…
THIS is what a woman needs!"

As you can't jump halfway into a swimming pool or press the pause button on an ill-advised leap of faith, I cup Jack's neck with one hand, grab my cowboy hat with the other hand, and shield us both from our audience.

From behind the relative safety of the hat's brim, I ask: "May I kiss you?"

Jack responds with a dazed *what* and inhales, lashes drifting down.

It's a sound-check kind of kiss, just making sure everything in the sexual chemistry department is good before I give in to the temporary need for some contact and comfort. That's all. It's not supposed to involve tongue.

But Jack feels so big and solid, so warm and inexplicably safe, his grip tightening with careful chivalry so that I don't fall off his lap and onto the sticky bar floor. He drags a warm hand down my back, pressing gently but firmly against the base of my spine.

It's the end-of-a-movie kiss, the best part of a book.

His lips part in either surprise or a manly grunt. He's out

of breath or I am because there's just so *much* of him. I press my lips against his in a butterfly brush, a quick taste to check if we fit together. But he looks amazed.

And amazing.

And—

I lick delicately at his bottom lip. *Open up. Let me in.* And the miracle happens and he does, leaning into me, his weight pressing me down into his hands as the barstool valiantly holds us both up.

His lips brush mine back and it turns out that the man can kiss. He can really, really kiss.

With each taste of his mouth, I learn bits of secrets, pieces of his day, of him. Secret the first: He owns mint toothpaste. Something green and crisp, with darker notes of coffee, bitter and black, not at all sweet.

He holds me steady, a big palm pressed against the small of my back, not moving, just right there, keeping me safe.

The small piece of my brain that remains online suggests this would make an amazing song. I can hear a tease of melody and the whiff of a refrain. It's good, so good, and he makes me want everything, right now—

Someone wolf-whistles. It's the giant bartender—Deacon—coming around the bar to stand next to us. He crosses thick, tattooed arms over his bear-sized chest, stretching blue-jean-covered legs out in front of him as he radiates don't-care.

"Hold that thought," I tell Jack's mouth. And then to Deacon, "Get lost. I'm trying to hook up here."

"Way to go!" Deacon slaps a big hand on Jack's back, laughing hard enough to bring on a heart attack. "Be gentle with him. Preacher's a dating novice."

"There's no audience-participation portion to this date," I say. "Plus, I'm a borrow-and-return gal. I don't date. And what's up with the nickname?"

Deacon winks at me. "It's not so much a nickname as a statement of fact. He's ordained."

Nope.

I've misheard.

Southern Comforts is loud and the kiss fried my brain circuits. Diverted all the blood from my ears to southern regions. Ordained is for priests, and priests are chaste. And in my very limited churchgoing, childhood experiences, they absolutely never come in hot, lumberjack-sized packaging.

But Jack isn't laughing or denying the accusation.

He just looks at me and waits.

"You're a priest?"

He shakes his head.

Thank GOD, my ovaries squeal. HAVE AT HIM.

"I'm a minister."

Three

Girl flirts with preacher

Jack

People love ministers—or hate them.

No in-between.

Either we save your soul, handing out free passes to the five-star resort of Heaven, or we're con artists who believe everything we read in the Bible and demand your hard-earned cash. Divinity school teaches how to memorize Bible verses but doesn't cover the way being a minister takes over every part of your life until there's no room left for anything else.

"Jesus Christ." Dixie sounds pricklier than a hedgehog and twice as defensive. "Did I just hump you in front of your entire congregation? Did an entire church's worth of people hear me proposition you for sex?"

I know a rhetorical question when I hear one. I stay silent and wait for her to jump off my lap like a scalded cat.

We've attracted enough attention to guarantee robust attendance at the Sunday church service this weekend, with everybody coming to see the preacher who'd gone rogue in the town bar. Opinions will be shared. My bishop may get an earful.

Worth it? You bet.

Dixie's hair spills over her shoulders and down the back of her leather jacket—which is black, as is her cowboy hat. The white dress is less goth, a buttery-soft material that hugs her curves and makes her look like the country version of Morticia Addams, if Morticia traded her mansion for a broken-down van and a dream. I remember one of those Bible verses that got drummed into my head: *Rejoice in hope, rejoice in hope.* Despite some dust from racketing around backcountry roads and deep shadows beneath her green eyes, she's strikingly beautiful—the grit-and-glamour package, with long, wild auburn hair that tumbles around her face beneath the brim of that black cowgirl hat. Her eyes sparkle, full of mischief, and freckles dust her nose and cheeks.

"Hold up a minute." Deacon slides his phone between my face and Dixie's, slow and deliberate as everything he does. "Reckon you might wanna explain why you're all over my YouTube recommendations, darlin'?"

Dixie's face pouts from the screen. In the photo, her smile is simultaneously sultry and carefree, despite the Y-shaped crack that splits the screen and transforms her into a Dali-worthy portrait. She's…a country music singer?

"Busted," she carols. Then her eyes narrow. I'm getting the feeling that's her factory default setting. "Although that goes for both of us."

I snag Deacon's phone and scroll. *Wow.* Dixie Jane Pearl is an up-and-coming country music singer who's written and performed her own songs for eight years. She has a bunch of songs on YouTube, some TikTok videos, and multiple Instagram shots of her wearing cowboy hats as she sings her heart out on top of a rusty truck, a hay bale, and a leather armchair. I don't recognize the songs, so I share the link with myself so I can listen to them later.

The information bursts the tiny fantasy I've had about tonight being the start of something. What's that saying about bright lights, big city? I'm small-town, through and through, and now I feel like a stupid moth flapping around the brightest light of all, the bold, bright, creative ray of sunlight that's Dixie. Okay. So she's more thundercloud than sunshine, but whatever.

The moth bites it. Every time.

"This is you?" I angle the phone so she can see.

"Uh-huh." She scoots around in my lap until she's straddling me, using me as her own personal piece of furniture. "But you don't have to take my word for it. Look at my bio."

She taps a button that proclaims MEET DIXIE! The words are inscribed in curly letters inside a hot-pink heart wearing a cowgirl hat.

"Wow," I say. "I guess I should have guessed based on how well you sing."

Deacon mimes what looks like "she's hot" over Dixie's head while giving an exaggerated wink. He makes a subtle nudging motion with his shoulder. *Come on.*

I try to brush him off behind her back.

She makes a face. "How can you be a preacher?"

"The usual way," I say as lightly as I can. "Lots and lots of summer Bible camp. A calling. Divinity school."

"But you do karaoke," she protests. "In a *bar*. How did this not come up when we met?"

"We met less than an hour ago and it's not my usual opening line."

Her frown deepens. "The minister thing should have been disclosed up front."

"Why?"

"Because—" She waves a hand enthusiastically, knocking Deacon's phone out of mine. He grunts and swipes it off the floor. "Just because!"

"I'm allowed out of the church," I say dryly. "I get that's a shock."

I know I won't spend the evening preaching at people or making them feel bad about their choices, but there's no good way to explain that. Tonight, I just want—

I'll stop right there. I blame the amazing kiss that relocated the blood from my brain to my dick for my inarticulateness. I'm at a critical disadvantage from blood loss.

At church or my office, leading a Bible study or heading up the billion ministries essential to church life, the expectations are crystal clear. My congregation loves me, and not just because I whoop their butts at karaoke. It's a pure, chaste, completely hands-off kind of love, though.

Those years of summer Bible camp followed by even more years of divinity school, however, mean I've learned a ton of Bible verses by heart. Some people think that memorization lands you a spiritual reward or is a piece of handy theological punctuation for shutting down debates. I think the words are an anchor. Reciting scripture keeps me from saying something else when I'm angry or overwhelmed or just plain frustrated. I won't put words out there that I'll regret later. Tonight's Bible verse is *create in me a clean heart*. If I say it enough, maybe it'll keep me from acting on my attraction to Dixie.

And from telling her that this minister has a working penis.

And isn't saving himself for his wedding night.

Despite being a big fan of two people committing to waiting for each other before they've even met, I get the argument that waiting is challenging and leaves you at an emotional disadvantage. Practice is good and people get lonely. They have committed relationships that end before ever reaching the altar. They like sex and don't believe it requires a legal and spiritual commitment.

Bottom line: You choose sex for yourself.

I'm not the only minister who believes it's up to my parishioners to decide for themselves whom they sleep with and when, but it's also not the most popular opinion. I keep it to myself unless asked.

Right now, I'm uncomfortably aware that Dixie is sitting on top of my dick. Wriggling. The *thinking about sex* part of things isn't presenting any kind of a problem for me.

It's more that up until now, I haven't spent a ton of time practicing it. Planning for it. Or doing it.

"Do you even——" She waves a hand.

I fill in that blank. *Do you EVEN have sex? Do you EVEN like it? Do you need a permission slip from your bishop before you can get naked?*

The answer is yes, of course, and no. Although the bishop might disagree, but never mind.

I remind myself that *clean heart* means *no thinking dirty thoughts about the lady.* "I feel like I should state for the record that sex is good."

"Great!" I get the feeling that she isn't applauding my sex positivity so much as affirming that if I'm ever lucky enough to find myself in bed with her that *our* sex will be great.

"Fuck." She scrubs a hand down her face. "This is so weird. I hit on a minister."

This is why my dick is rustier than my truck.

Dixie squirms on my lap. "So——"

She starts. Stops. While she figures out her sentence, I brush my thumbs over the silky curve of her waist. I'll take what I can.

"Are you okay?"

At the same time, Deacon sticks his oar in with: "Is the minister thing a deal-breaker?"

"Oh my God." She blasphemes with enthusiasm. "Do you really want me to answer that question? Yeees?"

She draws the word out like a lifeline and then leans away, almost overbalancing.

My gaze slides down her body before I can stop it, drinking in her long, almost bare legs wrapped around me, the way the soft fabric of her dress pools between her legs.

Her thighs tighten, holding me close.

Focus. I jerk my eyes back up to her face. Her lips are purple, a slick of deliberate color.

Dixie tugs on my arm. "Do you like having sex?"

"Yes. Do you like asking intrusive questions?"

She nods. "I have so many."

I'm not surprised. "Let me guess. I'm not a priest. I will not be taking a vow of celibacy, so I'm not searching for a sex marathon before I'm cut off forever. Sex *is* allowed, although my church strongly prefers that I be married before I have it. Agree to disagree. I am allowed to date and to have a girlfriend, and no, I am not 'weird' about sex."

"Wow." Dixie purses her lower lip, less impressed than McKayla Maroney spotting her vault score.

"I realize the minister thing was a bit of a surprise, but some people do actually enjoy dating me."

Granted, "some" might be generous. Maybe "a person." Singular. And she moved to Florida.

Behind the bar, Deacon winces. *Smooth*, he mouths. Or maybe *swoon*?

"Sure they do." She waves a hand. I'm the dating equivalent of a traffic accident or a spill: shit that happens and gets dealt with. She sweeps on before my ego recovers. "I would just corrupt you."

Is that a joke? Or please God—the next action item on tonight's agenda?

"Generally, I'm held to be fairly incorruptible."

True story.

"But I'm really good at it," she counters.

"Are you sure?"

"Absolutely. Yes."

"Really?"

"I'd be the devil on your shoulder." She states this with

utmost confidence. "You, obviously, are an uptight and rule-following individual, so your life would be far more balanced with me in it, but I do try to be responsible. On random, ill-selected occasions."

"We do seem like two unlikely people to date."

"Yep." She grins wickedly. "Come on."

She slips her fingers into mine.

"Where are we going?" I twine my fingers with hers, savoring the contact.

We can go wherever she wants. Her van if she needs a parking lot escort. The karaoke stage if she's decided to torture me further.

What I don't expect is—

"Let's go to your place," she says.

I can't tell if Dixie means the guest room I offered earlier or something else entirely. Either way, discussing the specifics in front of fifty pairs of ears seems like a terrible idea.

"Sure," I say, because what else do you say when the most interesting thing to happen to Wickham Hollow in a decade just asked to come home with you?

My phone buzzes in my pocket. Then again. And again. I don't need to check it to know what's happening. Deacon holds up his own phone, grinning like an idiot. The screen shows a meme of a cartoon preacher with hearts for eyes and "JUST SAY YES" in font big enough to read from space.

Dixie tows me through the crowded bar, past the Jenkins sisters who run the bakery and know everyone's business. Dee raises her phone, snaps a picture, and gives me a thumbs-up. We'll be on the bakery's Instagram account (@TwoTartsInWickham) by midnight.

Future Jack can handle the concerned phone calls and pointed questions. Present Jack is focused on not tripping over his boots as he follows Dixie outside.

"Watcha thinking, Preacher Man?" Dixie hums, her fingers dancing over my wrist as she picks out a tune against my skin.

"I—"

The bar door opens behind us and we both turn. Deacon hands over a bag of take-out containers. "Tonight's winnings."

Shoot. I forgot to feed her. I'm the world's worst date.

Then, when we both reach for the bag, Dixie intercepts it. "I can carry my own stuff." She turns back to Deacon with a grin. "I should give a victory speech! I beat Jack's butt!"

"Easy there, sugar." Deacon flashes her a slow grin. "You and Jack are co-winners. Means there can only be mutual, consensual spanking."

I try not to expire in flames of embarrassment. This is next-level dating.

"But I'm better at winning. You should totally pick me." She leans up to whisper in Deacon's ear, her fingers still threaded through mine, a big grin splitting her face. "PS, I have a secret: I hate losing."

"That's not much of a secret, darlin'." Deacon runs a hand down his beard and heads back inside Southern Comforts, still shaking his head.

Dixie guffaws. "I like him! And he pays way better than my last gig. I scored a Diet Coke and that was it.

"Lead on, Macduff," she misquotes happily, waving a hand at Main Street. It's small, but it's been home since the first summer I came here as a kid. "Are you close by? Do I get the town tour on our way to your place?"

I glance around as if a Hilton or a Holiday Inn might appear from nowhere. Not that offering to take her to a hotel sounds any better than *come home with me.* "There's no hotel in Wickham Hollow. We don't have a motel, or even an Airbnb. My offer still stands, though—you're welcome to my spare bedroom, no strings attached."

I suppose I should drive her to that motel off the interstate, but it's an hour away and skeevy as heck. Plus, she'll have to come back for her van.

"Oh, I'm going home with you," she declares. "Unless—"

She tilts her head back to…look at the moon? The stars. Maybe there's a comet up there or a new planet. It certainly feels like asteroid weather. Any minute now, a giant chunk of rock will crash-land in my life—I put it on the list for Future Jack to worry about.

She tugs her fingers free and throws her hands up. "You ever just look up and feel small? Like, in a good way, not a bad way? Like all your problems and plans are just the teeni-est, tiniest specks in the grand cosmic mess of it all?"

I follow her pointing finger. Star, star, star, cloud, plane. The plane chugs across the dark sky, its anti-collision lights a bright, white beacon. "I mostly look up and think, *God sure knew what He was doing.*"

"Right. *That* guy." Dixie twirls in a circle, hand over her head, skirts and the French fry bag orbiting around her. I drag my gaze back to her face. *Do not stare at her legs.* "See, I like to think that those stars have more say in things than some ancient dude with a clipboard."

God as a middle manager with office supplies wasn't exactly covered in seminary. "That's one way to put it," I say finally.

She's waiting for me to argue theology with her, but hon-estly? After tonight, I'm not sure about anything except that she makes me want to believe in whatever she's selling.

"You know, checking off names, deciding who gets what? Kind of like Santa Claus but instead of an annual, fun holiday, it's the performance review of a lifetime? 'Dixie Pearl, here's your starter dose of stardom, but let's balance it out with a side of chronic pain and a tendency to make really bad decisions about men.'" She thinks for a beat, while I tell myself not to ask questions about *chronic pain*. "And women. My romantic mishaps are very equal opportunity. Or divine retribution. My just deserts? I'm Team Astrology."

She grabs my hand briefly and I find myself holding the take-out bag she vowed to carry herself. I bite back a grin as she rummages inside it with a crow of delight.

"But really, I don't have a whole lot of quality relationshipping under my belt," she confides moments later around a mouthful of French fry. "So, it's not surprising that I'm not living my happily-ever-after. You gotta practice if you want to be perfect!"

I can relate. Dating as a minister comes with its own special brand of awkwardness. "Rough experiences?"

"Yes!" She waves a half-eaten fry. "It's not that I think the stars are a cosmic matchmaking service, but when you've spent enough time making bad choices in love, sometimes it helps to have a little celestial warning label. If Mercury retrograde can remind me to back up my hard drive, maybe it can also remind me not to text my ex."

I set my free hand at the small of her back and steer her toward the rectory. "So, you believe in karma? Or astrology?"

"I'm greedy! I believe in *both*, because I like to hedge my bets." Dixie taps a fry contemplatively against her lips. Her lipstick is miraculous, the color unsmudged. "But if I had to pick a favorite child, I'd trust the stars. I'm a Sagittarius, born under a fire sign—passionate, restless, a little reckless."

A little reckless is putting it mildly. The woman has zero filter and even less inhibition. It's fascinating.

She eyes me suspiciously and edges away. "Are you judging me? I've judged you to be the judgmental type, so now's the moment to live down to my expectations."

"I'm too busy being shocked to judge anyone," I say. "You've used up all my processing power."

"Phew. What's your sign? When were you born?" She drops the remainder of her fry in my hand.

I hook the take-out bag over my arm and pull my handkerchief out, handing it to her so she can wipe her fingers. "April."

This earns me a shocked face. "Oh no."

"What?"

"We're about to have a moment. I'm setting the mood. Dum-dum-dummmmm."

I smile despite myself.

"Good news, bad news, Jack. You're either an Aries or a Taurus. Aries would make sense—gruff, stubborn, takes charge. But if you're a Taurus, that'd mean you're a romantic at heart, love good food, and prefer stability over chaos. Possibly, you have the soul of a ninety-year-old man."

She waves my handkerchief pointedly and I burst out laughing. "Guess which one sounds more like me."

She grins. "You're a Taurus, aren't you?"

"I do like good food." I finish her fry, retrieve my handkerchief, and wipe my own fingers.

"Damn, that explains why you're built like a brick house and give off all that 'slow and steady wins the race' energy. But we're either about to succumb to irresistible attraction or total frustration. We Sagittarius types are a challenging romantic match for you Tauri."

"So, you actually make decisions based on a star chart?"

"You make yours based on an old book."

"The Bible."

"Tomato, to-mah-to."

"I think my ancient pieces of paper have a little more credibility."

"Burning bushes and talking snakes are not credible, mister." Her mouth curves up.

"And you've got…what was it, Mercury in retrograde?"

"Exactly. When things go wrong in my life, I get to blame planetary alignment. What do you blame?"

"Free will," I say dryly.

"Maybe." Dixie skips along at my side. "Maybe not. But maybe they brought me to this particular stretch of road at this particular moment. Maybe they lined things up just right. Maybe the stars think we should hook up."

I freeze. "That's…"

"Awesome. Spectacular. Probably proof that there is a God, after all—and she has a thing for hot, bearded preacher men." She fishes for her phone and I redirect my gaze toward the Gemini twins in the sky because she's stashed the phone inside her bra. "Did you check your horoscope for today? 'Stability is your strength, but today the universe nudges you to embrace a little spontaneity. A surprising connection could deepen in unexpected ways—if you're willing to let go of control. Love may be closer than you think and tonight just might be your lucky night.' See? You get a lucky night!"

I smile. "It sure is."

When we pass Deacon's auto shop, she detours and bee-lines toward her van.

"Deacon will check the van out first thing," I say. "He and his brother, Slate, are the town mechanics."

"I can handle my own van," she mutters, loud enough for me to hear, and yanks open the van doors.

The inside is a jumble of speakers and music stands, cables and power strips, electronic bits and pieces I can't identify. A guitar case sits on top of the mess, and an inflatable mattress is pancaked on the bottom. She rummages through the disaster, before dumping a monster-sized tote bag on the asphalt and slamming the van door shut.

"*Waste not, want not, that's what Mama used to say, Make the most of what you've got 'fore it fades away.*" She sings the way other people use their words. Her hands catch mine, tugging them out of my pockets as she twirls us in a circle. "Dance with me. *Don't spend your days just countin' dimes, let your heart do the spendin', too, 'Cause if you live for tomorrows, you'll find a little more to lose.*

"Okay. I'm all packed." She laughs, a little breathless. "Take me home, big guy."

Dixie is out of my league. Wickham Hollow is—*small*. Paint peels genteelly from the craftsman bungalows lining Main Street and the houses all have the slightly haunted look of a

Southern small town with more spirit than cash. It's pretty, though, in the moonlight. A silvery light stipples the deep porches with their thick, square columns. Ferns hang from the rafters and shrub roses invade the sidewalk. The Hargroves turned their porch into a spare shed two years ago and it's packed to the eaves with ancient appliances and cardboard boxes. I can't imagine Dixie here.

"I can crash at Deacon's if that makes you more comfortable. You'd be safe."

"I'm very picky about my accommodations." She winks at the van. "As you can see for yourself, I'm a five-stars-minimum traveler."

It's too cold to sleep in a car. I remember what that's like.

"I don't have any expectations." I sling her tote bag over my shoulder.

She looks at me, clearly debating grabbing her stuff back. "I, on the other hand, have expectations. *High* ones. Although you're right. I should ask some preliminary questions. Do you live alone?"

"Yeah. Well, except for Huck and Georgia Peach." I wait a beat, just to tease her. "Georgia Peach is the world's oldest chinchilla and Huck has sworn undying love and devotion to her."

"And you don't have any weird kinks? I don't need a safe word?"

"Not that I'm aware of."

She taps a finger against her lips. "That's what they all say and then it's here's my banana and the olive oil."

"I have no idea what that even means."

She feigns shock. "Is there a Mrs. Preacher?"

"If there were, there would have been no kissing in Southern Comforts."

We walk the three blocks from the auto shop to the church in easy silence, her fingers threaded through mine. Holy shit. I can't stop looking down at our joined hands like I'm sixteen and this is my first time holding hands with a girl. Which, considering my dating history, isn't that far off. Her grip is strong and warm, and she swings our arms slightly as we walk, completely unselfconscious about it. Meanwhile, I'm trying not to think about how this feels like the most natural thing in the world—walking through my town with this woman who showed up out of nowhere and turned my quiet life upside down in the span of an hour.

She stops. Looks up. Then up some more.

"So, you're definitely— Wow. That's definitely something. You could make a fortune renting this place out for movie shoots."

Wickham Hollow Chapel doesn't do subtle. Pointed arches, dramatic buttresses, and a bell tower that juts up into the sky like it's trying to poke God in the ribs. The roof—my nemesis—pitches at angles designed to shed shingles directly onto my head. Behind the church, weathered tombstones sprout out of the ground at random angles, half swallowed by beard moss and twisted cedar branches. The founding families either had a flair for the dramatic or watched way too many horror movies.

"This place is straight out of a Tim Burton movie." She eyes a tombstone. "I'm expecting skeletal hands to claw their way out of the ground any moment now."

"Judgment Day would be something."

"It would be awesome!" She shakes her head. "Zombies galore, arms falling off, missing eyeballs, lots of body rot!"

Like her fictional zombies, my real-life church is falling apart. The building shambles along, in dire need of a new roof and better plumbing.

"Do you live inside?" She gives me an enthusiastic thumbs-up. "I'll bet the acoustics are amazing!"

She is—*a lot*.

"I don't live inside the church. Do you sleep on the stage?"

"It's been known to happen," she mock-whispers.

I move on. "I have a rectory—and a life."

Out of habit, I give the roof a once-over (still attached, good) and pick a piece of shingle off the pavement (not so good).

Dixie snags a second shingle from the leafless hydrangea bushes lining the western side of the church and hands it over. "It's raining rooftop. Is that supposed to happen?"

"Not unless I want the congregation wearing raincoats to Sunday service." I lead her around the side of the church toward the rectory. "I'm working on it."

Working on it means finding forty thousand dollars I don't have. But that's yet another problem for Future Jack. My master plan involves winning the statewide church talent show, which sounds about as likely as divine intervention. Maybe less likely.

The rectory, at least, doesn't look like it belongs in a horror movie. Shingled and gabled, cozy instead of gothic. Mine, even if the church comes with it.

When I look over at Dixie, she's doing some kind of spy routine—darting between shadows, flattening herself against the church wall, checking corners like she expects snipers.

"What are you doing?"

"Making sure none of your parishioners are watching." She shudders dramatically. "They're like a panel of gymnastics judges, waiting to score your sex life. One-million-point deduction for stepping out of bounds!"

"It's none of their business and they definitely don't get to watch."

"Okay. Cool. But bummer because I've never starred in an orgy before."

She what—

She bursts out laughing. "Oh God, your face! Just kidding! As long as you're up for some fun and not worried about your immortal soul, I'm good."

I wrap my fingers around hers. "You're something else."

"I'm yours," she says.

"That escalated fast."

"For the night." She winks. "Just think of me as a one-night engagement, a limited-time opportunity. Sneak me into your rectory, big guy."

Four

Preacher gets an indecent proposal

Dixie

Jack freezes for half a heartbeat—blink and you'd miss it—but then he's all in on my ridiculous plan. And I mean *all in*.

We're practically sprinting toward his place like a pair of silly teenagers sneaking in after curfew, giggling and bumping into each other. His shoulder knocks mine, our hands brush, and there's a whole chaotic dance of trying not to trip over each other while also trying to stay close enough to do—well, whatever this is we're doing.

By the time we hit his front steps, I'm wound tighter than a guitar string and about twice as likely to snap.

He tosses the roof bits we collected into a small basket by the door, saying, when I raise my eyebrows, "Evidence. Every time the wind blows, I lose more of the church roof. I'm building a case to convince the council to fund a complete replacement before the whole thing caves in."

"Sounds expensive."

"You have no idea," he mutters, then opens the door—it's

unlocked—holding it for me and waiting for me to go first like the Southern gentleman he is. He searches my face, all careful glances and unspoken questions. *Are you sure? Do you want to change your mind?*

As if.

"Don't mind if I do!"

I feel like I could take on the world right now, and my plan is to *carpe diem* so hard it'll leave marks. Who gives a shit what tomorrow brings? Tonight, my body's finally cooperating with my brain, and we're both voting yes on Operation Jump the Preacher.

"Make yourself at home." His face goes pink again above his beard—that same adorable flush that makes me want to pinch his cheeks or maybe bite them. If I stuck around longer than it takes to fix my van, I'd buy him SPF 50 just to mess with him.

From where I'm standing, Jack's house strikes me as what would happen if a fairy-tale cottage got really into Goth architecture. All pointy bits and fancy trim, like someone took a normal house and decided it needed more drama. The kind of place where you'd expect a witch to lean out the window offering poisoned apples, not a minister sharing hospitality. But it's also got this pristine white paint job and black shutters that frame windows looking straight out at the church and—oh, great—a whole cemetery full of dead people.

Charming.

Whatever. I'm not here for the real estate tour.

I blow past him into the house before he can change his mind or remember he's supposed to be a respectable man of God or something equally inconvenient.

He strides after me and closes the door without locking it. Jesus Christ. Does this man just trust every random stranger who wanders into his life? Because that's either incredibly sweet or incredibly stupid, and I haven't decided which yet.

"Safe!" I throw my arms up like I just scored a touchdown.

"For a minute there I thought the locals were gonna form an angry mob and come after us with pitchforks!"

Jack's staring at me. When your audience doesn't appreciate a good metaphor, you move on, so I start snooping around his living room.

The place is trying hard to be a library—all bookcases with glass fronts that look handcrafted, shelves packed with more books than any one person could possibly read, and a well-used fireplace. There's a sad fiddle-leaf fig in the corner that's begging for a bigger pot, and a leather chair that's seen better decades. The walls are painted a rich navy so dark it's basically black, which should be depressing but somehow just makes everything feel cozy and secret. And when I glance out the window? Nothing but row after row of headstones.

"Okay, I have to ask." I turn to face him, hands on my hips. "Are you secretly a hot centuries-old vampire gift wrapped in flannel?"

A darker strip of pink colors Jack's cheekbones. "Sunlight doesn't fry me, and I have a distinct lack of fangs."

"The dark, broody aesthetic says otherwise. This is some serious 'eternal scholar waiting out the centuries' energy."

"I like books," he says. "And quiet. And chairs that don't fall apart when you sit in 'em."

Oh, the perils of being a monster-sized man.

I shrug off my jacket, dropping it onto his oversize chair. "See, that sounds exactly like something an ancient vampire would say."

"And here I thought I was more of a rock than a bloodsucker," he says, completely deadpan. But there's this tiny twitch at the corner of his mouth that gives him away.

"I don't know." I tilt my head, pretending to consider this seriously. "I've met rocks with more game."

Shit. Did that come out meaner than I meant it to?

But he just laughs—a soft, rumbly sound that does a number on my insides—and scoops up my jacket before heading toward what I assume is a closet.

"And yet," he calls back over his shoulder, "here you are. Standing in my allegedly game-less house."

I grin. "What can I say? I'm a *sucker* for a good mystery."

He has a massive Victorian dollhouse tucked in a corner. Which, okay, raises some questions. What grown-ass man keeps a dollhouse on display in his living room? It's giving some seriously disturbed vibes.

I drift closer to investigate and nearly jump out of my skin when I spot two tiny dark eyes and the fluffiest little ears peeking out from one of the miniature windows.

"Georgia Peach," Jack says from somewhere very close behind me. I get goose bumps. "I rescued her—" of course he did "—but that's one chinchilla who prefers to have her own space."

I poke a finger toward the little window. The glass is missing, so the chinchilla's not trapped—just antisocial.

"She's shy," Jack explains. "And she's not big on people."
Called it.

Georgia Peach makes a distinctly judgmental chittering sound, then disappears back into her tiny mansion, leaving behind tiny chinchilla hairs.

How is this man still single? He's got a job, he looks like God's apology for every disappointing Tinder date I've ever been on, and he comes with the cutest menagerie.

As if summoned by my thoughts, Huck appears around the corner. He eyes the dollhouse like he's trying to figure out the architectural requirements for squeezing his giant self through those tiny doors.

Jack shakes his head, running a hand over Huck's head. "The world's best watchdog. Where's your bark, man?"

His voice holds this wealth of love and understanding. Huck's the luckiest dog in the world: He gets to be himself, drool and all, and Jack loves him for it.

I drop to my knees to love on him. "Who's the sweetest boy? Yes, you are! The bestest boy in the whole damn world!"

Jack leans against the wall, arms folded over his chest, amusement lighting his eyes. He's too far away for my liking, but I'll fix that situation in a minute because right now Huck's doing this adorable thing where he butts his massive head against my palm like he's trying to push all the love back into me. The appreciation drool is just a bonus.

Huck gives me one more enthusiastic lick and rams his head into my hand like he's trying to high-five me with his skull, then apparently decides I've passed whatever test dogs give people and wanders off to do important dog business.

Now it's just me, Jack, and enough sexual tension to power a small city.

I lean back to get a better look at him. He hasn't budged from his spot propping up the wall. My stomach picks this exact moment to growl audibly, reminding me that a handful of fries isn't exactly dinner.

"Hungry?" Jack asks, his smile widening.

"Starving," I admit. "But not just for food."

I definitely wink at him. Sue me.

"We've got our winnings." He pushes off the wall and heads toward the kitchen.

Ten minutes later, I'm absolutely demolishing a plate of surprisingly edible chicken and dumplings while Jack watches with amusement. "What?" I say through a mouthful. "I need to keep my strength up."

"For?"

I give him my most wicked smile and push the empty plate aside. "Let me demonstrate. Bedroom?"

He makes this sound that's half groan, half laugh. *Christ, you're cute.* "Down the hall."

The hallway's narrow enough that two people can't walk side by side without bumping into the walls. I zip down it, and the whole situation hits me—this is officially the weirdest hookup of my life, and somehow I'm absolutely here for it. Ten of ten, would definitely do again.

Jack follows me, and God, he has the deepest, happiest laugh.

"In here?" I push the door open fast because from the outside, this house looks like it's one creaky floorboard away from a full-on haunting. There's the smallest hitch in my step, my knee deciding it wants to be a little bitch about the February cold. It's got opinions about pretty much every month that isn't July, honestly. Wants me to pack up and move somewhere tropical.

I ignore it.

I stretch, pushing my arms up toward the ceiling, working out the kinks as a familiar heat trickles through my body and my breathing picks up. It's been way too long since I last did this.

"That's a big bed, Preacher Man." I toe off my boots and dig my toes into the coolness of Jack's hardwood. Just a hint of stiffness in my joints, but we're still good to go. "Time to put it to good use!"

I dive onto the bed. It's not exactly graceful, but fuck it.

Jack watches me, breathing hard.

His eyes—

They're warm and intense, and my libido's sending up flares about how much we like the way he's looking at me. I find my footing on the mattress, bounce a little to test the springs, then find my balance and fist the hem of my dress.

Up and over my head it goes.

His smile does the hottest things to me—warm, electric, tingly things that make me want to yank him down onto this bed and skip straight to the main event.

But then I think maybe I want to play with him a little first. So I hum him a tune under my breath, doing a slow shimmy as I work my panties down my hips, over my thighs, past my knees until they're bunched around my ankles. It's not the most graceful look I've ever pulled off, but judging by Jack's face, he'll be leaving a five-star review.

I stretch some more, cup myself, fingers brushing over nipples that tighten because even though it's late February in Tennessee and definitely not beach weather, I'm burning up.

Not even a little bit cold.

"You're beautiful," he growls.

"And you're way too slow." I make grabby hands at him. "You get naked, too."

He nods—of course he does, because he'd give me whatever I want and we both know it. Then he strides over, wrapping his arms around me gently, pulling me into him. We're eye to eye now, and I'm on fire.

I cradle his face between my hands and kiss him.

He—

God. He *opens* for me.

He kisses me back, his tongue teasing mine so lightly, tracing my lips. *Hello. Come on in.* This is our second kiss, but our first without an audience, and his mouth feels like it's everywhere at once. I forget to breathe, forget that I should be touching him back—he kisses me and I lose my place in this whole song. His mouth is That Firm Curve of Him, and when he deepens the kiss I fall into That Irresistible Dip that peeks out from the corner of his beard. And then there's all That Edible Scruff along his jawline, rough and delicious.

He pulls back. "Is this too fast? Too much? Yes?"

"Unequivocally," I whisper against his mouth. "Yes, to everything you want to do to me. If you need suggestions, I have a list."

He curses roughly.

I feel the corners of my mouth curve up. "You have a wicked, wicked mouth, Mr. Carter. FYI? I'm taking those as promises."

Then we're kissing again, his hands sliding up, up, up into my hair, angling me, taking control. The brush of his flannel shirt against me is maddening—of course he's still dressed. He wears his self-control like armor, and the way he holds himself in check drives me wild, has me squirming against him.

I fall into him, already lost. I slide my hands behind his neck, down his back. *Come here, you.* He's frowning—fierce in his concentration, but also looking at me as if he—

I don't know.

But I like it.

His hands get busy, moving down to cup my ass and pull me up, my legs wrapping around his waist. I press harder against him, riding him, messing him up, arching my back. This is what I need, this connection, to feel like I'm fully alive and capable of flying for once. He groans, making these guttural sounds, and none of the words falling from his mouth are *stop* or *no* or *we should think about this.* Instead, he's saying things like *yes* and *beautiful* and *use me. Let me. May I? Like that?*

It's all urgent kisses and wet touches, sweet friction and breathlessness.

Except I'm naked, and he's still not, and I need him all the way close with no clothes between us. I lean back to yank at his shirt, undoing his buttons and pushing the sleeves down his arms. He's got a hand between my legs now—*so wet*, he growls, his fingers working—as I get his flannel shirt off and toss it on the floor.

He groans, setting me down on the bed. Steps back.

He fists the hem of his T-shirt and yanks it over his head. Beneath the flannel and cotton, he's a work of art, all slabs of muscle, a light dusting of hair, lines, and grooves worthy of a Michelangelo.

"Faster." I rise up on my knees, reaching for his belt buckle.

He's wearing too many clothes for the dirty plans I have, and I unbuckle, undo him, push his jeans and boxer briefs down. Our fingers meet because we both have the same fucking goal.

My hands stroke over his hot, bare skin, learning, taking,

and he lets me. He's mine now. I've claimed him. I kiss the strong line of his shoulder, kneeling up in front of him to lick his chest and slide my hands south to wrap around him.

"Christ," he rasps. And then, "Dixie."

He takes my mouth with his. His lips demand, open me up like a box of sweets, sweep inside to taste me. He kisses with unexpected hunger, bold and unrestrained. This is Jack unleashed. The preacher thing is false advertising—he's absolutely filthy.

He's all in, angling my face toward him with a big, sure hand, holding me tight. His beard against my face is an unexpected softness. His arm wraps around my waist, pulling me toward him, and my brain skips a track on this record, imagining his hands, his mouth, the goddamned beard elsewhere on my body.

He tears his mouth from mine, his chest heaving, eyes fierce. "Yes? Yes, Dixie?"

His voice holds the sexiest rasp.

"More." I kiss the stern line of his jaw, a little too fierce and not at all gentle. "I want all of you, Jack. Right now."

He grunts something softly—a breath of a sound, not quite a word. *Good? God?* I'm not here for conversation.

"I've wanted to get your clothes off you since we met."

He groans. "That was about an hour ago, Dixie."

"Yes! And we've wasted so much time. Your flannel shirt should be illegal. I need you naked all the time. Fuck me now, okay?"

"I—" His big hands palm my ass. "Okay. Yes."

He takes his cue, shifting me until I'm flat on the bed. He braces himself over me, one big hand planted beside my head. His thumb finds my cheek and strokes.

I explore his body with greedy hands. Muscled forearms cage me in. He's a perfect frame of steel and heat and strength. I want to bottle him up, drink him down like the vampire I accused him of being. He grunts, sliding against me.

"You're my silver lining." My voice is low and needy, and I can't catch my breath but I kiss him harder, deeper, because things between us can't be uneven, not ever. My mouth devours his, fingers tight in his hair, and I've never felt more alive.

Not ever. Not even onstage.

It doesn't take long before we're both done, panting and wrecked and tangled up together in his big bed.

When the afterglow fades, Jack's still braced above me.

His thick fingers thread through my hair, beard brushing my forehead. When he shifts, I feel the tug everywhere—regions south, my scalp, and everywhere between.

"Okay?" He rumbles the question, eyes searching mine as he pulls free.

I am. I'm fine. Great. Collapsed in a puddle of postorgasmic bliss. That's not what freaks me out.

It's not even the kiss he brushes across my forehead like we're some long-married couple or reincarnated Victorians. No—it's the way he rolls us both over and goddamned *spoons* me.

That's what bothers me. The tender grip. The care with which he holds on to me like I'm the best surprise ever and he can't get enough. He whispers things, compliments, praise, rougher sounds that aren't words but still say way too much.

I suck at this part of sex. The aftercare, the cuddling, the making-emotions-out-of-hormones bullshit. It's like a Magic Eraser for all the good parts.

Now I'm hot and sticky, with handfuls of my hair trapped under my shoulder. And I'm stiff everywhere. Activity's supposed to help with my RA, but I've overdone it.

I should go. Somewhere. Back to Nashville if there's an Uber that'll drive out this far for free.

And as soon as I try to plan my escape—Google Map a move to Mars—I realize shit, I haven't answered his question. He checked in about our sex, and I ignored him.

"Super! That was awesome, big guy!"

There. Feedback given, ego stroked. I'm the worst ever postcoital snuggler. I want to jump out of bed and get things done. Had it been sixty seconds? Ninety? Can I leave in two minutes?

When bells ring—twice and loudly, like the whole god-damned roof's coming down—I jackknife upward. Could be the harbinger of doom. Could be the ice cream man. Either way, it's GO time.

"Just church bells," Jack murmurs.

Out in the hallway, Huck bays his agreement.

"Every hour?" I need clarification because holy interrupted sleep patterns, Batman.

"Yeah," he grunts. He sounds sleepy. Oh God, he's one of those people who falls asleep after sex.

He surprises me by getting up to dispose of the condom, then comes straight back, cracking a window before sliding in beside me.

"You're—" he starts. "That was—"

"Yeah." I pat his arm, roll over. "Totally."

He pulls me back against his chest, trying to be the big spoon to my teaspoon. Joke's on him. I'm a knife—stiff and sharp. He settles himself carefully, one big paw smoothing my hair back from my face.

He established in the first sixty seconds of our acquaintance that he's a giver. He towed me, made room for me at Southern Comforts, offered up a bed. No questions asked. If I need it, he gives it.

He's one of the good guys. I'm not. Not even close.

"You okay?" he rumbles in my ear.

I yank his duvet—a *duvet* with *pinstripes*—up to my chin and squeeze my eyes shut. "Shh. I'm sleeping."

"That bad, huh?"

"No complaints. Five stars. Would sin again."

His hand brushes my shoulder. "Sleep tight."

When he goes to shift, to roll away, the words fly out of my mouth. "You're warm."

"You can stay, you know," he says quietly.

I tense for half a second.

"Yeah. Thought so," he adds, when I say nothing.

I pretend to be tired, to drift off in his arms, and then he gives up, tucking his chin into the space between my shoulder and my ear. His breathing evens out and slows.

I trace the muscles in his forearm as it loosens with sleep. There's a name for those under-the-skin pieces that I forgot years ago in high school biology, if I ever knew it. His arm's darker, sun-bronzed. I bet he rolls his sleeves up every month of the year, not just summertime. Drives around Wickham Hollow 10 percent naked all the time.

When the stupid church bell tolls three times, I get up, grab my clothes, and tiptoe into the hallway.

I'm shaking, but only a little. Just too much sex. No big deal. Huck raises his head to look at me.

"Don't look at me like that, mister."

His tail thumps.

I shimmy into my clothes and dart out the door without looking back.

Five

*Bridge (minor key): Girl has feelings.
Non-orgasmic ones.*

Dixie

"Goddammit!" I snap at the empty page. I really thought I'd beat my writer's block tonight, but it's five in the morning and my brain is officially fried. Pretty sure God's cackling up there in the sky and, seeing as I've just ditched his favorite kid, Jack the minister, I probably deserve it.

After the sneak of shame out of Jack's two hours ago, I've barricaded myself in my van, sitting cross-legged on the air mattress like some kind of broke meditation guru. My A/V equipment is shoved to the side, and I'm wrapped up in blankets like a mummy, waiting for the world to warm up (come on, global warming!) and the creative juices to flow.

It's been months since I've written a whole-ass song. My dad's professional take on this failure? "Just put your butt in the chair and write, Dixie!" As if twenty more minutes—or two hundred hours—will magically unlock my brain. Easy advice from a man who wrote one Christmas novelty hit twenty years ago and acts like he cracked the code to songwriting. My agent hasn't weighed in on the failure—she knows my mind is an empty sheet of paper. A single note plunked out on a piano.

I'm not going to cut it.

I stretch my leg out, trying to work the stiffness out of my hip. Jack is something else in bed (the adjective I'm looking for is devastating), so I totally don't regret the residual effects on my body. These include spectacular beard burn on my chest and thighs, the sexy postcard version of JACK WAS HERE. Or maybe X MARKS THE SPOT?

His prowess deserves to be immortalized in song. Right?

Except I have nothing. Nada. Zero inspiration despite getting thoroughly *inspired* mere hours ago.

Sweetgum Auto is darker than an auditorium in a blackout. I've dug out my tea lights and my current plan is to not set my van—and all my earthly possessions—on fire. February in Tennessee is colder than a witch's left tit. Come on, Muse! We're writing by candlelight! Don't you want to speed-write a soulful ballad?

"Oh, God," I say out loud, because Jack's a bad influence and has me praying. Sort of. I'd be more of a sacrifice-to-Diana pagan lover if I had to choose.

Great. Wonderful. Now I'm thinking about Jack. He's a hungry man, which is flattering. Or maybe it's just that it's clear he doesn't pick up women in a bar as a general rule, and I always like being an exception and a broken rule. It's a fabulous two-for-one.

There's more to him than just a broad pair of shoulders, although I definitely like the way his muscles come gift wrapped in flannel. He screams *I am a rock! Lean on me!* The half smile that he only half hides behind his beard promises that he's on your side no matter what. He's supremely capable of carrying and burying any bodies I might create.

I like how he thinks before he speaks, slow but deliberate, one word following the other in a neat, orderly train, in a way that says he's aware that people listen to him and, why yes, he has earned that trust. In short, the man is horribly, wonderfully capable, and it would be way too easy to lean on him like everyone else in this ridiculously small town probably does.

It's a good thing I'm out of here just as soon as my van is functional.

Plus, there's the whole man of God thing that I might, just possibly, have not come to terms with. I have no idea what draws me to him.

My phone buzzes loud enough to jolt me out of my brooding, and I nearly crack my skull on the van's metal ceiling when I sit up too fast.

It's Dear Old Dad. The Begetter. Sir Talks-Too-Much.

He'll lecture me about my life choices. Give advice that's on point but supremely annoying. Make me actually consider singing his stupid song with him.

I groan, flopping back onto my pillow (aka bundled-up hoodie). My joints feel like they've been stuffed with gravel overnight, and my fingers don't want to cooperate when I jab at the screen. If I let this ring through, though, he'll just call again. And again. And again.

I swipe to answer and press the phone to my ear. "Dad! This better be good."

"Dixie! Finally! Thought I was gonna have to send a carrier pigeon." Dad's voice is way too loud. "You sound like you're not awake yet. You gotta early-bird it if you want to get that worm!"

I'll get right on that. Maybe Hawaii or Arizona have viable country music circuits.

He clocks my answering silence as hostility and moves on. "You sleeping in your van again?"

I roll onto my side, curling into myself against the cold. "What do you want?"

"I wouldn't have to call at the crack of dawn if you'd answer your phone at normal hours." That's rich, considering the time difference between Tennessee and…

"Where are you?" I ask more to delay the inevitable than out of real curiosity.

"The Maldives." He announces this the same way he would say *that cute little coffee shop down the road* or *my McMansion that's twenty miles outside Nashville and sits on an acre but I pretend it's a ranch and I have horses because I am a Big Star.* "Beachfront bungalow. Five stars. Sun, sand, drinks with tiny umbrellas. You'd love it."

He's right. A giant, heated ball of gas sounds perfect.

"Anyway," he continues, oblivious to—or uninterested in—my irritation, "I've been thinkin' about this Christmas album, and I really believe you should do it. It'll be great for your career, give you some exposure. A nice cash infusion, too. You could use that, right?"

We both know the answer, but I won't give him the satisfaction of saying it out loud.

"Dad, I told you—I'm not doing your Christmas album."

"Come on now, Dixie, don't be like that. I'm just tryin' to help you out here. This is a real opportunity for you. A little boost from your old man won't kill you."

I stare up at the van's ceiling, counting the specks of rust along the edges. "I'm not singing 'Jingle Bell Dash' with you."

His version of that perennial Christmas favorite snuck onto the Billboard Hot Country Songs chart in the fiftieth spot twenty years ago in a true Christmas miracle. It's a hyperactive ditty about Santa street racing his sleigh and features such outstanding lyrics as "Reindeer hooves on the icy road, Santa's got a need for speed, lock and load!" and "Giddy-up, Dasher, don't be slow, we got presents to throw, let's go, let's go!" It has both an extraneous banjo solo and an *a cappella* section where Santa raps about "leaving Frosty in the snowdrift dust."

"It's a great song!"

"It's a terrible song."

There's a pause where we both silently admit that I'm right, then he leans into it. "Well, it charted higher than any of your songs ever have."

That lands like a kick to the ribs, seeing as how exactly none of my songs have charted. Even though I should be used to his criticism, I have to bite the inside of my cheek and take a steadying breath lest I go supernova on his oblivious, suntanning self. He doesn't mean to be cruel. He just is.

"You don't have to do my song." He's generous in victory. "We could pick something else. Or co-write! The point is, you need a push, Dixie. You're not a solo act—never have been. You need direction, a team. I mean, look at you—still spinning your wheels, still playing those same old dive bars after almost ten years on the road. You really think that's gonna lead somewhere? Those gigs are supposed to be the on-ramp to somewhere, not the only road you take."

My fingers curl into the blanket, the RA making my knuckles ache at the movement. "I'm fine."

"Look, honey, I get it. You're stubborn. You wanna prove something and you've got your old man's grit. But the reality is, you're running out of time. You're not twenty anymore. You're tired, you're broke, and let's be honest—you ain't makin' it big on your own. Just do the album. You need the money. And I could use a good singer on it."

He thinks he's helping. But every word out of his mouth is another cut, slicing away at whatever stubborn dignity I have left. The worst part is that I do need money. And exposure. And yet, the idea of tying myself to him musically, of stepping into the twenty-year-old shadow of his single, minor hit, makes me feel as if I'm drowning.

"Shoot," I lie. "My phone's about to die."

"Dixie—"

"—losing you—" I make static noises with my mouth. This is a shame-free zone.

"Don't hang up on me, baby girl—"

I end the call and then turn my phone off for good measure. How much longer can I afford to refuse? How much longer before even he gives up on my career?

I sit there for another minute, stewing in my own irritation and the lingering sting of his words. I do a quick search online for preacher erotica to check out the obvious answer to "Why are priests hot?" and discover multiple historical romances to add to my to-be-read pile. I realize it's not weird that I jumped a priest-guy! Not at all! I'm just living out a really kinky fantasy without the broody, half-naked-man-chest covers.

Jack is nothing like other guys I've hooked up with, who were mostly other musicians. I'd met them in smoke-filled bars where we'd knocked back tequila shots, licking salt off our wrists, laughing hard about nothing. We'd played tiny stages, split tinier door takes, and then stayed up all night to work out a new melody. Driven from one club to the next, crisscrossed the South in the van, and played anywhere and everywhere because musicians never had money. After a few gigs, we'd always parted ways.

What would have happened if I'd met a man like Jack, back when I was shiny-young and optimistic? What if I'd been as deliberate about my dating choices as I had been about my music?

A soundtrack to that thought pops into my head, a new melody playing in my imagination.

I bend over the guitar, coaxing the music closer until I can pick out individual notes and scrawl them down. It feels as natural as breathing, translating unwelcome, uncertain feelings into black notes on white paper. The words come fast, angry and honest and raw:

> "She's not one of those girls
> Who says yes to a preaching man
> Walks down the church aisle
> Wears white on her big day
> Could have been, should've been?

That's what they say
Ask her to be yours, she says, 'No'
Because she don't stick
No place for her in that life
No safe spot for her heart
Pretty preacher man makes her hot
But she'll keep on walking
Right on out of his life
Never gonna be preacher's girl
Not gonna wear his ring
Not gonna share his life, be his one and only
'Cause she's not one of those girls
That's gotta trust a man
Just gonna kiss him good and go
She's a once-upon-a-time girl
Who's gotta keep on walking
Right out of reach
Once upon a time she could have been preacher's girl
Could have been that trusting girl
No, no, no
She's not tryna fit that life
Now she's nobody's girl
Her own girl
Not one of those girls."

The melody's beats flow as I finger the guitar. Before I can lose the moment, I record it on my phone. The quality isn't ideal, but I need to know if it's any good. I upload it to my Instagram, along with a stock photo of a black sweater casually discarded on a bed and add a caption: "When you accidentally hook up with a preacher man and have to own your poor life choices. Am I hot for preacher?"

Boom. Click. Done.

Like my hookup.

Six

Preacher arrives. Girl says, "I had it handled"
(she did not).

Jack

Huck's gotta-go-hurry-it-up howl stabs through my head, straight into my brain. My body's sluggish, slow to respond, and I haven't slept enough. I was out late last night and then I brought Dixie home and then—

And *then.*

I don't regret what happened. Not her hands in my hair or the way she said my name. Not a damn second of it. But waking up to cold sheets? That sits wrong with me.

I drag myself up anyway, scrub my face with my hands. I should've known better. She'd made it clear what this was—and wasn't. But knowing something and feeling it are two different things.

Huck stares up at me from the floor. His mournful look is a decoy. He's chewing on something suspiciously feminine—a velvet pouch covered in tiny red cherries. My dog is a thief, which usually I accept, but right now I'm painfully aware that I'm alone in the bed.

"Huck."

Huck chews industriously on a soggy cherry.

"We've discussed this."

He flicks his ears but keeps right on chewing. He has a thing for stealing ladies' things and purses in particular. This means he's banned from church on Sunday. It doesn't bother him one bit.

I reach down, running a hand over his silky head. "That's not yours, buddy. You gotta return it."

Huck wags his tail and devours another cherry.

"Drop it." I tug gently on the purse, but Huck just huffs a sigh around the red string hanging from his mouth. "You know what that does to your digestive system. This is why we don't get invited to nice places."

Huck lets go just enough to bay, then lopes out the bedroom door with his loot.

"Huck! You little outlaw! Bring that back!" When I jump up to chase him, I step on wet rug. How can so much drool come out of one dog?

Huck careens joyfully down the hallway as I give chase. I'm about to admit defeat and make him breakfast when my phone vibrates with a call from Deacon.

"You gotta get over here." His voice is a low rumble, like he's trying not to wake someone—or trying to keep this conversation a secret.

The only reasons for Deacon to call me this early on a Saturday morning involve death. Doom. Car accidents.

"Who's hurt?" I shove my legs into my jeans, juggling the phone as I search for a clean shirt.

"No one—yet," Deacon drawls. "You, maybe, if you don't get your ass over here in the next sixty seconds."

"On my way." I get the shirt on and debate whether I have time for more than mouthwash.

"Dixie's here. Think she slept in her van last night. Way to go, man."

Mouthwash it is. I hate to think she slipped out because she didn't want to stay with me, but she's there and not here. Last night we'd had the whole town watching us, and maybe that was too much. But for a few hours, I'd thought things could be different.

Yeah. No rethinking my life choices before coffee.

I'm not in love with Dixie Pearl, cute and beautiful as she is. There hasn't been enough time, so my feelings are more of the pheromone kind. And it can't possibly matter anyhow because she's made her choice clear.

I'm a limited-time opportunity!

"Had some bad news for her," Deacon is saying as I step outside, Huck on his leash at my side. That protective streak of his is showing. "That van of hers needs a ton of parts, none of which I've got and two of which have to be drop-shipped from Mexico. It'll take weeks to get her running again, and she's bitching about the cost. Which—fair. It'll be astronomical, even comping her the labor."

Dixie strikes me as someone who suspects everyone. Maybe it's the angry crinkle in her forehead. The twist to her lit-up smile that I wish wasn't so cynical. She's been a hundred places I'll never go, and I'll bet she's seen a lot on the roads she's traveled.

"Would you believe an unknown mechanic when he claims your ride is on life support and needs foreign imports to survive?"

"I wouldn't trust me for shit," he says with a dry chuckle. "Hell, I look like I could part out her van and sell the pieces."

I cut him off. "I'll cover it. I'll be there in two."

I turn the corner and there Sweetgum Auto is, in all its greasy, gritty glory. The scent of motor oil, old rubber, and Slate's terrible coffee hits me first.

Slate himself rolls out from beneath a car like some kind of automotive cave troll—buzzed head, grease on his face and his coveralls, and a scowl that could strip paint. Where Deacon's got that full, thick beard and wicked grin that makes him look approachable, Slate's face is all sharp angles. He fixes me with a look and grunts.

Deacon has Dixie's battered van up on the lift. He's examining it with the sort of look brain surgeons reserve for baseball-sized tumors. From what I can see, the undercarriage is a mess—grease-streaked, rusted out, and dripping something that sure shouldn't be dripping.

Dixie stands just outside the work bay, shifting her weight impatiently from foot to foot. She looks like she just rolled out of bed. Sweatpants, fuzzy boots, and an oversize T-shirt with colorful flowers. Wisps of hair escape from her bun. She's laser-focused, though, on what Deacon and Slate are saying.

"She's seen better days." Deacon points his flashlight at a leak.

"She's doing fine!" Dixie waves both hands—which makes me remember where she put them last night.

Deacon shakes his head firmly. "Darlin', she's seen the grave and come back out of it."

"*She* is not a zombie," Dixie protests. "She's got character. And why is she a girl van? Is it because you boys are all up in her innards?"

Deacon valiantly ignores that question. "She's held together with prayers and zip ties."

"Slander! Lies!" Dixie mock-gasps. "I use duct tape, too."

"Christ." Slate slaps the rag in a bucket and strides off to the storeroom.

Deacon smirks after his brother. "We'll patch her up. But it's gonna take time. A month minimum. Honestly, you'll be lucky if you see the inside of the van again in two months. She needs a ton of parts that I don't keep here."

"*Weeks?* Seriously?" Dixie groans dramatically as Deacon

lowers the van back down. "Y'all are mechanics, surely you can patch her together."

"Your van's a corpse," Slate growls from the storeroom. "And there's only one person in Wickham Hollow in the business of miraculous resurrections."

I discreetly give him the bird. That's my cue, though, so I rap my knuckles on the side of the bay door. Dixie whirls around and sings a bar of something that sounds suspiciously like DUM-DUM-DUMMMMM.

"Hey, Preacher Man." She waves a hand. A little too casually to fool me, though. I have to work to not smile. "I'm so sorry I rushed out, but car stuff. Thanks for a great night."

Her eyes flick over me, fast and assessing, then dart away. Like she'd rather be looking anywhere else—at the van on the lift, at Deacon, at the busted socket wrench on the workbench—anywhere but me.

"I believe this is yours." I hand over the remnants of her purse.

Nice, she mouths at Huck. She shoves it under her arm, ignoring both its soggy state and me.

"Morning, Jack." Deacon puts a whole lot of emphasis on *morning*.

The devilment dancing in his eyes says he'll give me shit for days for how last night ended.

I don't answer, mostly because I'm too busy looking at Dixie. Her hair is messed up, her arms crossed tight over her chest. She's scrappy. A little too adorable to pull off the scary-business look she's wearing.

"Tell me the truth. Is she really on life support?" Dixie flashes an enormous grin at Deacon.

"She's a mess."

"The van?" She scratches the side of her head with her middle finger.

"Both of you." He smirks back at her.

From what I can see through the open van door, I understand her issue with Deacon's timeline. The van is crammed with more than just the music gear I saw last night. Pillows and blankets are heaped up on a futon thing. There are piles of dog-eared sheet music and notebooks. Cute plaid curtains cover the windows. She's strung twinkle lights where the walls meet the ceiling. It's clearly the home where she lives.

"Houston, we have a problem." She throws her arms out, indicating the van, Sweetgum Auto, and me.

"So," Deacon says. "Do you want to leave the van here and come back for it?"

"I'm the broke type of musician." She twirls theatrically. "Also, I'm itinerant. That's my house." She rummages around in the van. I avert my gaze when she starts shoving lingerie into a tote bag. "My palace. My tiny, four-wheeled kingdom. To sum up—I live here. There. Everywhere. Van life is really popular on Instagram."

Last I checked, Instagram doesn't need running water or heat. "All year round?"

She plops down in the open doorway. "Don't be so shocked, Preacher Man."

"Nope."

"It's fun." She waves a bra. "Unconventional, sure, but you have no idea how gross motels are when you're on a budget. My van is clean and it's safe." She thinks that over for longer than I like. "Mostly."

The idea of her sleeping in that van anywhere, like a random parking lot or God knows where, makes my chest feel tight.

"Stay with me," I blurt out. "Sleeping in the van isn't safe."

"Oh, and staying with you would be safer?" She stuffs more clothes into the tote. "Is Wickham Hollow a hotbed of desperate criminals now and I need protection from their felonious acts?"

"Yes, to the staying with me, no on the criminal population."

"You realize you're being illogical?"

"And you realize that you're out of choices?"

Deacon takes this as his cue to disappear into the back, but not before shooting me a look that says both *you're welcome* and *don't screw this up.*

"I have plenty of choices." She makes a face. "And I don't need saving."

"Didn't say you did."

A glare.

"Then why are you acting like a white knight, riding in with a grand offer to take in the poor, helpless musician who's stuck in your town?"

I rub a hand along my jaw. One night, I can explain away as basic hospitality. Any longer and the gossip mill will start grinding. But I can't let her freeze in that van. "I've got a guest room, Dixie. It's not an offer—it's common sense. Take the room."

"No."

"Take it."

"No."

We're not getting anywhere.

"Fine. You want to be stubborn? Here's the deal—I'll move out. I'll crash on Deacon's couch." I know he won't mind because he sticks his head out of his office door and flashes me a thumbs-up. His grin is pure mischief—he's enjoying this matchmaking opportunity way too much. "You won't be 'taking anything' from me, if that's what's bothering you. The rectory is yours for as long as you need it."

Something flickers across her face—something I can't name. "Why would you do that?"

I hold her gaze. "Because it's the right thing to do, Dixie."

She doesn't like my plan. I can see that in the way she shifts, how she bites the inside of her cheek like she's trying to stop herself from snapping.

"You'd actually move out of your own place?"

"If that's what it takes to keep you from sleeping in a broken van, yeah."

Dixie mutters something under her breath—it's blasphemous—then exhales. Frustrated. "I don't want your house."

I wait.

After another pause, she groans, rubbing her hands over her face. "I can't just move in with you. That's insane."

"Is it?"

Her eyes narrow. "Yes! We don't know each other. And there's the whole preacher thing, which—" She waves a hand. "The internet and my sketchy recollection of organized religion informs me that preachers aren't supposed to hook up."

She's connecting the dots—a preacher caught in a scandal could lose his job, his income, his ability to raise the money the church desperately needs. She's right. This is insane. I should walk away or drive her to that sketchy motel an hour away. Drive her to Timbuktu if she needs it. That's what a sensible man would do. But standing here looking at her, sensible feels overrated.

"It does tend to raise eyebrows when they do."

"And you've got your church roof to fix."

"I do."

"Right." Dixie stares at me for a long moment. "I need to think about this."

I nod. "That's fair."

"If—and I mean if—I were to consider this ridiculous offer, there would be conditions. And caveats. Lots and lots of legal fine print."

"I'd expect nothing less."

She's wavering. I can see it in the way she's looking anywhere but at me, the way her fingers are fidgeting with her rings.

"I'll… I'll let you know," she says finally.

"Take your time." I pull out the keys I never use, take off

the one to the rectory, and hold it out. "In case you decide yes."

She stares at the key like it might bite, then snatches it and shoves it in her bag. "This doesn't mean anything. I'm just keeping my options open."

Seven

*Girl's got coffee, no plan, and a preacher
in a tight spot*

Dixie

I have zero clue what I'm gonna do. Taking Jack up on his offer might buy me time to get my shit together, or at least make him stop hovering over me with those puppy dog eyes. Faced with all that bearded remorse, I can't think clearly.

Shoving his key into my bag, I bolt out of Sweetgum Auto like my ass is on fire.

Shockingly, Wickham Hollow hasn't grown larger overnight. Main Street's still a miserly three blocks long, although the end down by Southern Comforts has grown a Saturday farmers market where you can probably buy things like vegetables and homemade soaps. Organic goat milk caramels in recycled Mason jars. It'll be disgustingly wholesome and entirely boring.

Since every storefront I pass has CLOSED signs in their windows, the market's my only option. Coffee's a dire necessity. At this point, I'd even drink herbal tea. Plus, I need to find some free Wi-Fi and come up with alternatives to throwing myself on Jack's mercy while I wait for Deacon and his grumpy-ass sibling to fix my van.

At least the walk helps with my morning stiffness. Despite the breeze that seems to be coming straight from Alaska, I'm slightly warmer. And given the delicious smells wafting from the various stands, I figure I can lay my hands on coffee. I just hope they take Apple Pay out here in the middle of nowhere.

The coffee van has its pop-up side flung open like a wave hello. Painted in bold black-and-white cow print, it looks less like a caffeine station and more like a Holstein on wheels— udderly (pun fully intended) unmissable. A hand-painted chalkboard hung from the open hatch lists drinks with names like "Moo Brew" and "Udderly Delicious Cold Brew."

A brunette barista with a pixie cut has her back to me, doing something to the coffee machine. She waves a hand without turning around when I walk up. "Order away!"

"Black coffee with oat milk. Thank you."

"Honey, this is Wickham Hollow. We have three dairy farms. That means real milk, straight from the cows. You know—*moooo*?"

She makes an exaggerated cow impression that includes jazz hands as she turns around, eyes twinkling. Great liquid eyeliner, lots of freckles, and enough enthusiasm to power a small city.

"I'm gonna have to moo-ve right past that offer." I tap my phone to pay, hoping it won't be declined. "Black coffee."

"Coming right up! I'm Deirdre. Call me Dee! I make the coffee. And half the sweet stuff. Owner, baker, and caffeine dealer! Welcome to Wickham Hollow!" She bounces from one sentence to the next like a kitten chasing a bug, examining me with unabashed curiosity. "You visiting? You have the look of someone who needs something iced, sugared, or smothered in cinnamon. Or all three. I'm not judging but oof, black coffee's a stare-down kind of order. You okay?"

The flood of questions makes me freeze. Shit. My previous coffee-buying experiences involved fewer words, more cash. This woman thinks we should exchange names. Possibly addresses, likes, dislikes, and our astrological signs. She's total Aries energy.

"I'm fine." I take the coffee cup she hands me.

"That song you sang at karaoke last night was amazing. Did you make it up? Because I didn't recognize the words at all. Deacon says you're a professional singer and travel around the country singing? Or was it country singing like the noun? Either way, I need to hear all about it, please."

She hands me a Danish in a bag—that I have very much *not* paid for—and points to a wrought iron table and chairs beside her cart.

"I borrowed the music, improvised the lyrics." Willing to be bribed with delicious pastry, I sit. "Consider them copyrighted."

"Are you famous famous? Like, have-you-met-Beyoncé famous or just the kind where people scream in Cracker Barrel?"

"Famous?" I laugh. "Dee, I'm lucky if I get fifty people at a show. I'm nobody."

Dee closes her eyes dramatically. "Let me imagine that for a moment." Then she snaps them open and gulps her coffee. "Okay. I have the mental picture. Next question—have you ever dated a professor-prince like the guy from *American Royalty*?"

Blue eyes twinkle as she thumps a dog-eared paperback down on the table. A hottie in a military uniform with lots of gold braid is sniffing the hair of a gorgeous woman in a red dress. To be fair, her hair is amazing. To be less fair, Dee apparently thinks fiction's a blueprint for real life.

"Sadly, no. There's an aristocrat shortage in the South, although I've met a lot of super-entitled men." The Danish is almost delicious enough to compensate for this interrogation. "Closest I've come is a drummer who lived in his mom's basement and claimed to be descended from the guy who invented Pop-Tarts."

"Not the same vibe at all."

"No, but he did try to tattoo my name on his calf with a needle he bought at a gas station, so romance is alive."

Dee snorts her coffee. "You're hilarious. You're hereby invited to Dirty Girls."

Say. What?

"Garden club!" she clarifies. "We meet weekly. Mostly we plant things and yell about men, fictional or otherwise."

"Fictional men are vastly superior to real ones."

"Amen, sister." Dee taps her cup against mine. "Except maybe Reverend Jack?"

"Off-limits." I give her a look. "Don't start."

Dee grins, undaunted. "Too late! He's like if a lumberjack and a rescue golden retriever had a baby. And you are clearly having a Time."

I ignore that. "This coffee's actually good."

"Duh. Wickham Hollow may be tiny, but we know how to bake and eavesdrop like champions. You're gonna be fine. You just need coffee, a plan, and probably one more Danish."

"I never say no to Danish, but I'm not sticking around for long. You Dirty Girls will have to meet without me."

She shrugs. "I'll save you a seat anyway."

To my surprise, Slate strides up to the coffee cart. Dee makes a face and launches herself off the chair to go and take his order. He doesn't bother studying the ridiculous menu, ordering black coffee (shocker). Unexpectedly, however, they get into it about a brioche. Slate has *thoughts* and can speak in full paragraphs when motivated.

I watch their exchange while my mind wanders back to last night. Back to Jack.

I'm stuck between a rock and a hard place.

Except, in this case, it's a broken-down van and some really impressive dick. The kind that makes a girl see God and bless the Devil.

My options suck. I check on rideshares, but even if I can find a driver willing to drive four hours one way, it's out of my price range. Which gives me plenty of time to notice that my Instagram notifications are lighting up like a Christmas tree. The song I posted earlier this morning—the throwaway track I recorded in a stupid moment of post-hookup angst—has jumped from my usual two likes to over two thousand.

What the hell? I scroll through comments ranging from fire emojis to "WHERE IS THIS PREACHER?" to "Girl, you really said 'Just gonna kiss him good and go' and thought we wouldn't LOSE OUR MINDS."

My phone buzzes with a text from my agent: Let's talk Monday.

I stare at the screen, heart hammering. My agent never texts me. Ever. The last time we spoke was three months ago when she instructed me by email to "keep grinding" after yet another venue passed on booking me.

I consult Mrs. Google, who informs me that if I start walking now and don't stop, I'll reach Nashville on Tuesday. Pass. The Greyhound bus also connects nowhere near Wickham Hollow and it turns out that Amtrak has a single route to Memphis that's also far, far away from me.

The nuclear plan is texting my dad. He'd come, or more probably transfer money into my account. I'd have to say *yes* to singing "Jingle Bell Dash" because no one gives you something for nothing. But it's an option. It'll just cost me the hit to my pride and my dignity.

Except I can't. Not again. I crawled back to him twice last year, and I'm pretty sure there's a three-strike rule on pathetic daughter bailouts.

So that leaves me with the last-ditch option: I'm going to have to give serious consideration to moving in with a judgmental preacher. Not that he's offered his opinion on my life choices, but I know his type. He believes in rules that some guy wrote down on a stone tablet.

I get up without having made a decision and head down the street. Dee's finally finishing up her argu-versation with Slate and I'd prefer to figure my life out without accepting anyone's help. Help's never free.

It doesn't take long to walk to the edge of town. Wickham Hollow just stops. A block of pretty, Southern homes with front porches, ferns, and rocking chairs, then BOOM. Nothing but train tracks the grass has grown over. From the bird's nest in the crossing guards, I can eliminate hopping a train from my list of escape options.

By the time I drag my sorry self back to the rectory, I have a golf-ball-sized knot in my back and the straps of my bag have dug a furrow into my skin. My bag knocks against my knee with every step and I'm one step away from ditching everything in the street.

"Dixie?" Big, firm hands pry the bag off my shoulder.

Those strong hands shouldn't feel so good skating over my shoulder, not after our disastrous meetup this morning and his patronizing offer to shelter an unhoused stranger. But they do.

A wave of heat sweeps through me—and not the fun kind. Well, okay, there's definitely some sexy heat mixed in there because the man's got those hands. But mostly it's pure aggravation. Irritation. All the shittiest-tion words you can think of. There might be relief buried in there, too, but I'm taking that little secret to my grave.

"Reverend." I scowl. "Don't you have sermons to be writing? Souls to be saving?"

His clothes are dusty and he has smudges of what looks like tar on his forearms.

"Nope." He jogs up the steps and into the rectory.

"Hey!" I bellow after him. "That's my stuff."

He disappears inside, leaving the door wide open. It's a

trap. One of those honeypot things. I'll go inside and gotcha! Humiliation galore.

I hate that I'm checking him out while he's stealing my luggage, but damn if he doesn't still look like he belongs in the Tennessee mountains with their granite rocks and jutting peaks. All broad shoulders and flannel, beard hiding that mouth that does interesting things when he smiles at me. Not remarkable at all except for how he's completely messing with my head.

I need to remember that when he looks at me, he sees someone to fix. Homeless? Find her housing! Check!

I do not want to be a box on this man's to-do list.

He comes back out empty-handed. If he thinks he can move me around like a Monopoly piece, he's about to find out that I'm not the boot or the cute Scottie dog. I'm the freaking battleship.

He's tall, broad, and far too steady for his own good. The kind of man who looks like he's been preparing his whole life to disapprove of someone like me. His arms are crossed, his shoulders squared, and that quiet, unreadable face is set to preacher-neutral, which somehow feels more damning than a full-blown scowl. He has slow, serious good looks—the kind that sneak up on you. Not movie-star handsome, but solid. Reliable. Those brown eyes see more than they miss, and the way his jaw tightens when he's thinking makes me want to rattle him just to see what else he's holding back.

And yet.

Something about the way he stands there—calm and unbothered, like nothing I throw at him can shake him—makes my skin buzz in places it has no business buzzing. I hate that my body hasn't gotten the memo: This man's a walking, talking reminder that I don't belong here. I'm a mess while he's the kind of person who files receipts and flosses nightly.

I stomp up the steps.

"Down the hall," he calls. "Last door on the right."

The guest bedroom screams granny chic—white chenille spread, milk-glass vase full of droopy purple flowers, and a water glass painted with ladybugs. My temporary prison, but whatever. It'll do.

When I trudge back outside, he's leaning against his truck waiting for me, mouth set in a firm line. If I hadn't kissed him last night, I wouldn't know how soft those lips get when he stops being so damn serious.

"Let's get the rest of your things."

"I've got it." It'll take me a dozen trips if I carry everything by hand, but that's a reasonable compromise if it lets me avoid his company. "Or did you not meet your good-deeds quota for the day? You don't have to help me."

"I know." He opens the passenger-side door.

I stomp over and get in. "Then why are you?"

"Because everyone needs a place to land sometimes." He waits for me to buckle up, even though we're driving two blocks at five miles an hour. "Even people who don't want one."

Why does he say it like that? All gentle and sure, like I'm not some train wreck. Just a person with a bag full of crap and nowhere else to go.

I don't know what to do with kindness I haven't paid for.

"Fine, but I'm not staying long."

"Didn't think you would."

He drives down the street like a turtle. It feels like I'm riding a parade float. He waves a hand at someone on the left side of the street. Then at someone on the right. We're nodded at, hollered at, and get the one-hand lift. The honk-and-wave combo. There's absolutely nothing discreet about my move-in.

I slump lower in my seat. "Wow, you're really leaning into this."

"We're getting your stuff."

"You're gonna have so much explaining to do."

When he pulls into the parking lot at Sweetgum Auto, I all but throw myself out of the truck.

The top of my van's grown a potted marigold. The succulent-shaped sticky note stuck to the side says: *For our newest Dirty Girl!*

Two years ago, I was living and playing from this van. A year ago? Same story. Last fucking week? Same song, same refrain. I've always been on my way up but not there yet. Making it big(ger) in the country music world. I'd been sure I had a musical future. A recording contract coming my way and people who'd love my music. Now I'm stuck in Nowhere, Tennessee, and my only career path forward is partnering with my *dad*. I have an empty bank account, a maxed-out credit card, and nothing whatsoever to show for eight years of hustling—except, maybe, just maybe, a half-thought-out song on Instagram.

Jack comes around to stand beside me. "Point out what you need. I'll grab it."

The fight drains out of me like water from a backed-up toilet that finally unclogged—sudden, messy, and with an undignified gurgle. Pride's a real luxury commodity.

"You know what? Fine." I throw my hands up. *You win, Jack. You win.* "I'm accepting your help because I literally have no other options. But don't expect me to be all sunshine and gratitude about it."

Because my whole damn life I've been told that needing help means you're weak, that it means you're not trying hard enough, and I'll be damned if I give anyone—especially Jack with his good intentions and perfect shoulders—the satisfaction of proving Dear Old Dad right.

"Never," he says solemnly, but there's a smile hiding in his beard.

"And I'm going to be a terrible houseguest. Just awful. Singing at all hours. Using all the hot water. Leaving my stuff everywhere."

"I'm trembling with fear."

"You should be." I grab the guitar case from him. "And I always carry my own guitar."

He inclines his head. "As you wish."

And damn him, that almost makes me smile back.

"Do you have anyone else to call?" He grabs a music stand and tilts his head at me.

"I know tons of people! I can have a phone conversation anytime I want but that's very nineties of you." *And none of those conversations would include the words "Hey! Can you be my unpaid moving and pickup service?"*

Jack's obviously big on relationships. He knows everyone we passed. I bet he could knock on any door and whoever answered would happily drive hours and hours to Nashville for him. He's disgustingly friendly.

He shrugs one big shoulder. "And did you call these people?"

"No." *A point to you, Preacher Man.* My soul resists the demand to confess more than a couch potato asked to run a marathon.

"So let's get you moved in. I can find ways for you to help out. I have a whole talent show act to plan."

"Singing?" My ears perk up despite myself. Performance is my turf. My jam. My superpower.

"The choir." He gives me an assessing look. "You know, you could actually help with that. You being a professional singer and all."

"You want me to work with your church choir?" I can't hide the horror in my voice. Hell, I don't *want* to. "I'm a solo act, Jack."

"They need help," he says stubbornly, looking toward the church where a tarp flaps in the breeze over one section of the roof. "We need help, mostly in the form of the prize money from the talent show. It's our best shot at fixing that roof before the whole thing collapses."

Even from here, I can see the missing shingles, the uneven patches, the spots where water damage shows on the eaves.

"I don't do backup vocals—" *anymore* "—and I definitely don't do gospel. Just how terrible are they? And how much money are we talking?"

He doesn't deny they suck. Just smiles that infuriating smile.

"For the roof? Forty thousand, give or take. For the talent show? First prize is fifty."

That's a lot of money.

"I'd rather eat glass than coach church music," I mutter.

After his first trip from the van to the truck, Jack stops to strip off his flannel shirt and toss it in the front seat. He shifts my huge suitcase, plus the plastic bags with the overflow clothes, and then he climbs all the way in to go for the huge box of sheet music crammed in the far corner.

Slate frowns at me from across the lot. He and Deacon have their hands on the back of a rusty old car.

"Gotta roll this old Buick past you and into the bay—y'all mind scootin'?" Deacon asks.

I wave an acknowledgment and watch them lean into the car, muscles straining as they get the heavy beast rolling. The Buick starts creeping forward with a metallic groan. They'll need room to maneuver, so I hop into the van and slam the door shut.

Eight

Girl's in the van. Preacher's in his head.

Jack

It's a harmless sound. A door closing. No big deal.

But the second the van door slides shut with a familiar clunk, I stop breathing.

Dixie makes a joke about carrying her own gear, stepping over a laundry basket and a collapsed pillow. "You've got more biceps than brain if you think you're hauling all this solo."

Her voice sounds like it's coming from underwater.

It's not dark. Plenty of sunlight comes through the windshield and the side windows. I can see fine. And it smells faintly of coffee and lavender dryer sheets. Old dust maybe. The mattress eats up most of the floor space, so we've been grabbing stuff from the edges. We've cleared a path. It's fine. There's another guitar case balanced on a pile of books, and a stickered cooler wedged in the corner. It's cozy, lived-in. Home, in the way a van can be.

And yet—

The air feels thin. My chest pulls tight like I've wrapped

an old seat belt around my ribs, clicked it in place, and then it's locked up the way belts do at the worst possible time. I'm pinned here.

I try to move, but my hand is stuck, braced on the metal lip of a shelf above the back wheel like it's the only thing holding me upright. Great. Now I'm guy who needs rescuing instead of doing the rescuing.

"Jack?" Dixie leans toward me, a frown in her voice. "You okay?"

I blink. And I'm eleven again.

We're parked behind a gas station somewhere outside Asheville. It's cold. My little sister is crying, and my mom's trying to sing her to sleep. There's only so many times you can hear "Hush Little Baby" before you scream. That's what my dad says. Like it's a joke except Mom's shooting him dagger eyes and no one's laughing. His mouth is pulled all tight. He shuts up and goes back to pretending like everything's fine—like soup on a camp stove is a grand adventure, like the car isn't our home now.

There's no room to stretch out. No room to breathe. I can't get out because we're all stuck together in a big knot. My knees are jammed up against the back of the front seat, and I'm trying not to panic because if I panic, my mom will panic, and if she panics—

"Jack." Dixie's voice. "Talk to me."

I swallow, try to look at her, but end up staring at the floor instead. Ridges and grooves. *Cool.* Gray, not super exciting, all as expected. Rust spots run along the seams, kind of like a map—the jagged edges are coastlines, with little "islands" branching off. I should seal those for her, or she'll have bigger problems than a broken fuel pump.

"Can we open the door, please." It's not a question.

There's concern on her face as she reaches for the latch, cracking the door.

The air isn't fresh, but it's air. I breathe. Once. Twice.

Be still. The words come automatically, a Bible verse I learned long before seminary. *Be still, and know that I am God. Be still and know that I am God. Bestillandknowthatiam—*

I force myself to slow down as the front half of an old Buick rolls past the passenger-side window. It's close enough to scrape the van's paint. Dixie shrugs. *It's fine.*

The driver's side window is down, a hula girl on the dash bobbing wildly with each bump. Then the trunk drags past— heavy, dented, with a crooked dealership badge barely hanging on. A metal-on-metal clunk comes from somewhere underneath.

Slate's leaning all his weight on the frame, sweat darkening his shirt, jaw set like he's moving a mountain instead of a Buick. He's favoring his left shoulder. Probably tweaked it again. Deacon pushes from the other side.

The whole thing coasts on and on and on for what feels like forever before Slate snarls, "Clear."

"You want to sit this one out?" Dixie asks, shoving the door all the way open.

She doesn't sound freaked out. Or sorry for me. She doesn't pepper me with questions or try to fix my shit. She gets it.

"I'm good." I think I mean it. It's stupid to fall apart over a closed door but I don't linger inside, either. "But I'll take that hand with the rest of the boxes."

It's not pride talking—I know my limits, and I'm back within them.

She smirks. "Guess that makes me your roadie."

I huff a laugh, the knot in my chest loosening. Dixie hops down from the van and grabs a box like nothing happened.

"Here." She passes me the lighter box with a wink and takes the heavier one herself, her hair twisted up into a messy bun that's lost the battle to contain her auburn curls. Little pieces have escaped to frame her face, and the whole chaotic mess makes her look adorable in a way that would annoy the hell out of her if I said so out loud.

Focus on the fresh air. Open space. Trucks with doors that stay open.

By the time we reach the truck, the panic has faded into something warmer. Something off-limits. She's just seen me fall apart and somehow made it okay.

Thank God for beards. At least she can't see how completely gone I am.

Nine

Refrain: Every love story needs a slow burn

Dixie

It's the day after Jack moved me into his place. To celebrate my near death by exposure yesterday, I dress for spring break in Miami so I can pretend it's a humid hundred degrees out. I'm wearing a cropped T-shirt and a pair of pink-striped boxers. There's plenty of midriff exposure happening, plus there are rhinestone horseshoes over certain areas of my chest. It's very *Girls Gone Wild* for Sunday morning in a parsonage. Or monastery. Whatever. Do I care?

Nope.

My phone buzzes with a list of dates and a message from my dad.

Pick one. See you in the studio!

Delete.

Other people think my dad's super supportive. My sister,

my brother. All my family's myriad Facebook friends. He's a loving father, someone who wants what's best for me.

That's such bullshit. It's a constant emotional tug-of-war between love, resentment, and exhaustion. He wants to know why I won't sign with his label? Maybe because I don't want to spend my life singing backup in someone else's dream.

My dad's an emotional vampire. Drains you dry, then drop-kicks your husk to the curb.

We did a project together when I was fifteen. He offered to let me sing backup vocals on a new album. I sang *ooh* a billion times, and not one of them met his exacting standards. He replaced me and I vowed never again. The album tanked because Karma's a bitch like me.

Except now I'm a bitch with followers. Holy shit. I refresh Instagram and the numbers keep climbing—20K, 25K, 30K views on my song about Preacher Man. I keep screenshotting because what the hell? I post song snippets all the time to see what sticks, but nothing's ever blown up like this.

The smell of coffee eventually propels me, unwilling and half dead, away from my phone and out of the bed. Somewhere in the house—*my temporary house, definitely not my home*—Jack Carter's awake. Doing things. Probably being competent, responsible, and making drinkable coffee.

I hate him.

I hate morning.

I hate everything.

Dragging myself upright, I rub my face, wincing as my joints protest. There's the usual shitty dull stiffness in my fingers. It isn't super bad, but "not bad" turns into "very bad" fast if I don't take care of myself. One of the many reasons I'd agreed yesterday to crash in the rectory rather than my van. I shuffle out of the room on pure caffeine-seeking instinct, following the scent like a bloodhound.

Jack Carter, *Preacher Man*, stands in his kitchen, crisp white T-shirt stretched over broad shoulders, dark hair mussed from sleep. He's barefoot, cradling a coffee mug, bathed in golden morning light that makes everyone look good. Georgia Peach has parked her furry behind next to the fruit bowl, gnawing on something that's either an apricot pit or the bones of Jack's last houseguest.

Could go either way.

"You are way too awake." My voice is still rough with sleep.

Amusement flickers over his face. "Good morning to you, too."

If he calls me *sunshine*, I'll kill him and bribe Georgia Peach to help hide the body.

I grunt. Squinting at him through my bed-head chaos, I point an accusing finger. "How. How are you like this? It's *early*."

"It's six thirty." In his world, normal humans wake at sunrise on Sunday. I bet he sets New Year's resolutions and keeps them.

"You disgust me."

Jack chuckles, filling a second mug that reads *Episcopalians Do It Liturgically*. "Coffee?"

I snatch it and take a cautious sip. It's good. Annoyingly good. If the whole preaching thing falls through, he could become a barista at that local coffee van, charming church ladies with his voice and muscled *forearms*.

Unfortunately, the caffeine means I'm now awake enough to notice how his dress slacks cling to his muscled thighs. Twelve out of ten would recommend looking again.

I hate that, too.

Jack leans against the counter, arms crossed, watching me guzzle his peace offering with trademark easy patience. "How are you?"

Hookup or not, we aren't friends. I'm not oversharing about my RA or my well-founded fear of homelessness. Ergo, I roll my eyes. "None of your business."

His expression doesn't change. "That bad? I just figured I'd ask."

I wish he wouldn't.

I take another sip. Caffeine will make me less irritable, right? Long shot. I might have to settle for a warm feeling in the pit of my stomach (absolutely unrelated to proximity to Jack). The barest loosening of my bad mood. Not enough to make me *pleasant*, but enough that I realize I need to counteract this moment of human decency before things get out of hand.

I set my coffee down. Time to be *annoying*.

I march to the fridge, yank it open, start pulling out the eggs, cheese, and butter I bought in Wickham Hollow's one and only grocery store yesterday, depleting my cash reserves to four bucks in the process. It's also the bait, beer, and general store. Everything's cheap, generic brands. Apparently, the fish aren't any pickier about their worms than the fishermen are about their beer.

I flash him a grin, spin toward the stove, and crank the burner on high. Then, I take a deep breath and belt out the raunchiest country song I can make up on the spot. Hey, if it's any good, I can post that on Instagram, too!

"I wanna sin, I wanna pray,
I wanna have the devil's way
With my preacher man..."

Jack scrubs a hand over his face, mussing his beard. Bits stick out in a way that's adorable if you like your guys hairy and wild.

"Dixie."

"Told me meet him at the altar—" I crack an egg with gusto *"—but I met him in the back pew..."*

Jack groans. His misery makes me smile. That, and the intensity with which he watches me.

"You don't like my music, Preacher Man?"

You're welcome, Jack. You'll never look at the back pew the same way again.

"I have to go lead a church service at eight."

I drop the spatula and whip around. "Oh, *right*! Sunday! *Your* fun day! You tell people how to be good and decent and not take strange women home from bars!"

He laughs. "Dixie—"

I cut him off. "Wait. Are you running out the door to avoid setting house rules? Because if we're going to live together, I need to know what I'm not supposed to do. Imagine how I could go wrong. Just lay them on me. Here's a story prompt. Thou shalt not—what?"

He looks from me to the pan, where my eggs are now burning, and reaches over to turn the heat down. His arm almost touches mine and he smells good. Cedar and laundry detergent? Does white cotton have a special scent? Can I bottle it? Fuck eggs. Fuck church. This makes me want to throw my arms around him and eat him up.

Abort, abort.

He nods. Agreement with the eat-him-up plan? Great! "One, no stealing the last cup of coffee. Not unless you make a new pot."

Oh, *riiiiight*. I arrange my face into over-the-top listening.

"Sounds reasonable," I say. "Agreed."

"Two, respect the quiet hours."

He rinses his mug, sets it in the sink. I make a show of writing a note with my invisible pen. "Preacher Man needs sleep, and so does the country star. Midnight jam sessions and five a.m. Bible studies are hereby banned. Got it."

The corners of his eyes crinkle. Can't. Look. Away.

"Three, do not, under any circumstances, let Huck sneak into the bed. He will act innocent. He is not. You will regret it."

"Wow… I'm not sure what to say. I've noticed zero bad behavior from Huck. He's a perfect angel."

"Four, no passive-aggressive notes. Texts." He thinks. "Or songs."

Seriously. *Songs?*

"Give me an example. Also, I'm gonna need alcohol for this conversation."

I whip out my phone and text Deacon. Or Slate. One of the two. Those two are practically interchangeable, and I'm not sure whose phone gets the Sweetgum Auto texts. I'm sure it's one of them. Doesn't matter—

I'm not leaving my alcohol needs to chance.

Need emergency tequila delivery. Will also take Bailey's. Or anything that goes in coffee.

Alcohol's a terrible coping mechanism, but today's an exception.

Whoever's manning the phone returns a middle-finger emoji. My money's on Slate.

Jack's amused expression tells me he read my text. "It's not ten a.m. You can't buy alcohol yet. State law."

"Someone must have a personal stash." Which would work better for me, seeing as I have super-limited cash. "And you shouldn't be so judgy about drinking. We did meet in a bar."

When he gives me a look, I lean into it. "I bet you've heard worse in your confession booth."

"That's private. Plus, reconciliation is optional and there's no confessional. This isn't reality TV. Five, as noted yesterday, no breaking each other's hearts. No sex."

I wink. "I believe I only mentioned sex. Your heart's one hundred percent safe. Fine."

"Fine?"

"Fine," I repeat.

I look down at a tug on my coffee cup. The handle has

grown a chinchilla and Georgia Peach is slurping my coffee like it's hers.

"Your chinchilla is possessed. Have you considered an exorcism?"

Jack's mouth curves up. "Not that kind of preacher."

"Sure?"

"Very." He eyes me calmly. "If you're concerned, I can call a Catholic friend. They teach demon exorcism in seminary. I also know an evangelical who does deliverance."

I'm almost sure he's teasing.

"I notice she drank my coffee and not yours."

Jack shrugs. "She's got a caffeine problem."

"Or a boundary problem."

He strokes the fluff demon like a Bond villain.

The chinchilla glares at me. I've eaten bigger burritos.

As if she read my mind, she starts barking—loud, sharp sounds I translate as *I see you, I do not like you, and I will scream about it.*

I concede the mug but meet her beady gaze. "I don't want your man. You can keep him, honey."

Jack gives in and laughs. Just lets go and bellows, a full-on, belly-shaking laugh.

"I'm leaving," he wheezes, grabbing a button-up shirt from the back of a chair and shoving his feet into a pair of shiny dress shoes. He's forgotten his socks and he's super early for his church gig. I win!

"You mean you're *fleeing*," I correct.

"I'm *going to church*. To do my job."

"Uh-huh. Running away from temptation, just like the Bible says."

Jack levels a long, unreadable look at me, then—because he's *infuriating*—smirks.

"Enjoy your breakfast, Dixie," he says, voice low, full of something I *don't* want to name.

Because he can't stop being a nice guy, he puts Georgia

Peach back in her mini mansion on his way out. I shamelessly stalk him to the door because if I'm being abandoned with a one-pound psycho killer, I'll have to take steps.

I stand there, watching him lope down the stairs and head over to the church. Best commute ever: short and quick. The view's amazing. Not just his long legs and lumberjack shoulders eating up distance like it's nothing. His outsides are pretty, but his insides—those are the true prize. He won't ever change. Doesn't have a deceptive bone in his big, beautiful body. What I see is what I get. With him, I feel safe.

The parking lot's filling up with cars. Ladies in hats go up the stairs where Jack disappeared. Someone hammers on the organ, a wheezing, out-of-tune rendition of… I haven't got a clue. Could be music. Maybe.

My phone buzzes. Pick a date, my dad writes. You wanna do that preacher song of yours? I could be convinced.

I leave him on read but if Dad's heard about it, that means the song's getting even more attention than I realized.

I can't help myself—I open Instagram to recheck the numbers on my post. Holy shit. The view count has exploded since I last looked. Comments are pouring in faster than I can read them, and my DMs are packed with heart-eye emojis and fire symbols. My follower count has jumped by thousands, and there's some kind of official Instagram notification with a blue badge that I should probably check out.

People aren't just listening to the song—they're obsessed with it. With him.

With *us*.

Ten

Interlude: One guitar and a Plott hound

Jack

"Jesus Christ!"

I freeze in the doorway, hands up. Dixie's got Huck in a protective grip and hairspray aimed at my head.

"Sorry." I keep my voice low. It's been days since she moved in—you'd think by now she'd realize I do come home. "Didn't mean to scare you."

"I'm fine." The glare she shoots me could strip paint. She sets the hairspray down but doesn't ease up on the attitude. "You nearly got an eyeful, Reverend."

I step into the living room—carefully, because apparently I'm the intruder here. Dixie's clearly been camped on my floor for who knows how long, guitar across her lap, fire crackling behind her. Her hair's a disaster and there's tension in every line of her body. She looks like a hedgehog that's been poked one too many times—all spikes and defensive posture, daring the world to try her just one more time.

I probably shouldn't poke the hedgehog.

But then again, when have I ever been smart?

My phone buzzes in my pocket. Again. It's been going off all day—people asking about some "internet situation" that I haven't had time to check on yet. In my defense, I've been busy trying to keep the church roof from becoming an impromptu skylight. Still, as I haven't posed for any nudes—that I know of—or accidentally livestreamed myself in my underwear, whatever this is, it probably isn't my fault. Which, in my experience, means it'll definitely be worse than if it actually was. When you screw up yourself, you know what you're dealing with. When other people drag you into their chaos? That's when things get really interesting. And by interesting, I mean the kind of interesting that makes you change your name and move to Alaska.

Instead, I look at Dixie, sitting in my house. I love those walls behind her. I almost fucked her up against the one by the front door and it deserves to be memorialized. Maybe I'll buy a bronze plaque. I could have it inscribed:

ON THIS WALL
circa three hours after meeting
DIXIE PEARL, COUNTRY MUSIC
SENSATION-TO-BE,
and
REVEREND JACK CARTER, VERY MUCH
NOT THAT KIND OF PREACHER,
did nearly engage in
SACREDLY QUESTIONABLE BEHAVIOR
between the hours of 11:00 p.m. and 03:00 a.m.
before being interrupted by a judgmental dog and/or crippling
panic on the part of said star.

If I hang it where my visitors can see it, it'll save me answering their questions. PLEASE RESPECT THE WOODWORK would also work.

"Sorry," I say again, because what else do you say when you walk into your own house and get threatened with Aqua Net? She stares back without answering. From the wreck of her hair and the way she's holding herself, whatever she's working on isn't going well. I hazard a guess. "Writing?"

"Trying to." She gets to her feet—she's super careful, like her joints aren't cooperating. "Not having much success."

She walks over to the front door and reaches for the lock. We haven't talked about it, but she only locks up when I'm not here. When her eyes meet mine, I can read the question clear as day: You gonna freak out if this is locked?

"Please," I say, and she leaves it unlocked without a word.

Smart woman. Multiple exit points are my favorite thing in the world.

"Long day?" I settle on the floor next to where she'd been sitting.

"You could say that." She drops back down, cross-legged, settling her guitar across her lap again. Huck cuddles up against her, the traitor. "Yours?"

"Church council meeting. They're real concerned about my 'living situation.'" I make exaggerated air quotes.

Her mouth quirks up. "Scandalous."

"That's one word for it." My phone buzzes again. I ignore it. "They also failed to come up with money for the roof, so there's that."

"How much do you still need?"

"The entire forty grand. Give or take about two hundred bucks."

She whistles. "That's a lot of bake sales. I can see why you're all in on the talent show plan."

"Tell me about it."

We sit in comfortable quiet for a minute. It's weirdly nice. The fire pops and settles. Huck sighs and sprawls across both our legs like he owns us (he totally does). Outside, I can hear the wind picking up—probably more rain rolling in. Perfect. More holes in the roof to patch.

"I was thinking," I say, because I've been worrying about her all day and can't help myself. "You're going to be here awhile. Maybe we could figure out some work for you. If you want. Dee mentioned the bakery could use some help."

The temperature in the room drops twenty degrees. "You think I'm lazy?"

"What? No. Not at all."

She points her guitar pick at me. "You think I just loll around in my van all day, eating gas station snacks and waiting for a recording contract to fall through the sunroof?"

"That's incredibly specific. Also, no."

She's on her feet again, pacing. It makes her boobs bounce beneath her tank top. I hate myself for noticing. "I've spent the last eight years sleeping in bars, hustling gigs, burning through voice memos and vocal cords and pairs of boots, trying to make something out of nothing. I've played in ten states and half of them paid me in beer and exposure. But sure, Jack. Let's talk about how I should get a real job so I can be a respectable adult."

Well, shit. This took a turn.

Her whole body's wound tight—arms crossed, chin up, feet planted like she's waiting for a fight. It kills me, seeing her like that.

"I didn't say you needed a real job," I try. "I'd like to see you safe—"

"Well, guess what? Safety's not exactly guaranteed in the music industry, Jack. It's rejection and heartbreak, singing in smoky bars where nobody gives enough fucks to even clap. So sorry I'm not living my life according to your neat, orderly rules."

I hold up my hands. "Dixie—"

"No, really." She gives me a sweeping, sarcastic bow. "Apologies for not living up to your small-town-preacher standards.

I should've gone into accounting. Or pottery. Something wholesome and quiet, right?"

I stare at her—this beautiful, exhausted, firecracker of a woman who somehow thinks I'm judging her when all I want is to make sure she has a pillow and a place to breathe.

"You think I'm judging you?"

She scoffs, but it sounds less sharp now. "You chose the ministry, Jack. That means you think you know what's right for everyone."

"That's not why I chose it." The words come out rougher than I mean them to. "I chose it because I want people to know they're enough. As they are. That they're not alone. That there's always room for them."

Something shifts in her face. The wall cracks, just a little.

She slumps down on the floor and rests her elbows on her knees. "My dad wants me to sign on to this Christmas album. Wants me to join him, sing backup like I'm still seventeen and lucky to be there. Says I need to do it. That I'm going nowhere on my own. Maybe he's not wrong."

"Like hell he's not."

She glares at me. "I don't know if I can do it anymore, Jack. All of it. The push, the hustle, the proving. I don't know if I'm enough for that kind of life."

And there she is—the woman beneath the armor. I want to wrap her up and keep her safe from every person who's ever made her feel like she had to prove her worth.

"Maybe I'm here because it feels so good to just stop. To not have to claw my way forward every second of the day. To just exist without selling a version of myself that people will clap for."

"Dixie." I lean toward her. "You are enough."

She doesn't call me out for sounding like a cheesy Instagram quote. "But I'm tired, Jack. Sick and tired."

"Of what?"

"Of always having to be on. Of hustling every damn day just to prove I deserve to take up space."

My phone buzzes again, insistent. This time she hears it, too.

"Popular guy," she says, but there's something off about her tone.

I pull it out, meaning to silence it, but the notifications keep rolling in. Missed calls from two members of my congregation, Deacon, even Bishop Morgan. That's a whole lot of outreach. My stomach drops. Maybe it's not accidental nudes but my shacking up with a lady? I knew it wouldn't be a popular decision.

"Jack." Dixie's voice has a real careful edge to it. "You might want to not check your phone for a while."

Guilt's written all over her beautiful face. Plain as day.

"Dixie. What did you do?"

She pulls a face. "It's not... I mean, I didn't think... Nothing big. Just posted something. Online."

I suspect I'm about to find out what my *internet situation* is. "Posted what?"

"A song. I wrote a song and I shared it. With my very small number of followers."

"About what?"

She messes with her guitar strings. "Just about feelings. It's a really good song."

Despite everything, I almost smile. "That supposed to make me feel better?"

"Maybe a little?" She shrugs. "Or we can commiserate with each other about our dismal career prospects and wallow in despair. Up to you."

"You know what the worst part is?"

"I'm sure you're about to tell me," she grumbles.

"I don't care about the song."

She frowns. "So either you're dismissing my life's work, or

you're totally cool with not going online and looking it up? You have zero feelings either way?"

"About whatever's blowing up on my phone? Nope." I shove my phone back in my pocket. "I care that you think offering you work means I see you as some kind of charity case."

"But you totally do."

"Dixie." I scrub my face with both hands. "You've been in town for four days. Living in my house for ninety-six hours. I have not had time to develop a savior complex. I offered you work because you're stuck here and I thought you might be bored. Stressed about money. Willing to help Dee and her sister out because they actually do need a hand. Pick one or all of those, okay?"

"Huh."

"Yeah. Huh."

We stare at each other across my living room. The fire pops. Huck sighs dramatically in his sleep, like he's disappointed in both of us.

"This is so weird," she says finally.

"What is?"

"Having an actual conversation instead of just…" She puffs out her cheeks. Exhales.

"Instead of what?"

"You know what."

I do know. *Sex*. And now I'm thinking about it again, which isn't helpful when I'm trying to have a serious conversation with boundaries and expectations and all the grown-up stuff that comes after you sleep with someone you barely know.

"Should there be a next time," I start. Stop. Yeah. I don't want there to be a next time, right? That's a terrible idea. "If you feel the need to process your feelings some more about our…whatever this was…could you please talk to me before broadcasting it to the internet?"

"Where's the fun in that?"

"Dixie."

"Fine. Point taken," she says, strumming the guitar. "For what it's worth, I really didn't think anyone would pay attention to some random song from a nobody musician."

"I should probably…" I wave toward the door.

"Yeah. You go work and stay off the internet." She settles back down with her guitar. "I'll just be here. Not writing any more songs about recent life events."

"Appreciate it." I head out, then pause in the doorway. "Dixie? Next time you have an existential crisis, you can always just knock on my door."

"Noted."

"I'm a good listener. Occupational hazard."

"I'll keep that in mind, Preacher Man."

I step out. Through the wall, I can hear her start playing again—something about bright lights and the big city that 100 percent doesn't sound like it's about me.

Which is probably for the best.

Because four days in, the last thing either of us needs is more complications.

Eleven

Girl to the rescue!

Dixie

"Hey, sunshine. Miss me?" I stroll into Sweetgum Auto on Friday. The place smells like oil, despair, and tire rubber. *The Great British Bake Off* plays on a cracked iPad. Paul Hollywood is judging a sad croissant, which feels like a metaphor for my life.

Slate grunts from under an ancient Chevrolet. Classic.

"I see you're not a Friday Friyay! kind of person."

"No."

"Do you like any of the days of the week?"

Pretty sure he flashes me the bird from underneath that car.

It's only been a week since it died on me, but I miss my van. We've slept together, been through shit together, broken down together. I can't just abandon her, so I've popped by the auto shop unannounced, fully prepared to annoy the ever-loving grump out of Slate until he coughs up an update.

My phone buzzes—another Instagram notification. Ten thousand likes. Fifteen thousand. Someone screen-recorded my post and slapped it on TikTok with: "POV: You accidentally wrote a thirst trap about your small-town preacher." The comments are getting wild. My favorite so far?

Girl said "bless me daddy" and meant it.

I shove the phone back into my pocket. What started as a throwaway post is spiraling completely out of control. My agent called Monday morning, practically vibrating through the phone. "Whatever you're doing, keep doing it. Your engagement is through the roof—labels are paying attention. Is he real? Can you get photos together?"

What am I supposed to do, follow Jack around with my phone like some stalker? Turn every moment into content? Jack said he's not going to listen to the song, but come on. Someone's definitely played it for him by now, right?

"I thought I'd check on my girl." I walk over like I own the place. "Y'all feeding her? Letting her watch her stories?"

"Still dead." Slate wipes his hands on a rag that looks suspiciously like a flowered dish towel.

Deacon leans out of the office. "Don't be dramatic. Technically, she's in a medically induced coma. Plus, her parts are in Memphis. Or maybe Mexico. Depends on which tracking number you believe."

"So, she's on a spiritual journey. Finding herself. Maybe learning Spanish."

Slate shrugs. For him, that's basically a sonnet.

"When do I get her back?"

"Maybe next month," Deacon says. "Maybe ten years. Depends on the international supply chain and God's will."

"Ten years?" I mock-gasp. "Lord, I'll have to marry the preacher just for a ride to Kroger." Slate's look could etch glass, so I turn to leave. I've got my update. My work is done here.

"If my van ends up in a dramatic cross-border car chase, I want her back with at least one bullet scar and a heroic backstory."

"No promises," he grumbles.

Armed with caffeine and a mission that's only half about avoiding my viral preacher problem, I march across town (all two blocks of it) to Jack's office.

I kick open his office door with my boot. "SHOWTIME, PREACHER!"

He looks up from a mountain of paperwork, hair mussed where he's raked a hand through it and beard sticking out sideways. "Is there an emergency?"

I slide a coffee to him. "Don't be ridiculous. I come bearing solutions and delicious pastries."

He pours half the coffee into his own mug and hands it to me. "What is this?"

"Sweet salvation in a cup." I plant myself in the beat-up armchair, toss the doughnut box on his desk, and kick my boots up on a pile of DIY construction manuals. "Black coffee, two shots of espresso, and a lemon-glazed cruller to ease the burn."

His eyebrow arches. "You went to the bakery? About that job I mentioned?"

I snort. "God, no. I've got bigger plans than bagging muffins. Besides, Dee was way more interested in telling me about your boring coffee habits. 'One sugar, splash of cream, and a cinnamon twist'—same order every time. You're living in caffeinated Groundhog Day."

He takes a cautious sip and winces. "Wow."

I pull out a crumpled flyer and slap it on his desk. "We need to talk about this talent show you mentioned in deeply disappointing undetail the other day."

"We?"

"Did you or did you not hire me to help out?"

"I asked if you would help."

"Right. So you've got me working for free for a good

cause." I shrug. "You need help, I'm living in your guest room, and I brought pastries. We're officially collaborators. Now tell me—what exactly do I have to work with, and what's at stake? I wasn't really paying attention when you tried to run me through it before."

"Raise the Roof is an annual talent show for participating churches. The top prize is fifty thousand dollars. Thirty for second place and fifteen for third. The money goes to your charity or organization of choice. Five judges score each performance—usually a mix of local music teachers, choir directors, and community leaders."

I snag a maple-glazed doughnut. "So that's roof money."

"If we win."

"We'll win. Manifest it, baby. Tell me about the choir. You have a song picked out?"

He hesitates. "They're enthusiastic? And 'How Great Thou Art'?"

I scrunch my eyes shut, running scenarios. Someone will crack on the first note. Half the choir will sing it like their grandpa, the other half like a funeral dirge. And the second we hit "Then sings my soul," everyone in the audience will sing along in different keys. It's the kind of song where everyone thinks they know it, but they're all remembering different versions.

"Bless your hearts."

Jack goes for fatal optimism. "Did you hear them in church on Sunday?"

"I did. But I was unaware you were banking all your hopes and dreams on that exact set of people." I shove the rest of the doughnut in my mouth. "Tell me your competition is equally bad."

"They're excellent, and they need a fellowship hall." Jack, being Jack, is scrupulously fair.

I don't think he's going to be open to sabotage.

"Dee gets scared and can't sing in public. Slate can hit one note perfectly, but it's a note that makes him sound like Huck's twin." He pauses. "Your help is definitely needed."

I press my palms to my face. "We're gonna need to take Huck for the cute vote."

I'm painfully aware of my phone's weight in my pocket. Jack hasn't mentioned my viral moment again.

Fine. If he wants to forget I've accidentally made him internet famous, I can play along. We'll focus on the choir, win his roof money, and speak no more of the song that has twenty thousand likes and climbing.

I can keep my mouth shut. Probably.

Twelve

Girl panics

Dixie

"I'm not going."

"You said you would." Jack leans against the doorframe of the guest room, arms crossed over his chest. The Monday afternoon light catches in his beard, turning it from dark brown to something warmer. His look says he's trying not to smile at my refusal and it's annoying.

"I said I'd think about it," I correct. "What kind of name is 'Dirty Girls' anyway? Sounds like the world's most disappointing stripping troupe. 'Watch as Marjorie removes her gardening glove…very…slowly.'"

"It's a garden club." The corners of his mouth twitch. "They plant things."

"Revolutionary." I flip through my notebook without reading it. I'll be honest: it's surprisingly hard to write when people actually *like* the last thing you wrote. "Do they also water them? Groundbreaking stuff."

He doesn't take the bait. Just waits. Patient as a saint, which he basically is.

I hate that I like that about him.

"Fine." I slam the notebook shut. "But only because I've written zero songs today and need human interaction that doesn't involve a preacher or his judgmental chinchilla."

"Georgia Peach will be devastated."

He does *not* say that he will be devastated. Duly noted, Jack. Duly noted.

Twenty minutes later, we're walking down Main Street. It's quiet except for the occasional truck and I'm feeling twitchy.

"They've been meeting for years," Jack says. "Dee wanted to beautify the town but couldn't get funding, so she rallied friends."

"Vigilante gardeners. Do they wear masks and carry bolt cutters to 'liberate' plants from corporate nurseries? 'This petunia deserves to be free!'"

He laughs. "I once watched Dee go full John Wick on a squirrel that was terrorizing her hydrangeas."

His hand brushes mine and I get that stupid electric shock feeling. My body is apparently sixteen years old.

"The choir needs something special for the talent show." I'm desperate for safer topics that don't make me imagine him touching more than my fingers.

"They'll have you."

My heart does a stupid somersault. "I'm serious. Your competition has been doing this for years. I googled them."

"So what do you suggest?" His voice sounds closer, like he's stepped in nearer. Or maybe I drifted toward him. That seems likely—Jack's the magnetic north for my compass.

"Something unexpected. Something that makes the judges sit up and notice."

"Like 'Highway to Hell'?" he deadpans.

I bark out a laugh. "That would shake things up."

"We're here." He stops in front of a bungalow with fairy

lights and way too many plants on the porch. "Run your ideas by the girls. They're all active in the choir, except for Dee—she hides in the back and mouths the words."

"You're not coming in?"

"Ladies only. I'll pick you up at nine."

Ladies only is as outdated as garden party gloves, but I'll save that revolution for another day.

"I can walk myself home. I'm not five."

"I know." He runs a hand through his hair, looking like he's fighting some internal battle. "But maybe I want an excuse to find you under the stars later."

Whoops. There goes the careful distance we've been maintaining. Our eyes meet, and I watch him realize exactly what he just said. His cheeks turn pink and he looks like he wants to crawl under the nearest rock. For a second I think he might actually kiss me right here in the middle of Main Street anyhow. Part of me wants him to, part of me wants to laugh my ass off at how mortified he looks. I don't think he meant to say that at *all*.

Then the front door bursts open.

"Is that our country star?" Dee calls out. "Get in here! We need your opinion on cocktails!"

Jack steps back quickly. "Nine o'clock."

"It's a date," I say without thinking, then wince.

"Yeah. It is." His smile could power the town.

I'm screwed.

"Ladies!" Dee announces as she drags me inside. "Our newest Dirty Girl! And yes, I saw that moment with the Reverend. We're not discussing it until wine."

The living room is packed with women of all ages. Tilly, Dee's twin sister, waves from a corner where she's arranging pots in precise rows of four. Where Dee's hair bounces in its pixie cut, Tillie's longer brunette waves are pulled back in a complex braid, and she's wearing a soft green cardigan that's got flour on one cuff. The coffee table is loaded with wine bottles, cheese plates, and what might be gardening catalogs but could be porno for all I know about plants.

"We're not actually that dirty," says a woman with silver hair, handing me a glass of the aforementioned wine. "More dirt-adjacent."

"We also gossip, drink, and make questionable plant purchases at two a.m.," Tilly adds calmly. Where conversation with Dee is like being hit with a fire hose, Tilly's more of deep, slow river. "I now have seventeen different kinds of hostas." She holds up a small potted plant. "This little guy was inspired by a romance where the heroine was a botanist. Completely unnecessary purchase, but the book made me do it."

"Don't forget man-bashing as an alternative to plants," someone calls out. "That's forty percent of today's agenda. Fifty percent in the summer when they all refuse to wear shirts while mowing lawns but still expect dinner at six."

The room erupts in laughter.

"Dixie doesn't need to bash men," Dee says with an aggressive wink. "She's got our resident holy man wrapped around her finger tighter than clematis on a trellis."

"Wait a minute—" Tilly squints at me over her wineglass. "Are you the one who wrote that song? About the preacher? I've been playing that on repeat!"

Half the room starts humming the melody, and someone calls out, "Sing it!"

"Absolutely not." I'm grinning despite myself. My first fans!

"She's living in the rectory," someone stage-whispers.

"In the guest room," I clarify. "Different zip codes. My vagina's Fort Knox. I sleep with the door locked, a chair under the knob, and a moat full of crocodiles."

"Mmm-hmm." Dee's eyebrows disappear into her bangs. "How's that working out? Need some chicken? A drawbridge?"

"Can we talk about plants instead? I was promised dirt."

They mercifully change subjects. For the next two hours,

I learn more about plants than any human should know. To-matoes have feelings and hate peppers. Some soil is fancy five-star hotel dirt, some is the equivalent of a highway rest stop bathroom and we do *not* go there.

Weirdly, I don't hate it. Plants don't care if you chart on *Billboard*. They grow—or die—regardless of your Instagram following or how many venues you play. They have the au-dacity to exist without a five-year career plan.

"So," Dee says, sliding next to me as I murder a succulent with my repotting skills, "what's your next move?"

"Not killing this plant."

She swats me on the arm. "With Jack."

I focus on my dirt. "There's no move. I leave when my van's fixed."

"That's what you keep saying. But I see the way you look at him, too."

"Like he's my temporary landlord. A breathing, walking rental agreement with excellent beard conditioner."

"Sure, Jan."

I snort. "Did you just meme me?"

"I'm young and hip," she says mock-seriously. "I know all the cool-cat slang. Yeet. YOLO. The kids still say 'on fleek,' right?"

"Every day." I grin despite myself. There's no way she's older than me. "But I'm not in the man market. I'm more window-shopping. From across the street. In the dark. With no plans to ever buy."

Someone across the room squeals, "Look who's here!"

Slate looms in the doorway. He's holding a toolbox and scowling. Apparently, he's the exception to the ladies-only rule.

"Slate!" Dee goes pink. "I didn't expect you tonight."

"Sink," he grunts, holding up the toolbox like a shield. "Leaking."

"Right. The sink." She tucks hair behind her ear. "That I mentioned."

"Three weeks ago," Tilly observes quietly. "She's mentioned it approximately forty-seven times since then."

Dee skips toward the kitchen. "Ladies, don't wait for me. This could take a while. Slate is very thorough."

The moment they disappear, the room erupts.

"Ten bucks says he needs to order a part."

"Twenty he stays for dinner."

"You're both wrong," Tilly says matter-of-factly. "The sexual tension is thick enough to frost a cake with, but it's been going on since high school. Sometimes I think about locking them in the walk-in freezer at the bakery and not letting them out until they've worked through whatever's keeping them apart." She frowns contemplatively. "There's an emergency latch but he won't know that. It would be safe."

I smile into my wine. Church ladies have zero chill.

The doorbell rings, drawing everyone's attention.

"Nine o'clock already?" Tilly checks her vintage floral watch. "Your carriage awaits, Cinderella. Try not to lose a shoe on your way out—though it might be fun to see Reverend Jack going door to door with a strappy sandal."

I roll my eyes, but my heart does stupid backflips as I collect my jacket and the potted succulent Tilly insists I take home. "It's an elephant bush," she says, handing it to me. "Practically indestructible. Just ignore it and it'll be fine."

Jack's waiting at the bottom of the steps, hands in his pockets. When he sees me, his chagrined smile could stop traffic.

"Have fun?"

"It wasn't terrible. Don't tell them I said that."

"Your secret's safe." He eyes my plant. "Nice succulent."

"It thrives on neglect and is hardy as fuck. We're perfect for each other."

We start walking back. Close but not touching. Look at us putting our walls back up.

"Learn anything interesting?"

"Tomatoes and potatoes have a whole Romeo and Juliet

thing going on. They die if you plant them next to each other. Also the whole town thinks we're sleeping together."

He misses a step. "Does that bother you?"

"Not really. For tonight at least, the big scandal is Slate fixing Dee's sink."

"That's been going on for years."

"Sounds exhausting."

"Sometimes people need time to figure things out, even if it seems perfectly obvious to everyone else."

He stops walking, turning to face me. The moonlight makes him look less minister, more dangerous.

"We should probably talk."

"About Slate and Dee?"

"Dixie."

"Probably." My brain's waving a dozen red flags. "But talking's overrated."

His eyes go dark. Once again, he's going to kiss me. Right here where anyone could see.

A car drives by, headlights sweeping over us. He steps back quickly and I nearly drop my plant.

"Let's get you home."

The word feels weird. Temporary. Like borrowed clothes that fit but aren't mine.

We walk in charged silence. When we reach the rectory, he holds the door like the gentleman he is.

"Thanks for the escort." I'm aiming for lightness and missing by a mile. "Very chivalrous."

"Anytime." His eyes hold mine too long. "Dixie, I—"

"Good night, Jack."

I cut him off before he can say anything more and hotfoot it to my room. Am I the murderous potato or the invasive mint in this little garden metaphor? Definitely team potato. I'm gonna kill the sweet tomato preacher if I stick around much longer.

Thirteen

Choir practice and other disasters

Jack

Today's been two thousand hours long and it's not over yet. I've checked in on elderly parishioners, visited the hospital, helped Mr. Jackson with his fence because arthritis makes holding tools difficult. Lots of people have asked about Dixie. Most are curious, but some are pissed.

Mrs. Lancaster cornered me after the hospital visit, lips pinched like she'd been sucking a lemon. "I need to express my concerns, Reverend. About the young woman living in the rectory. It sets a certain tone. People talk."

Translation: Shacking up with a singer who doesn't even do Christian country doesn't align with her vision of proper ministerial behavior.

Then Walter from the vestry committee ambushed me at the hardware store to remind me the rectory is "church property, not some kind of…temporary housing solution." The pause is loaded. He doesn't say "hookup," but his eyebrows do the heavy lifting.

On the flip side, Margaret Jenkins pressed a casserole into my hands while grilling me about my "intentions." She's worried I'll let Dixie leave before "sealing the deal." Three generations of Jenkins women have been trying to marry me off and they see Dixie as their best shot.

Both camps think they know what's best for me. Neither bothers asking what Dixie wants.

I should be focused on tonight's choir rehearsal because if we don't win the talent show, I'm screwed. But mostly I just want to see Dixie. She's been holed up recording all day—I've heard her guitar through the walls, snippets of her voice trying different approaches to the same lyric. It's something her agent asked for, which sounds promising.

She's gotten creative with recording spaces. The guest room closet is her "budget vocal booth" with blankets on the walls. The bathroom provides "indie-folk gold" reverb. I even found her in the linen closet singing into her phone propped against my laundry basket. "Makeshift reflection filter," she'd grinned. "The things we do for art."

My phone buzzes. Bishop Caldwell.

The Right Reverend Dr. Morgan Ellery Caldwell is a former theology professor turned parish rector turned bishop. Her election surprised a few people, but she energizes the younger clergy and lay delegates. High church, but low tolerance for nonsense—in her own words—she's got a well-earned reputation for striding around our diocese wearing limited-edition Doc Martens and a sincere smile.

"Jack," she says when I answer.

"Bishop Morgan."

Usually she reminds me to use her first name. Not today. Message received.

"I wanted to check in. I've been hearing interesting updates from Wickham Hollow. Thought it best to go to the source. Have you been on social media lately?"

"No," I say mostly honestly, conscious of my half promise to Dixie. "I've been too busy with the roof to check social media."

"Maybe sit down for this one." She pulls something up on her phone, grumbling about *too-small buttons*. "Your houseguest has written a rather interesting song about a 'pretty preaching man who makes her hot.'" She pauses. "There's also some kissing, a strong implication of fantastic, consensual sex, and the preacher ends up ghosted. I'll send you a link. Forty-seven thousand likes and counting. Hashtag Preacherman. Someone posted a Google Earth screenshot of Wickham Hollow Chapel."

I pull into the church parking lot, engine running, while I check my phone. The Instagram link shows nothing but a generic stock photo—a sweater tossed on a bed—but when I unmute it, Dixie's voice pours out, guitar and all, singing about a preacher man. The caption reads: "When you accidentally hook up with a preacher and have to own your poor life choices. #preacherman #oops."

I jam my thumb on the mute button. "Jesus Christ."

"That's exactly what half the comments are saying. You made her see God, Jack, and the whole world knows it."

Despite everything, I almost smile.

"My take is you're a grown man and a minister, not a monk. But gossip fills silence faster than truth. Whatever's happening between you two, your community deserves honesty."

"We're not involved. Not in the way they think."

Great. Now I need to have *that* conversation with Dixie.

"Keep me posted, Jack. And honestly? I'm rooting for you."

After she hangs up, I sit there staring at my phone like an idiot. I knew Dixie had written something about me and posted it online—she'd told me that much. What I hadn't fully comprehended was just how big it had gotten. Apparently I'm internet famous for a song I've never even heard. I'd told her I wouldn't go looking for it, but maybe that was a stupid promise to make. How am I supposed to deal with this if I don't even know what everyone's talking about?

Huck's waiting on the church steps like he knows I need backup. He gives a mournful woof when I get out.

"I missed you, too. I think I'm in trouble with my boss." When I reach over him to push open the door, Huck tries to nudge me back home. "Smart dog."

Inside, it's chaos. At seven, Dixie still isn't there, so I get the choir started on warm-ups.

At 7:19, she blows through the door dressed like it's summer— cutoff shorts, fuzzy boots, that black sweater. Her hair's falling out of whatever she did to pile it up and she looks beautiful. Which isn't helping my focus any. The choir stares. Phones come out. Murmurs ripple. Can't say I blame them.

"It's that girl online—"

"I didn't know she was *real* real."

I really should find out more about that song.

Dixie grins. "Hey, y'all. Ready to get started?"

In the first ten minutes, she's got them doing more vocal warm-ups and teaching them how to breathe properly. She drops her voice low, doing some growly impression of Slate that has Dee cackling. *"Again. Add FUCKING feeling."* She's good with them. Real good.

I should've known it wouldn't last.

An hour later, I'm trying not to fall asleep as the choir massacres three different hymns. When Dixie calls a break, she saunters back to the organ where Toby's hiding-slash-hanging out. He's shy but his mom drags him along with her every week because it's that or leave him home alone. He's been half-heartedly poking at the organ keys, which hasn't helped the choir's performance any.

"Hey, superstar. Wanna learn the most dangerous, scandalous piano duet of all time?"

Toby jams another key down and nods.

"Alright. It's called 'Chopsticks.' Fancy, right?" She wiggles her pointer fingers. "You only need two fingers. These two. Not the fun middle two. Put up one on each hand and finger-gun me, my man."

Toby focuses intently on his fingers and mostly succeeds in imitating her.

"You got it. So now you're gonna start right here— middle C. That's home base. Press this one—" Dixie taps a key with her finger "—and then skip one and bang on the next. Boop. Boop."

Toby copies her.

"Good! Now go up, like you're climbing stairs. C and G. D and A. E and B. Just bounce your fingers outward like you're shooing flies." She scoots onto the bench beside him and plays along. "And…we add attitude!"

Toby lights up like a Christmas tree and bangs away at the keys while she sings a goofy, bluesy "Ooold Mac… Don-ald… had…a faaaarm… E-I—E-I—Ooooo…"

Dee laughs. Then—God help me—starts clapping along.

"And on…that faaaarm…he had…a goat—E-I—E-I— Bleaeaaat…"

Dixie stretches the "bleat" like she's belting out a love ballad, wailing theatrically as Toby pounds away.

"Bleat-bleat!" Slate growls. His sheep has anger management issues.

"And on that farm, he had a…chinchilla?"

This woman. I can't even.

After Old MacDonald has populated his farm with more animals than Noah ever crammed into an ark, she turns back to the group. "Okay. Let's try our talent show hymn. But we're gonna give it some Tennessee flavor. Ready? One, two, three, four!"

What comes out isn't the stately hymn we've been butchering all night. Dixie's got them clapping offbeats, adding twang to "O Lord My God," and turning "Then sings my soul" into something that belongs in a honky-tonk. Some of the choir looks shocked, but they're convinced after the first sixty seconds. Slate's boot slams against the floor keeping time.

It's irreverent as hell. It's also the best they've ever sounded. Maybe we're not totally screwed?

After rehearsal, a handful of church ladies circle Dixie like floral-scented hawks, making pointed comments about "special men" and "settling down." She deflects like a pro.

When everyone's gone, I find her on the front steps. My heart pounds, which is stupid. I gave her a tow and a bed and somehow she's become the center of my world.

She hops down when she sees me, keeping one hand on the railing. Something's off in the way she moves, but I can't put my finger on.

"We're getting somewhere," she says. "They'll do good at the talent show."

"You were amazing."

I want to wrap my arms around her, swing her in a circle, ask her what she needs and how I can make everything right for her.

"Flatterer." She sticks her tongue out. "I'm officially promoting myself to Music Angel of Wickham Hollow Chapel. I want business cards and a sparkly halo."

"I mean it," I say and she makes a face like compliments are wool sweaters in July. "I see what you do."

"Uh-oh. Empty compliments portion of the evening? Dude. I'm mean! Kick ass! Do not mix me up with one of your church ladies."

I nod at the stack of sheet music under her arm. "Why rewrite that song?"

"Because it sucks and it's boring!" She pauses and then sounds only a *little* sullen when she adds, "It was out of Mrs. Appleton's range. When her voice cracked, she was embarrassed."

"So you're really doing it for her."

"My ears still hurt. I'm at least thirty-percent self-motivated here—you realize you're annoying, right?"

I smirk. "Or right."

We walk to the rectory, arms brushing. She's moving slower tonight, missing her usual bounce.

"You okay?"

"Sure. I'm fine."

I don't believe her, but I can't exactly call her a liar.

At the door, her gaze shifts to my mouth. I lean in.

Almost.

"Good night, Preacher Man." She slips inside.

I'm left on the porch, heart thudding, staring at the door.

Almost.

Fourteen

Bonus Track: Gossip, casseroles, and almost-kisses

Dixie

We run the choir through its paces on Tuesday and Thursday evenings. We're on our third rehearsal and I'm still not convinced that we've made progress. At least we're not worse.

My countrified "How Great Thou Art" is getting better—if you can call adding banjo fingerpicking to a sacred hymn "better." The sopranos survive when we hit the twangy parts, and Slate is actually keeping a steady beat. But I still feel like I'm putting rhinestones on someone else's wedding dress. This isn't my song, isn't my style, and definitely isn't going to win us anything. I'm just adding glitter to a safe, boring choice. We need something with actual teeth to beat the competition.

Although what if I sent a clip of this to my agent? She's been working her contacts since my preacher song went viral, setting up meetings with A&R reps who want to hear "what's next." Maybe they'd eat up this whole small-town-girl-does-gospel thing. There's something sneaky and hopeful threading through my chest—what if this is it? What if opportunity knocked and I actually answered? What if I'm headed back to Nashville and stardom sooner than I thought?

But no. One look at the ragtag choir and I know better. This isn't gonna be my ticket out of here.

Tonight, I lead them through warm-up exercises and pass out sheet music. Jack hangs back—*way* back, like in the pew nearest the door. He's ready to escape if the locals turn on me. Hopefully he's got an escape route mapped out in case they show up with pitchforks and torches like some religious zombie apocalypse, and maybe he'll grab me on the way out. He greets everyone as they walk past. He knows their names, how their days went. He's calm and interested even when an old guy with the bushiest beard to ever beard overshares about his IBS. I doubt Jack's interested, but boy can he fake it. He also keeps trying to put the brakes on the conversation by interjecting "Walter" every three seconds, but Walter is unstoppable.

"You feel better now, Walter." Jack finally gets a word in halfway through our warm-up. His best wishes sound sincere. He's way too nice. I'd have walked away from that monologue two bowel movements ago. Lucky me, I don't have a problem being rude. Maybe I'll rub off on Jack.

Walter, being Walter, just moves on to another (and equally annoying) line of conversation. Which contractor won the roof bid? How much lower than the other bids was the winning bid? What did the inspector say and has Jack checked references yet? He rocks back on his heels, tucking his thumbs into his belt, and opines about the roof. He runs a hand down his beard, nodding at the sage words coming out of his mouth. He's the world's leading expert on all things roofing because he's done stuff to not one but three barns out on his dairy farm. He needs to get up there and straighten things out because *back in his day* he could fix a leak and poop rainbows. Simultaneously.

He asks whether Jack (just Jack!) plans to pay for the roof

in cash or if the church will be financing. He then worries that Jack will take out a loan and that would lead to interest payments. My eyebrows fly up.

While I walk the sopranos through a verse, I overhear Jack reassuring Walter that he has the roof repairs under control, punctuating his explanations with funny stories about the contractor ("Family business, they attend church two towns over"), the roof's current state ("Need to get a new tarp up there before next week's antediluvian flood, which gives me a much greater appreciation for Noah's challenges"), and the unexpected aerodynamic qualities of roofing materials ("I've been picking shingles out of the hydrangeas for weeks"). But, despite the sure rumble of his voice and the calm competence with which he tackles the questions, you can't color Walter convinced. He's always got one more question.

Yeah. I should put that motor mouth to good use.

"Walter!" I bellow across the sanctuary. "Get your backside over here. Since you like to talk so much, I've got a solo with your name on it."

Walter's bushy eyebrows shoot up to his hairline. "A solo? Me?"

"You heard me. Come on over, and we'll see if you can do something other than ask questions."

Walter huffs audibly. I make big, WTF eyes at Jack, but he just gives me back his small smile. He's trying to telegraph *All's good*, but he'd do the same if the Four Horsemen of the Apocalypse parked themselves in front of his church.

He drops onto a pew and makes a carry-on gesture with his hand. I stick my tongue out at him, tell my ladies and gentlemen to take five, and park my ass next to him. He looks like he's been through the wringer—hair all messed up, shirt coming untucked, that slightly glazed expression of someone who's been patiently answering stupid questions for way too long.

"Are you okay? Need me to run Walter over with my van?"

A smirk. "Your van still doesn't run."

I shrug. "I bet Slate will give me a push and I aim real well."

"You don't need to commit a felony on my behalf." He stretches his legs out, somehow fitting them under the pew in front of us. It looks uncomfortable but he settles in like all that polished wood is the world's best mattress and he's about to take a nap.

"The offer's good indefinitely." I don't recognize that weird note in my voice. It's almost protective.

At Jack's feet, Huck woofs his support.

When the ladies regroup and stare our way, I get up and go back to my impossible task. Fifteen minutes in, someone's giving me stink eye because I told her to "try singing like you're not trying to scare baby Jesus." Our sole tenor is flat, Slate hasn't shown up, the altos are whispering like this is middle-school homeroom, and Jack keeps making encouraging noises that I'll smother him for if he doesn't stop.

But also—he lets me run it. No back-seat directing. No correcting me. He's slouched in the pew with Huck at his feet and that steady look on his face, like he believes in me more than I believe in myself. It's super annoying.

"Okay, okay." I clap my hands to get their attention. "Let's try that again, but this time, pretend you like the song. Maybe even like each other. Radical idea, I know."

Someone mutters something that sounds suspiciously like "heathen," and I flash her a grin. "That's Music Angel Heathen to you, ma'am."

Jack coughs, definitely covering a laugh.

We start the song again, and this time it's better. Not good, exactly. But less like a group of cats being exorcised and more like a choir. I tweak the harmony, bump up the tempo, and suddenly it clicks.

They sound…okay.

Jack's watching me like I'm the miracle.

I shrug, trying to play it cool. "Not bad for a bunch of tone-deaf Methodists."

"We're Episcopalians," he murmurs, stepping up beside me as the ladies start gathering up their stuff and saying goodbye to each other.

"Tomato, tomatoh."

We're standing close now. His arm brushes mine. I should step back. I should make a joke. Or, in case Jack is right and God is both real and omnipotent, drop to my knees in his church and pray for the miraculous resuscitation of my van and my career.

Instead, I blurt out, "Thanks for asking me to do this."

His smile fades. "You're the best thing that's happened to this choir in years."

"Desperate times, eh?"

"The best thing," he repeats.

The last of the choir trickles out with a chorus of good-nights and "See y'all Sunday," leaving behind the lingering scent of drugstore perfume, Dove soap, and a half-empty thermos of chamomile tea in the third pew.

I wind mic cords and stack music stands while Jack moves chairs back into formation, like he's restoring order to the universe one metal folding chair at a time. The sanctuary is quiet now, but I hum with leftover energy.

I hit the floor to coil the last cable that somehow ended up under a pew. My joints pop audibly and Jack glances over.

"You okay?"

"Just a little snap, crackle, and pop. Nothing a hot bath and a shot of whiskey won't fix. There's rain rolling in—I'm better than a weather app."

He chuckles and puts his hand down to help me up from the floor. *Really?*

"I know you don't want to lose that." I get up all on my own, thank you very much.

"Sorry, Dixie."

He doesn't look sorry, though, and promptly sets off for the door at a sprint, where he ostentatiously holds it open for me even when I make a dramatic *such a gentleman* face at him. We spar briefly over who carries my guitar case—I win and sling it over my back—and then we race each other across the parking lot toward the rectory.

His legs are longer than mine—so unfair—and he easily stays ahead. Being Jack, however, he repeatedly catches himself and slows down so I can keep up and feel like I have an actual shot at winning. He tries to be sneaky, slipping sideways peeks at me from the corner of his eyes, but he sucks at subterfuge. Plus, he's constitutionally incapable of not helping others. He smiles about it when they turn him down, but inside he worries. I'm still not signing up to be one of his projects, but I get it.

On the other hand, as I'm totally not averse to cheating—only one of us is morally upright—I grab his hand. Human anchor! And then after I've slowed him down, I swing our hands dramatically and belt out the opening lines of "Amazing Grace."

He shakes his head but lets me. Hopefully, the church's spy ninjas are safely tucked up in bed.

I probably would leave it at that because I have some dignity left, but then he raises our joined hands and spins me in a circle. I add a heel click at the end of the verse because this song needs help.

"Was blind but now I seee-eee…and honey, it's youuuuu."

I pump my free hand dramatically skyward.

He groans but squeezes the hand he's holding. "Did you just turn 'Amazing Grace' into a pickup line?"

"Not just a pickup line." I spin (smash) into him and catch his other hand. "Dance with me."

He mock-glares, but lets me take the lead, because of course he does. Preacher Man is steady as a stone, but he has rhythm, and when I guide him into a slow two-step, he follows, setting a hand on the small of my back. Our bodies snap together like puzzle pieces.

"You're dangerous."

"You let me two-step you," I counter.

"You started it."

We sway-dance up the path toward the rectory, quick-quick-slow-slow. Absurd and corny? Sure, but for some reason Jack always does what I want.

He leapfrog hops me up the steps to the door, wrapping his warm hands around my waist and lifting me up. I make ballerina arms, holding an enormous, imaginary beach ball over my head. I don't feel like going in just yet, and if we do, he'll just say good-night and that'll be that.

He sets me down on the top step and then rummages in his pocket for the key. After the second time I made him check the rectory from head to toe for burglars, he agreed to start locking the door on select occasions. You never know who's hanging around or what they want. He puts the key in the lock and pauses.

Maybe the lock's warped. Stuck. Out of order and non-functional. Good job, lock!

"Let's stay out all night." I'm close enough to smell his soap—it's clean and simple, all cedar and Sunday—and close enough that my breath hitches.

"Dixie." I love the way he growls my name.

I tilt my head. He leans in because he's the best at taking direction. Our foreheads brush.

And then—

A porch light flicks on across the street.

Jack freezes.

"This is the least private place in Wickham Hollow," he mutters.

I can think of worse. Like his pulpit. The church steps. The middle of Main Street. "And?"

"So, I'm kissing you—" he's already tugging me through the front door "—but not with our audience across the street reporting on tongue angle and hand placement to the choir."

I'm laughing when he kicks the door shut behind us, and then I'm not laughing anymore.

He steps closer, close enough that I have to tip my chin up to meet his eyes. Those blue eyes—wait, no, brown eyes—are studying my face like he's memorizing it. Like he's been thinking about this moment for weeks.

"Tell me you want this," he says, voice low and rough. He's already sliding the guitar case off my back, setting it down. Somewhere. Anywhere.

My heart happy-hammers against my ribs. It's not stupid. YES. "I want this."

That's all he needs. His hands frame my face, thumbs brushing against my cheekbones, and then his mouth is on mine.

The kiss starts gentle—a question more than a statement. But when I rise up on my toes and press closer, when my hands fist his shirt and pull him down to me, everything changes. His control snaps like a rubber band, and suddenly he's kissing me like he's been starving for it.

His lips are warm and sure, moving against mine with a confidence that makes my stupid knees weak. When his tongue traces the seam of my mouth, I open for him without hesitation. The taste of him—coffee and something purely Jack—floods my senses.

I should worry about the betraying sounds I make, but I'm too busy drowning in the sensation of his hands sliding into my hair, angling my head so he can kiss me deeper. His body presses mine back against the wall beside the door, and the solid warmth of him is everywhere—his chest against mine, his thigh between my legs, the rough texture of his beard against my skin.

"God, Dixie," he breathes against my mouth, and I love how wrecked he sounds. How undone.

I nip at his bottom lip and he shudders. "Don't stop."

He doesn't. His mouth moves to my jaw, pressing hot, open kisses along the line of it. When he finds that spot just below my ear, I gasp and arch into him. He takes advantage, one hand sliding down to grip my hip while the other stays tangled in my hair.

"You're going to be the death of me," he growls against my throat. *You feel plenty alive to me, Jack.*

"What a way to go, though," I manage, then lose the ability to snark when he sucks on the spot where my pulse is trying to beat its way through my skin. Jack's got points of his own to make.

We're all hungry hands and breathless kisses, the kind of making out that belongs in the back seat of a car or against a bedroom door. My fingers work at the buttons of his shirt while his mouth devours my neck. He's got me memorized now. *Me, too, Jack. Me, too.*

But then he pulls back, breathing hard, his forehead resting against mine.

"We should…" He swallows. His eyes are dark and intense, the pupils blown wide. "We should slow down."

I can practically see his self-control tank running on fumes, the little red warning light flashing like crazy. "Should we?"

His smile is soft and devastating. My hammering heart switches to a mournful key. "Yeah. We should."

"Okay," I blurt out.

He takes a step back, running a hand through his hair where I messed it up. There's a canyon's worth of space between us.

"Good night, Dixie," he says, and I don't know what name to put to the emotions I hear in his voice. I'm gonna need a field guide to reverends, because apparently they come with a whole set of feelings I can't decode.

He turns and heads toward his room, leaving me standing there against the wall, lips swollen and heart racing.

"Yeah, well," I call after him, pushing off the wall with more force than necessary, "don't flatter yourself, Preacher Man! It wasn't that good!"

He pauses at his doorway, glancing back with that mad-
deningly knowing smile. "Sure it wasn't."

Maybe he's not taking things any further tonight (cheater),
but I sure want to.

I'm in so much trouble.

Fifteen

Preacher nearly drowns. Girl dries him off and definitely catches feelings.

Jack

The rain starts early Wednesday morning. First it rains all morning. Then all afternoon. Now, with the sun just down, it's *still* raining.

I run for my front door. There's a moment of forward momentum—followed by confusion—when it doesn't open.

"She locked me out." I slap at my jeans pockets for a key.

Deacon hoots with laughter somewhere behind me.

We've spent the last hour up on the church roof, hammering on a tarp while it rained hard enough to make me wonder where I parked my ark. I'm soaked. And apparently locked out of my own house by the woman I'm falling for, which seems about right for how this day's been going.

"See you tomorrow," I holler and Deacon honks the horn of his truck as he drives past. He doesn't even wait around to make sure I get in safe—he's a terrible date.

I end up having to fish the spare out of the key frog sitting on the top step. As soon as the lock turns, I barrel inside. I'm more interested in being somewhere less rained on than in playing it cool, which is probably good because I'm about as far from cool as a man can get right now.

The second I step inside, I discover my living room's been replaced with a tropical sauna. Georgia Peach is wilting in her dollhouse. She barks a cranky hello as I shut the door behind me and halt on the doormat. If I track mud and water all over the house, I'll have to clean it up. And explaining to Dixie why there are boot prints on her freshly mopped floors would require admitting I noticed she mopped them, which would require admitting I notice everything she does, which is a conversation I'm not ready for.

So, it makes sense to strip down by the door, except I'm not alone and Dixie and I have established a no-one-gets-naked rule. A rule that seemed sensible when we made it but feels increasingly stupid every day I live with her. Walking away from last night's kiss wasn't my smartest move.

I toe my work boots off while I debate how far I can push that rule. Boots, yes. Socks, 100 percent. But what about my flannel or my T-shirt? Pants, I decide regretfully, have to stay on. Pants are a roommate requirement.

Speaking of which, where *is* my roomie?

She's hard to overlook, thanks to the constant singing and chaos. The house feels different when she's not in it—quieter, sure, but also emptier in a way that makes no sense given I lived here perfectly happily for years before she crashed into my life.

It's possible she's gone to bed. It isn't even eight but she's not feeling 100 percent today. She's held herself extra carefully and fine lines dig into the corners of her mouth when she thinks no one is looking. She's keeping herself together, but something hurts, and the fact that I can read her pain now should probably worry me more than it does.

A shower. That's what I need. All the hot water in the

world. Use the menthol shower steamers I stole in last year's Dirty Santa gift exchange. Take a cup of tea in there and the crossword because all that roof time has turned me into an old man.

The bathroom door opens with a bang, bouncing off the baseboard I repainted last month.

"Strip!" Dixie shouts, loud enough to be heard in the parking lot.

I blink at her like an idiot. "I'm asleep on my feet," I mutter, which isn't entirely true. I'm definitely awake now.

There's a whole lot to see. Her kimono is pinky, silky, and clings everywhere except her cleavage, where it parts like the Red Sea. I can tell she isn't wearing a bra—or panties. Noted. Noted again. Definitely filed away in the part of my brain that's going to make sleeping hard tonight.

Her legs are bare. She is, however, wearing a fuzzy pair of flip-flops because Dixie has never met a faux-fur animal that she didn't want to wear.

"Are you okay? Do you need me to repeat myself? Got water in your ears?" Dixie frowns at me. Her hair is swirled on top of her head and anchored with a handful of clips that kind of remind me of Georgia Peach when she gets her wrath on.

I blink at her. Maybe I'm not dreaming. Maybe this is just what my life looks like now—coming home to a woman who yells at me to get naked while wearing next to nothing herself. My dream is *awesome*.

My Dixie dreams have never included four-legged mammals before, so when a towel suddenly soars toward my face, I know this is real.

It's scorching hot. She must have run the dryer, which means… She planned this?

"You look like hell," she says way too cheerfully.

The towel in my hand is definitely one of mine, but it smells like the fancy fabric softener she uses, not the generic stuff I buy. I like her version better.

She mimes rubbing herself with a towel, and I force my-self to look away before my imagination gets the better of me.

"You been doing laundry?"

She shrugs. *No big deal.* "I'm taking care of you, Preacher Man. You shouldn't climb around on roofs in a rainstorm. You might fall off."

"You watched that?"

"I had 911 on speed dial the whole time. Now take your clothes off." The briskness with which she says this is less sexy, erotic demand than practical concern, but it still makes me want to tease her just to see how she'll react.

I reach for the first button on my shirt, moving deliberately slowly. "Right here?"

She rolls her eyes, but her gaze dips to my hands. *You feel it, too, Dixie.* "You want to track that through the house? You're wet all the way through."

That she manages to say this with a straight face while I'm standing here in soaked clothes, looking at her in that barely there kimono, is a testament to her commitment to pretend-ing we're just roommates. We both rock that particular lie.

"Yes, ma'am." I yank my flannel off. It isn't the sexiest strip-tease ever, but her eyes widen slightly, so maybe I'm doing better than I think.

"Dude!" She points a finger at me. "Warn a girl to turn around!"

"You've seen it already." I drop the shirt on the floor be-cause I'm committed to living dangerously and go to work on my T-shirt. It's clammy and stuck tighter to my chest than plastic wrap on pie.

She flounces herself around to face the kitchen, but her gaze goes straight to the kitchen window, and I realize she can see my reflection. I should probably tell her. I definitely don't.

Instead, I fist the bottom of my shirt and pull it over my head, hyperaware she's watching.

Yank off my undershirt.

They land in a wet heap by my feet, and I'm deeply grateful for all those years of manual labor that's kept me in shape. Not that I'm trying to impress her. Much.

When I start on my belt buckle, I definitely catch her peeking over her shoulder.

"What do you think you're looking at?" I pop the button on my jeans.

"Absolutely nothing," she says. As if I'll believe that.

I shove my jeans down my legs. They hit the floor with a sodden thump. I may groan as I straighten up—partly from the cold, partly from the way she's looking at me like I'm something worth looking at.

"You're stiff." She turns around to look at me properly. My boxer briefs are cold and clammy, but I'm about to have a different kind of *stiff* problem if she keeps looking at me like that. "Stiff makes a person clumsy and that's an excellent way to die, Preacher Man."

I wrap the towel around my waist. "Someone's got to do it."

"Well, it shouldn't be you. You're not a contractor, Jack."

"Someone has to, and it's my responsibility."

She's shaking her head as she grabs my soggy clothes, and I want to tell her that this is what I do. I fix things. I take care of people. It's who I am, even when it's probably stupid.

"Shower." She points toward the bathroom. "Go. It's pre-warmed. You're welcome."

She pushes me into motion and I go, mostly because arguing with her when she's being nice to me is counterproductive. The bathroom is foggier than the Great Smoky Mountains and I can barely find the shower curtain but when I do the water is perfect—hot enough to strip the chill from my bones.

As my brain unfreezes and the steam starts to dissipate (the curse of a very small hot water tank), I realize that Dixie has been busy. There are tea lights on the bathroom counter, next to a stack of fresh towels that smell like dryer sheets. A pair of my sweatpants and a clean shirt set out. A beer.

I'm pretty sure that for the rest of my life, I'll get hard when I smell raspberries, and that's going to be a problem when she leaves and I'm stuck with the memories.

Don't think about her leaving. Don't think about her at all.

Except I can't stop thinking about her, about the way she looked at me, about the fact that we kissed each other last night and now she's out there doing God knows what—but I think it might be taking care of me. I can't remember the last time someone did that.

By the time I come out, she's dragged my reading chair in front of the fireplace. Huck's flopped on the rug, paws twitching like he's chasing something in his sleep. Georgia Peach is nowhere to be seen, which probably means she's plotting the next battle in her anti-Dixie campaign. Or maybe she's given up and accepted that Dixie isn't going anywhere.

Does that make Georgia Peach smarter than me?

"Dinner is served!" Dixie winks and points to the dishcloth draped over her arm like she's working at some fancy restaurant instead of serving Cup Noodles in my living room. "I'm your fancy French waiter. Tip me on the way out."

There's a whole picnic set out on the rug—two bowls, two spoons, and two linen napkins that haven't come from my kitchen because I don't own linen napkins. Another tea light flickers in a Mason jar, and suddenly my living room looks like something from a Pinterest board.

She grins at me as she empties the plastic Cup Noodles containers into the bowls and then bows. "Bon appétit!"

She points at the chair and sits down cross-legged on a pillow I also don't recognize. It must have come from her van, along with the napkins and probably half the other things that have slowly migrated into my house since she moved in. I should probably be bothered by how easily she's made herself at home here. Instead, I'm bothered by how much I like it.

"Eat up, monsieur."

"*Avec plaisir.*" I'm flirting with her. It's my new default.

She pulls a face. "The only other French I know is *voulez-vous coucher avec moi?* And crepes! Baguette?"

"You forgot escargot and croissant." I settle into the chair and vow never to get back up again. I'm so tired, and this is the first time in months that tired feels good instead of overwhelming.

She points her spoon at me. "Brioche."

"We'll be polyglots if you keep this up."

"We're Americans. We're perpetual monoglots." She spoons noodles into her mouth. "So is the roof really bad?"

"It's a disaster," I admit. "And I only had, like, seventy percent of a roof to begin with."

She grimaces. "Yikes."

"Yeah. And the church council told me there's no money in the reserve fund." I stir my noodles, avoiding her eyes because talking about my failures isn't exactly romantic dinner conversation. "Not that I'm surprised. If they had cash, they could've hired their own vicar and skipped involving the bishop altogether."

"You mean they wouldn't have ended up with you?"

"Exactly." The admission tastes bitter. "Which wouldn't have been their worst outcome."

"You don't believe that."

But I do, a little. I've been trying so hard to be what they need, to prove I deserve to be here, and all I have to show for it is a leaking roof and a congregation that's probably questioning whether they made the right choice.

"You want to talk about it?" She hands me the rest of her noodles when I finish mine. "If not, consider the subject changed."

"No, thank you. Although—" I glance at the setup she's created. "Thank you for this."

She shrugs, but there's a flush creeping into her cheeks. "Whew. Hot flash." She fans herself with a noodle wrapper. "I'm really bad at sympathy."

"Could've fooled me." I thought I knew what kind of person she was when I first met her, but she keeps surprising me with moments like this.

"I mean, I *am* one of the world's leading experts on illness." That gets my attention fast. "Shit. Really?"

Her mouth quirks. *It's a test, Jack.* "No. Not really. But I get sick a lot. Plus, I'm great at malingering."

I've seen the pill bottles. The long sleeves, even when it's warm. The way she winces when she thinks no one's looking. The careful way she moves sometimes, like her body is betraying her.

"I have rheumatoid arthritis." She spits the words out like they taste bad, like she's daring me to flinch or run or start treating her like she's made of glass.

"That sucks."

It's not eloquent, but it's honest. And maybe that's what she needs, because some of the tension leaves her shoulders.

"Yeah, well. I don't need a fixer or special consideration. Just to malinger on occasion."

"And to rock on," I suggest.

She grins and the sun comes out from behind the clouds. "Yes! But it means I know what feels good when your body's cold and stiff."

I force myself not to think about the word *body.* Or *stiff.*

"Thanks for the noodles," I say because it's that or do something stupid like tell her I'm falling for her.

She launches into a story about a terrible dive bar where she and the other musicians lived on ramen and the bathroom had three sinks but no toilets, and I let her voice wash over me while I try to process what just happened. She told me something personal. She trusted me with it.

I tell her about the roof, about how hard it is, holding it together with duct tape and prayer. About how I hate that this place—this chapel where I spent a few summers as a kid and discovered I had a calling—is falling apart on my watch.

"I'm not a billionaire," I mutter. "I can't fix it the way it needs fixing."

"Yeah," she says quietly. "Asking for help is the worst."

Sixteen

Girl gets a gift. And a date.

Dixie

Thursday morning brings more than sunshine.

"Is it Christmas?" I holler, grabbing the tissue-wrapped package on my pillow. Santa hasn't come in years, seeing as how I'm on the naughty list and have a lifetime supply of coal.

"Still working on Easter," Jack bellows back. "Just say thank you."

Pffft. Not on my watch.

Someone (whose name begins with J) has folded the shirt like a pro and set it on my bed. Marie Kondo, eat your heart out at those sharp lines and the perfectly centered rectangle that declares ANGEL in glittering, gold letters.

I undo all his good work, holding it up to read the whole message:

Wickham Hollow Chapel Music Angel

And then underneath, in smaller but no less true script:

Staff (Unpaid, Mouthy, Highly Effective)

Accurate.

I wipe the smile off my face in case he's lurking nearby. He doesn't need encouragement.

"Pretty sure the only lap I've sat on recently was yours," I yell. "Not a fat white guy in a red suit with morally reprehensible fur cuffs. You didn't tell me you were granting wishes."

"It's your lucky day." He bangs around his office some more before I hear him head out. Once the coast is clear, I give in and read the sticky note in Jack's scrawl: *In case you want to dress appropriately for your position.-J.*

The shirt smells faintly like his laundry soap—clean and woodsy—and even more like him. I *love* it.

My phone's face down on the bed, notifications silenced, but it's buzzing like an angry wasp. The song hit 100K streams on Spotify. A music blogger wants an interview. Someone created a "Hot for Preacher" playlist on Apple Music.

So I've got what I want—people listening to my music. But it was supposed to be earned by my talent, not by accidentally turning my one-night stand into clickbait. *Fuck.* Jack and I will have to *talk* about it. Under no circumstances does that sound like a good idea. I'll accidentally overshare about my feelings.

I put my new shirt on while I check my socials and it's even worse (or better) than I thought. A notification pops up on my screen from my agent: Do you want me to pitch your originals to other artists? How much more do you have?

My dad posted four thumbs-up in the comments section, along with a tiger emoji (no clue). He's tagged it #HankPearlsKiddo and #ChipOffTheOldPearlBlock. I'm definitely pretending I didn't see that by hearting cute cat videos—ostensibly to train my TikTok algorithm—when Jack texts:

You doing anything tonight?

That's a loaded question. Georgia Peach, who's taken up

residence on my dresser, pokes her head around the milk glass vase filled with yellow flowers I found in a ditch. Jack says they're pissweed. I say he's deeply unpoetic.

"Your person wants to make plans with me," I tell her. On the off chance she does understand English, this will irritate her and I can award myself a point in our ongoing battle. Georgia Peach retaliates by eating a piece of my wildflower arrangement with her teeny fangs.

It's been sixty seconds tops since Jack texted, which is enough time to not seem overeager, right?

ME: Define "anything." I might be reorganizing your books alphabetically. Washing my hair. Flat ironing! Big plans.

JACK: Cancel them.

He's unimpressed by my bibliographic threats.

JACK: Go to the February Frost Fair with me?

February. Frost. Fair. With Jack.

Not overthinking this is important—we're both pretending our last kiss never happened. Even though there's zero chance I forget it since it's burned into my ovaries and my synapses, my skin and several other organs. Basically my entire body is Jack's personal welcome mat. I try to pretend it isn't so. He makes coffee. I drink it. We talk about the choir, trade barbs about my taste in floral arrangements—the usual stuff. Mostly, though, I try not to think about Jack.

Or to remember how he kisses. It's just that his muscled, broad body makes me feel needy. He works a lot with his hands and it shows. It would be rude not to admire the effort he's put in. Or the heat of his back beneath my fingers, the calloused touch of his hands on my body. The rough, raw way he shared how he felt. *You're so wet. That feels…yeah, do THAT again.* He checked in, praised me as his *good girl.* I really need to stop thinking about how he comes, the way he just stops and I become the focus of his everything.

Three dots bounce up and down like angry ocean water on my phone.

JACK: Are you in? Yes?

Preacher Man is feeling impatient today.

Dude. I count to twenty before adding: Don't you have to work? Smiting? Soup kitchens? Soul-saving?

Look at me, alliterating.

I've been let out of preacher jail early for good behavior. And also…

And then *he* counts to thirty. Asshole.

"He's onto me," I tell Georgia Peach.

JACK: I've got plans for some low-level espionage. One of the other groups that's competing in the talent show is doing a dry run of their act.

I throw myself backward on the bed, typing furiously.

ME: Think BIG! Let's go for high-level. Universe-level? Whatever! LEVEL UPPPPPP!

It takes him a second to process this.

JACK: So, you're in?

ME: You bet your sweet ass I am. Do I get to wear a trench coat and sunglasses?

More texting dots. Then:

JACK: Only if I get a code name.

He makes it too easy.

ME: Done. You're now Agent Holy Smokes. I'll be your handler.

He sends a groaning-with-an-eye-roll emoji and then: I'll pick you up at 6.

ME: Rock on, Espionage Man. It's a date.

Shit. I try to take that message back, but fumble the phone and then it's too late. He's read it all, adding a thumbs-up, and I have no idea what that means. Are we going on a date? Or is it on the calendar and we friends will go eat fried things on sticks?

"I suck at this," I say to Georgia Peach. She barks softly, the high-pitched, rapid noise sounding suspiciously like a vindictive heh-heh-heh.

So. The fair.

With Jack.

Technically, we'll be "spying" on another group in the regional talent show. I reread his texts in case I've missed something. Nope. Just scouting the competition. Church-adjacent. Entirely innocent. Nothing to see here, folks.

But…

He texted *me*.

Not someone from the choir. Not Deacon. Not one of his overenthusiastic Sunday volunteers. Just me. The pit of my stomach performs a somersault. It hasn't been properly briefed on whether to be nervous or excited.

I head toward the closet, open it, and stare like the right

outfit might leap out and explain things. I should wear something casual. Chill. This isn't a date.

Except I *want* it to be. Or I think I do. Probably. Maybe.

Dammit, at the very least I want to go uncover all the secrets of this other choir so we can beat the pearls off them at the talent show.

"Okay." I tug a shirt off a hanger. "Calm down. You're going to a fair with a preacher. For espionage. Nothing romantic about deep-fried dough and livestock barns."

Georgia Peach chitters from the top of my dresser like she doesn't believe me.

Neither do I.

Seventeen

Did girl just ask preacher out on a date?

Jack

Dixie's text is pretty obvious. Right? It's a date.

The dinner-and-a-movie kind of date, not the fruit.

Is she hoping that this is a date? Am I? It's only been a hand-ful of days (twenty if you're counting) since Dixie and I met, the night we dueled on the karaoke stage and she went home with me. Other than our kissing, she hasn't hinted that she wanted more than friendship. But kissing's a big clue, right? It's just that, since she's my houseguest with nowhere else to go, asking her out is inappropriate. I'm afraid she'll feel un-comfortable or as if she can't say no. *Please choose us, Dixie. It's okay to like me.*

Not that Dixie gives two shits about saying no.

She uses the word all the time. But still.

Still.

Are our kisses a hint? A flat-out admission? She's killing me. After I kissed her and walked away, I've kept myself busy doing preacherly things. This means I check on the roof (still full of holes). Touch bases with Deacon about the van parts (still in Mexico). Write a sermon and draft the church budget for the coming year. Try, and fail, to find cash for the roof. You'd think Dixie would be glad to have me out of her hair, but she's crankier than Georgia Peach. I've also been pulled aside multiple times by people who feel called to express their concern for me. Do I believe cohabitating with Dixie is a good idea? Can she stay somewhere else? Am I aware that people are talking? What about that SONG?

The answers to these questions are no, no, yes, and my best blank face. And yeah, I'm uncomfortable with the attention we're drawing, but that feeling fades real fast. Then I look at her and she snarks at me. Smiles or sings or just kind of breathes in my general vicinity. And I know I like that way more than people's good opinions.

I think she likes me. She's just allergic to having emotions.

So while I'm waiting for her to come around to having me around, I put in a lot of hours in my office. It's made me super productive. The budget's done, for example, so I've got plenty of time to watch the steady drip from the ceiling into the bucket on the corner of the desk. Thanks to all the rain we've been having, it's more than half full.

You could even say that my cup overfloweth.

I give YouTube a shot, in case roofing can be picked up from online videos, and watch a promising video of a twenty-something couple who bought a Victorian villa in Wales. They don't have a ton of cash, so presumably they're DIY fixing the holes in the villa's roof. Based on their drone shots, that roof is missing a significant number of shingles.

I also half-heartedly google *Episcopalian ministers in Wales*.

Turns out there aren't any job openings for me in Wales, but my roofing-related concerns must go out to the universe like a bat signal because my phone buzzes with a call from Ted, my wanna-be roofer.

"Look," he says when I answer, "I'm gonna level with you.

I've got three other jobs lined up. My crew has a window to work on your roof, but if I don't have a *yes* from you by the end of next week, I've got to move on."

I pinch my forehead. This works for people in books but does nothing to alleviate my stress headache. "I understand. Believe me, I'm trying. We're still short on the fundraising, and—"

Ted sighs. Loudly. He's a bit of a drama queen. "I get it. I do. But I can't float this job on a handshake and a prayer. Materials have gone up, and I've people to pay. You want the roof done, I need a deposit and a start date. No hard feelings if it's a *no*—just tell me."

"It's not a *no*. It's a *not yet*. I'm working on it. We've got a talent show coming up—"

He doesn't even try to hold back his snort. It's insulting. "Jack."

"Yeah?"

"You really think a talent show's gonna make you forty grand in cash?"

The grand prize is fifty, but I know better than to tell him that. The price of my new roof will shoot up 10K. "I think it's our best shot."

"Jack." More sighing. It's gustier than the Atlantic in a hurricane. "I want you to get your miracle. I'm praying on it hard. But you've got until Friday of next week. After that, I'm booking those other jobs and we're busy for the next six months."

I send up a quick prayer of my own and thank Ted for his patience. "I appreciate it."

"Alright," he says, then bellows something about *that is NOT a ladder* and *OSHA's gonna kill me and then I'll be resurrected on the last day and I'll kill you.* I forbear from pointing out that traditional Christian dogma does not suggest that resurrected people get to indulge their murderous impulses on the still living. "Sorry. What were we saying?"

"That I'll commit by next Friday." I thank him again and hang up. I have a maybe-date with Dixie to prepare for.

Dixie's sprawled on her back on the porch, one knee bent across the other, wearing worn-out blue jeans and a soft flannel shirt that looks suspiciously like one of mine. The heel of her cowboy boot taps to a melody only she can hear and I'm sure it's a lively one. Her hair's come loose from whatever she did to it earlier, falling around her face like she doesn't have a care in the world. I'd like to join her. *Let's lie here and you can tell me about your day!* I'm not sure she knows it's six o'clock.

"Ready?" I ask. Only when she startles do I realize she has earbuds in.

"Jesus, Jack." She gives me an upside-down glare. "Don't scare a girl."

I know better than to tell her she can do whatever she wants with me, so I tell her instead that we need to get going and then wait as she swaps out the flannel for a jacket. As soon as we're in the truck, she puts the radio on with a not-so-*sotto-voce* comment (*A radio, Jack? Are we reliving the 1950s?*) and then sings along for the entire thirty-minute ride to the county fairground. I know she's not a fan of talking and that she prefers to save her words for songs. Going by the town's reaction, she's done that a little too much already, but I can't help wishing that we could turn the music off and talk to one another. I know it will be okay if she just lets me have a chance.

Still, the February Frost Fair's promising. The air smells like fried dough and hay bales, wood smoke drifting from the barrel fires scattered among the red barns and twinkling pavilions. Despite the February chill, every single person we met is aggressively enthusiastic about the competitor choir's upcoming performance—Pine Grove Baptist has been practicing since Thanksgiving and this is their big dress rehearsal before the regional competition. I feel Dixie's tension, and it's so hard not to tell her that I don't really care if we win or lose. What I want is to spend time with her.

We've got time before the performance, so we walk around the fairgrounds. Couples stroll hand in hand past booths selling hot cider and mittens, while kids run around with bags of kettle corn. String lights hang overhead, and someone's tuning a fiddle near the craft barn.

We don't exactly blend in. There's plenty of side-eye from the locals. Word's gotten around that the preacher from Wickham Hollow brought his "city girl," and in a place where everyone's business is, well, everyone's business, we stick out like Christmas ornaments in July.

I should have got us matching T-shirts: NOT A DATE. Or maybe: THIS ISN'T WHAT IT LOOKS LIKE. Even with a foot of space between us, people keep looking. I've never minded before, but I live in a fishbowl. *Is this okay, Dixie?*

She notices because she wrinkles her nose, which is, all things considered, a pretty mild response from her. "This is a whole other level of stardom, Preacher."

It's something alright. "There's no such thing as a stranger in a small town."

She laughs. "Or secrets, if you believe Netflix."

Her smile makes me feel better. She doesn't totally hate this. I can deal with the staring, but she deserves a great night. She's just visiting (and down on her luck). She doesn't need their intrusive interest in her life. No staring. Yeah, I'm doing a little of that myself. Looking at her. Stealing glances.

She looks good. Really good. Bright in a way that makes everything else fade out a little. Her jeans fit her just right, and that brown duster coat she's wearing swishes when she walks. The coat ends in a waterfall of ruffles and she's wearing a dark brown cowboy hat and leather boots, none of which have seen a day of ranch work. It's like she stepped out of a country music video.

She's glamorous in a way I will never, ever be.

"So, what's the plan?" She buries her nose in her scarf like we're heading into a blizzard. Must be cold, though it feels fine to me. "When do we get our espionage on?"

I point to a nearby poster. "Show starts in ten minutes. We can grab seats or stand."

When she glances at the fried dough stand, though, I slow down and get in line. The pink-and-white sign's promising SUPERSIZED something, and the smell of hot oil is hard to resist.

Dixie raises an eyebrow at our detour but doesn't complain. I wonder if she'd take the same approach to other things. Like kissing.

I think about that more than I should while I hand over cash for a greasy paper plate of fried dough. It's already covered in powdered sugar, but Dixie's a *more* kind of person and heads straight for the condiment table. She dumps on more sugar until the thing's buried in white powder.

She laughs when it gets all over her hands and brushes it off like it's nothing. Doesn't bother her to get messy.

"Bite?" She holds the plate up, daring me.

"Sure." When I lean down to take a bite, her fingers brush my lips.

We share it as we walk past the booths toward the stage. There's only one chair left when we get there. I make Dixie take it. She offers to sit on my lap, but I shake my head. Half the crowd's watching us like their favorite soap opera.

The other choir's really good. They've got matching robes and hair that hasn't moved in decades. When they start their opening number—some complicated Bach thing—they move together like they're connected by invisible strings. Perfect symmetry, voices blending smooth as butter. It's like watching a very religious boy band.

Dixie's sinking lower in her chair. "We're gonna have to up our game."

"Or pray for a miracle."

When she laughs, I feel better. She's not giving up on us yet. I shouldn't be so relieved, but I am. She's frowning and muttering under her breath, trying to figure out if we quit or fight harder.

We get out of there fast when they're done.

"They're horrifyingly good," she rails. "Our choir can't compete with that."

I like the way she says *our.*

"So we need more showmanship!" She makes enthusiastic jazz hands. "You know how to do that?"

"I'm afraid to ask."

She elbows me. "You pick a song like 'Jingle Bell Dash.'"

"It's February."

"You can do Christmas year-round—it's like having breakfast for dinner. Everyone loves it. Plus, you can have audience participation."

I steer her back toward the truck. We shouldn't be planning strategy in front of our biggest competition. "Usually, the choirs pick something a little more classical. 'Ave Maria.' 'Amazing Grace.' That sort of thing."

She pulls a face. "Boring!"

I guess that makes sense. She'd never sing someone else's words if she could make up her own. It's like karaoke night: She borrowed the tune, but the lyrics were all her.

"You don't want to write a song for us yourself?" *Please.*

Another face. "I've been battling with writer's block. But I might be over that. Maybe. Fingers crossed!" She squeezes them together ostentatiously. She has powdered sugar on her index finger, which makes me smile. *I probably shouldn't lick her. Not in public.*

"Plus, I think we should lean into the fun," she continues. "So, we really kind of want exactly 'Jingle Bell Dash.' It's so awful that it's great. Very aggressively cheerful. Full-body choreography. Sleigh bells. Kazoos. There's an entire verse that's just shouting reindeer names to a techno country beat."

There's only one possible response to that. "Wow."

Dixie pulls up a video on her phone and hands it to me. I can't help but notice that she has a massive number of social media notifications.

Hank Pearl's song is something else. Once I get past the eyeball-bleeding horror of his backup singers (in their sexy country elf costumes), I can see Dixie's point. The song relies on enthusiasm, not musical talent. It's also loud and unhinged, but we do that well, too.

"You think we could get permission to sing that Christmas song?"

Dixie's grin gets wider. "For a licensing fee and a promise to mention his name in the program, the songwriter would absolutely agree."

We walk some more, brainstorming a possible performance. I'm not quite ready to commit, but she makes a good point. I should probably know what kind of performer she is.

"Do you usually sing with others? What were they like?"

She shrugs. "Not usually. The one duet I did, the guy split to do a solo act and he charted. Now he's got a big contract and is touring across the country. He's not booking arenas yet, but he's bigger than a bar even if he's not quite stadium ready. His last concert in Utah sold out and there were five thousand seats."

When she pulls the guy up on her phone, I recognize the name. The air goes right out of me. Dixie's a professional and she hangs out with guys like her. Driven. Talented. Urbane.

Not a small-town minister.

"So that's what you want? A record label and to fill arenas?"

Her smile dims some. "Those would be awesome opportunities."

The way her energy flags makes me wonder, though. Does she even want to hit the road? I don't know how to ask her, not when the first thing that comes to mind is that if she tours, we'll be in two very different places. Wickham Hollow doesn't have five-thousand-seat arenas. I tug her toward the rides instead.

Her face lights up when I buy us ride tickets. There's a Ferris wheel with the old-style metal cages for seats, a Tilt-A-Whirl, a run-down carousel, and some chipped-looking teacups swooping around a metal track.

"Ferris wheel!" She claps her hands enthusiastically. "That one, for sure."

The seats are shaped like a clamshell, rounded at the back and with high sides to make the riders feel safe. Or, you know, *trapped*. The mesh walls look like a ginormous tea ball but far more disturbing.

"Scared of heights?" she says.

"No."

She tilts her head. "Not even a little?"

"Nope."

She smirks, already climbing into a cage. I have no choice but to follow.

The seats are supposed to be big enough for two, but I'm tall. When the guy running the ride swings the metal bar down over our laps and locks it, we're forced to sit really close together. This part is my favorite.

The wheel starts to move, slow and creaky, lifting us up into the night sky.

"Pretty view," Dixie says, pointing over the fairgrounds.

I'm not looking at the view. The cage presses in around us and I think it's shrunk in the last sixty seconds. *It's fine. We'll be down in a few minutes.*

But when we hit the peak and the wheel pauses because the ride dude is a psycho, swaying in the breeze, something shifts inside me. The cage is definitely way too small. The mesh blurs, turning into the interior of a cramped van. The fair lights below become parking lot lights beaming through dirty windows.

We're parked behind a gas station somewhere outside Asheville.

It's cold. My little sister is crying, and my mom's voice cracks, trying to sing her to sleep. There's only so many times you can hear "Hush Little Baby" before you scream.

I keep my eyes on the safety bar—but I'm not sure where I am.

There's no room to stretch out. No space to breathe. I can't get out because we're all stuck together in one big knot.

"Jack?" Dixie's voice comes from far away. Real, real far away. "You okay?"

Shoot. The cage sways again and sweat beads on my forehead despite the cool air. I'm back in my head—even though I can tell Dixie is still right here beside me.

Eleven years old and waking up in the dark, can't breathe, can't open the door, can't get out.

"Hey." Dixie's hand covers mine on the safety bar. Her fingers are warm, real. It's exactly what I need. "Look at me."

I force my eyes to focus on her face instead of on the mesh walls closing in around us.

"We're on a Ferris wheel," she says quietly, matter-of-fact. "At a county fair in Tennessee. You can see the whole fairgrounds from up here—look, there's the stage where our rivals sang. There's the fried dough stand where you bought me enough sugar to kill a horse."

Her thumb rubs across my knuckles. I'm not sure if sugar and equines are mortal enemies or not, but I appreciate her thought.

"The wheel's moving," she continues. "We'll be down soon. You breathe with me, okay? We're safe. It's all good."

I nod like an idiot, trying to match my breathing to hers. In and out. Slow and steady.

The wheel lurches back into motion a thousand years later, and the tension leaks out of my shoulders like air from a balloon. By the time we're at the bottom, my heart rate has stopped imitating a jackhammer.

When the ride operator lets us out of our cage, I stumble

out onto solid ground. Dixie follows more gracefully, wrapping her arm through mine.

"You want to sit for a minute?"

I shake my head. *You're an adult, Jack.* "I'm fine."

She stops walking and turns to face me fully. "It's okay. Whatever just happened up there—it's okay."

I'm not sure it is. "Sorry. I don't usually—that doesn't happen very often."

"You don't have to apologize." She studies my face in the carnival lights. "Small spaces?"

I nod. "Sometimes. It's stupid."

"It's not stupid." Her voice is firm. "Just human."

She doesn't ask for details. Thank God.

"Thank you." I have to say something. "For—up there. You didn't have to—"

"Yes, I did." She squeezes my arm. Pats it. Her cheeks are a little pink. "That's what you do for your friends. For the people you care about."

There's something in the way she says *friends* that makes me want to push. Just a little. Just to see if I'm imagining the way she was there for me up there.

"Friends," I repeat, and I know she hears the question in my voice. "Is that what this is?"

She rolls her eyes. "What else would it be?"

"I don't know." I step in closer, enough so that she has to tilt her head up to look at me. "You tell me if I'm wrong, but that didn't feel like friendship."

"Jack!" She growls my name and tries to wriggle backward, but I catch her hand. *You're mine.*

"You feel something for me." It's not a question this time.

For a second I think she might actually answer honestly. Then her walls slam back up. "You're imagining things, Preacher Man."

"Am I?" I search her face. I want all her secrets. "Because if you were feeling something and you're scared about it, or worried about timing, or thinking I'll get spooked—I'll fall first if that's what you need."

Her breath catches, and I see something flicker in her eyes—I'd like to think it's want, maybe, or hope—before she shakes her head. *Yeah. I'm still taking that as a MAYBE.*

"You're ridiculous," she says, but her voice is softer now, affectionate in a way that tells me I'm not wrong. "And you must have hit your head up there."

She tugs me toward the game booths, ending the conversation before I can question her understanding of head injuries—or do that falling.

"Come on," she says, back to her usual breezy tone. "Let's see if you can win me something ridiculous at the shooting gallery. Can you ask God for a divine assist?"

I'm going to let her deflect because I've pushed enough for now—but I'm not letting go of her hand.

She cares about me. Not Jack the minister, not Jack the man who supposedly has his life together—just me, panic attacks and all. And maybe, if I'm patient enough, she'll stop being scared of it.

"You want the giant yellow banana stuffie or the tiger wearing sunglasses?"

"Both. And that inflatable guitar. Go big or go home, Preacher Man."

An eternity later—or maybe just twenty minutes—I manage the banana but that inflatable guitar's rigged six ways to Sunday. The bear, though? That one I can handle. Plus, I see her sneaking peeks at it. She takes them both, eyeing the bear suspiciously. "Your hirsute friend here wasn't on my list."

"You kept looking at it."

"I did not."

"You did."

She huffs but doesn't let go of the bear. Shoot. Whatever happened on that Ferris wheel—the panic, the vulnerability, the way she stayed present and was there for me when I wasn't at my best—has shifted something between us.

I'm not just falling for her anymore.

I'm already gone.

Eighteen

Girl rolls down the window and lets it all out

Dixie

"You know," says Jack, turning the truck down yet another no-name country back road. He's driving one-handed with a sexy confidence, his other, flannel-covered arm resting on the open window. It's a much better view than the trees, cows, and shadows outside my window, although let's hope he's not about to repeat the questions he asked earlier tonight. *You feel something for me*, he said. Yeah, Jack. I do. Attraction. Desire. The deadly, deadly sin of lust. It's nothing more than that. I won't let it be.

"You were right about needing something more interesting than 'Amazing Grace' for the talent show."

I'm safe. He's not asking to rethink our relationship. In fact, he's finally coming around to my way of thinking. This totally works for me. It's not like words can change anything and the talent show is coming up fast—that's the whole point of my leading the choir rehearsals, to drag them to greatness. Or at least the grand prize. And yet… I want to make things easier for Jack. *What is wrong with me?* Merle Haggard sings on Jack's ancient radio about how hard it is for everyday folks to get by. *I feel you, Merle. I feel you.*

"Finally," I say. "Safe is for suckers, Jack."

"Yeah." He turns right onto another dark road. Jeez. Why does one tree-lined lane look like another? "After seeing that group tonight, it's obvious we can't outsing them. So we do need something that'll make the judges remember us."

"I'm not saying talent doesn't count." *Talent matters, Jack. It MATTERS.* "But they didn't feel hungry. They weren't singing like their lives depended on it."

"Is that what it's like for you?"

"Yeah. It's not just about playing for me. It's about winning over the audience. About making them feel. It always has been. I know that sounds arrogant."

"No," he says. "It sounds honest."

"I used to tell myself I just wanted to be heard," I go on, because apparently there's no pause button for my mouth tonight, "but that's a lie. I want to *matter*. I want people to stand up after a set and say, 'That woman? She's the best I've ever heard.' Not just 'That was nice' or 'She's not bad.' I want the blue ribbon."

Jack's quiet, but it's the good kind of quiet. A listening quiet.

"I recorded my first demo when I was nineteen. Sold my first guitar to do it. My granddad's guitar."

His eyes flick to me. "That the same granddad who taught you to play?"

"Yeah. It was this beat-up old Gibson, missing a knob, duct tape holding the pickguard on. Had his name and mine carved on the back and it was the ugliest guitar ever—but it sounded like magic."

"You miss it."

"Every damn day. But I needed studio time. I thought if I could just get one clean demo, someone would hear it and sign me on the spot. That didn't happen, by the way. Plot twist!"

He smiles. "Still. That's a big sacrifice."

"It felt like trading in a part of myself," I admit. "But it also felt like the price of admission. Like maybe that's what success costs."

He nods, thoughtful. "Sometimes it is. I didn't always want to be a preacher."

I glance at him, curious. "What was baby Jack like?"

"Angry," he says with a rueful smile. "Joined the Marines right out of high school. Thought I'd serve my country, get my head on straight, maybe push myself into being someone better. It didn't work because it turns out, you can't outrun yourself just by wearing a uniform."

"So, what changed?"

"I stopped thinking about who I wanted to be. Started asking how I could help. *Who* I could help. Ministry isn't about perfection. It's about showing up. It's patching a roof, delivering groceries, sitting with people when they're scared. It's about being useful."

"You're good at that showing-up thing."

"So are you."

I laugh. "I literally showed up because my van died on Main Street."

"Still counts. You ever think about getting that guitar back?"

"I tried, once. Called the pawn shop, but it was long gone. Probably sitting in someone's closet now, collecting dust."

He reaches over and squeezes my hand gently. "I'm sorry."

"Me, too. But, you know, *choices*. I made them, I live with them."

I can't stop stealing glances at Jack. The dim dashboard light catches the strong line of his jaw, the way his beard has gotten ever so slightly mussed during our reconnaissance mission. He looks relaxed for the first time all week—pulling off low-level choir espionage is apparently exactly what he needed.

"So." I shift in my seat to face him better. "You ready to

hear more about 'Jingle Bell Dash'? Because here comes the tell-all."

He chuckles, a low sound that does things to my insides. "Tell me everything."

"It's actually my dad's song. He's the Hank Pearl who wrote it. It was his minor hit twenty years ago. So yeah, he'd probably let us sing it. Hell, he'd drag us into his studio and make it a whole production if I agreed to come along."

"Why's that?"

"Because he wants me to come home and do a Christmas album remake with him. Keeps calling and texting about it." I pick at a tear in my jeans. "Which is a hard no from me."

Jack's quiet for a moment. "Then why would you want to sing his song with the choir? Wouldn't that just encourage him?"

I grin. "Because it ticks our boxes. It's fucking ridiculous, but you can't stop listening to it. It's like a car wreck on the highway—everyone slows down for a lookie-loo and then talks about it later."

"Why not write something of your own?"

"You want me to write you a song, Jack?"

"Yeah." He nods enthusiastically. "Screw your dad's song. Do something different."

It strikes me like a fiddle bow hitting the right string. I've been trying to make myself fit the music—first with Dad's expectation, then Nashville's, and now with Jack's safe hymn choice. But that isn't how it works. The music has to fit us.

Safe is for suckers.

"If I do it," I say, sitting up straighter, "you have to promise me that you'll actually let them sing it. No backing down because it's too loud or too much."

He nods slowly. "Deal."

"Good." I grin. "Chaos. Pure, beautiful chaos. We lean into what makes us different—we're scrappy, we're loud, and we sure as hell aren't afraid to make fools of ourselves in a good cause."

That makes him laugh—really laugh, his shoulders shaking, his eyes crinkling at the corners. Of course he's not afraid and he's all in.

My mind reminds me what he looked like, navigating the fair like he owned the place. Charming the ring toss guy, making small talk with complete strangers, winning me the bonus bear that's on my lap and telling me he did it because he could see me looking at it. My face warms remembering his words. I didn't have to tell him anything. He just watched and learned me. How do I even begin to date him for real? I'm about to go back to Nashville. I'll be on tour, making albums, hundreds of miles and light-years away from him. It would be crazy for a preacher and a country music star to have a thing. Wouldn't it? But… He's not just a preacher and he definitely sees *me*. He seems to like that woman. So what am I supposed to do?

"You know," I say, voice pitched lower than it needs to be because fuck all these emotions he's stirred up in me. I'm picking the only one that's familiar: lust. "You're different when you're not being all ministerial."

He slides me a wary glance. "Different how?"

"Looser. More…" I drag my gaze over him deliberately. "Dangerous."

He chokes. "Dangerous?"

"Mmm-hmm." I lean close enough to smell his soap and something that's pure *Jack*. "Like maybe you've got some secrets tucked away under all that flannel and good behavior."

The truck slows. I think he's frozen. "Dixie…"

"What?" I trail my finger over the back of his neck, just barely grazing skin. He shivers. "I'm just making conversation."

"That's not conversation. That's trouble." His voice goes all stern.

"I like trouble." My hand drifts down to his shoulder, fingers finding the edge of his collar. Bad fingers! "Question is, do you?"

There's only the rumble of the engine and the whisper of tires on asphalt for a second. Then Jack yanks the wheel hard and pulls over, bringing us to a whiplash-inducing stop.

He aggressively puts the truck in Park, unbuckles, and looks at me. Calm Jack has vanished. His eyes are dark, pupils blown wide. I'm riding shotgun with a caveman.

"You know, you should probably practice your emergency stop. I bet you could do it smoother if you tried."

"Okay," he growls. Growls! I'm under his skin, worming my way inside him. "Cards on the table. You're staying in my house. You're my guest. And I've tried really hard to be respectful about that."

And that's a good idea why?!

"Wait! Jack, Jack, Jack," I complain. "Are we not having sex because I'm living down the hall from you and you think it's *disrespectful* to put the moves on me?"

"I want you so bad it's making me insane." His jaw ticks— or does something. Whatever, Preacher Man's definitely getting his feels on and is trying real hard not to show it. "I'm telling you that every morning when I make you coffee, I think about backing you up against the counter. Every time you steal my shirts, I think about taking them off you. Every goddamn time you sing in my kitchen, I want to—" He stops, running a hand through his hair. "But you're stuck in Wickham Hollow. With me. And that's not a level playing field."

"You think I can't consent because my van's broken?"

"I think you might feel obligated—"

"Jack. Jack, Jack, Jack." When I put my hand on his thigh, the muscles jump under my palm. "I'm a grown woman. I make my own choices. And right now, I'm choosing to be very, very interested in what you were about to say you wanted to do."

"So?" He's adorable when he's so worked up.

"Come on." I pat his thigh. "Don't leave me hanging. You want to what?"

His eyes go all hot and hungry, and when he speaks, his voice is rough as gravel.

"I want to kiss you until you can't remember your own name. I want to get my hands all over you and find out if you taste as good as I remember. I want to hear you make those sounds you made that first night, when you—"

"When I what?" I'm leaning in so hard that our faces are mere inches apart.

"When you came apart in my arms like you were made for it."

Holy shit. Where has this Jack been hiding?

"Okay, then." I'm so breathless now. "Good thing we've got a truck bed and some privacy."

Something shifts in his expression. The careful control he wears like armor just cracks. Peels right off. And underneath he's absolutely wrecked.

"You sure?" he asks.

Instead of answering, I grab his shirt and pull him to me.

This kiss is filthy from the start—all teeth and tongue and the taste of funnel cake and want. His hands fist my hair, angling my head where he wants it, and when I moan into his mouth, he makes a low, growling sound that goes straight through me.

"Finally," he rasps, like he's been holding himself back for weeks. "I've been thinking about this all goddamned day."

His mouth moves to my jaw, my neck, biting down just enough to make me gasp. He's all unleashed hunger now, the careful preacher mask completely gone. This Jack is a barbarian, a lumberjack beast who's been hiding behind Sunday sermons.

"God, I love the sounds you make," he growls against my throat. "You're gonna make them all night long for me."

When he captures my mouth again, it's demanding, desperate. His hands roam everywhere—down my back, gripping my hips, pulling me flush against him until I can feel exactly how much he wants this.

"I've wanted to get my hands all over you since the moment I met you," he says, voice rough as gravel. "Wanted to taste every inch of you. Wanted to find out if you sound as good as I remember when you come apart for me."

I reward that awesome confession by trying to arch against him as best I can, but the stupid front seat's cockblocking me.

"Truck bed," I gasp when we finally come up for air. "Now."

We fumble out of the cab like teenagers, all urgent hands and breathless laughter. Jack drops the tailgate and spreads out the blanket he keeps behind the seat—because of course he has a blanket, the Boy Scout—while I try not to combust from anticipation.

The night air is cool against my heated skin, but Jack is warm and solid when he pulls me against him. We're surrounded by darkness and cricket songs, the kind of silence that makes you feel like the whole world has paused just for you.

"You have any idea what you do to me?" His beard scrapes deliciously against my skin.

I pull him closer. "Show me."

I'm demanding, but he doesn't seem to mind. His hands are everywhere—skimming up my sides, tangling in my hair, mapping the curve of my waist like he's memorizing me. When he peels my shirt over my head, he doesn't go slow or gentle.

Instead, he kisses me like he's drowning and I'm air. His mouth moves over my collarbone, pressing hot, open-mouthed kisses to my skin while his hands make short work of my bra clasp.

"You taste incredible," he tells my shoulder, then bites down, making me arch against him.

I pull his head back up to mine, needing his mouth on mine again. This kiss is filthier than the others, full of promise and heat. When I nip at his bottom lip, he makes this low sound in the back of his throat that goes straight through me.

"Fuck, Jack—"

"Language," he warns against my lips, but he's grinning.

"If you want me to mind, make me," I snark back.

The look he gives me is pure sin. "Challenge accepted."

What follows is a master class in dirty talk delivered in that slow, honeyed drawl of his. Jack Carter, it turns out, has a mouth on him that could make a saint blush.

"I've been thinking about getting you naked in the back of this truck for days," he says against my ear, his voice rough with want. "About laying you down just like this and tasting every inch of you until you're begging me to stop."

When I shiver and press closer, he continues, his hands roaming over my bare skin. "You have no idea what you do to me, walking around my house in those little shorts. I've wanted to bend you over my kitchen counter and show you exactly what happens when you tease me like that."

"Jesus Christ, Jack—"

"I want to hear you say my name when I make you come." His fingers move between my legs. "Want to feel you fall apart under my hands, then do it all over again with my mouth."

His dirty promises keep coming in that slow Southern drawl, each more explicit than the last. He tells me how he's imagined taking me against his bedroom wall, how he wants to watch my face when he fills me completely, how he plans to make me scream his name until the whole town knows who I belong to.

And when I give it right back to him—telling him what to do and how it feels, he just kisses me harder.

"Jesus, your mouth," he breathes, hands stripping off my jeans. "You'll be the death of me."

"It's the best way to go," I say before he also strips me of the ability to form coherent sentences when his fingers find their mark.

He takes his time with me, calloused hands mapping every inch of skin like he's trying to memorize me. But it's his mouth that undoes me completely—pressing kisses to my wrists, the inside of my elbow, the hollow of my throat.

"I fucking adore your freckles," he growls and then loves on each one, his lips mapping constellations on my skin I didn't know existed.

When he settles between my thighs, looking up at me with those dark eyes, I nearly come apart from the intensity of his gaze alone.

"Jack—" The rest of that sentence dies on my lips because he puts his mouth on me.

He's thorough, deliberate, using his lips and tongue like he's conducting a symphony and I'm his instrument. Every sound I make spurs him on, and when I tangle my fingers in his hair, pulling him closer, he groans against me.

"God, you taste even better than I remember." The rough honesty in his voice makes me arch off the truck bed.

By the time he finally heads north to kiss my mouth, I need him now. I can taste myself on his lips.

"Look at me," he demands as he deals with the condom. "I want to see you."

When he moves inside me, it's slow and deliberate, like he's savoring every second.

"I've been thinking about this," he says against my ear, his breath making me shiver. "About you. How you'd feel, how you'd sound…"

"How do I sound?" My voice comes out breathless and wrecked.

"Perfect." His hips rock against mine, finding a rhythm that makes my toes curl. "Like you're made for this. Made for me."

Then he pauses, his hand stilling on my hip. "Are you

okay? Your joints—is this position working for you? We can change—"

"Jack." I grab his butt, urging him on. "I'm good. Really good. But thank you for asking."

His control finally snaps, movements becoming urgent, desperate. But even then, he never stops watching me, never stops whispering sweet, filthy things that make me arch and gasp. Make me forget my own name.

When I come apart in his arms, it's with his forehead pressed to mine, our breath mingling in the tiny bit of space between us. And when he comes a heartbeat later, calling my name like a prayer, something fundamental shifts between us.

Afterward, we lie tangled together under the stars, my head on his chest and his fingers trailing lazy patterns on my bare shoulder.

"So." I still can't breathe quite right. "That happened."

His chest rumbles with quiet laughter. "Yeah. It did."

"Any regrets, Preacher Man?"

He's quiet long enough for me to start to worry. Then his arms tighten around me.

"Only that we waited this long."

I lift my head to look at him. "Really?"

"Really." He brushes a strand of hair away from my face. "You're not just staying in my house, Dixie. You're not just my guest. You're…"

"What?"

"Mine," he says simply. Like it's that easy. That clear. "If you want to be."

Something warm and terrifyingly wonderful blooms in my chest. Joke, I tell myself. Deflect and keep things light. Instead, I hear myself say:

"Yeah. I want to be."

His smile is soft and devastating. "Good. Because I wasn't planning on letting you go anyway."

Jack

It's been a great twenty-four hours. The best. Red-letter day all around. The drawbridge to Dixie's castle is at least halfway down. She's letting me in, and I appreciate the gift.

Except something she said yesterday keeps echoing in my head, and I'm thinking I need to do something about it. There's an opportunity here for me to fix something for her.

"I recorded my first demo when I was nineteen. Sold my first guitar to do it. My granddad's guitar. It was this beat-up old Gibson, missing a knob, duct tape holding the pickguard on. Had his name and mine carved on the back and it was the ugliest guitar ever—but it sounded like magic.

"It felt like trading in a part of myself."

I get out of bed carefully. After we came back here last night, she got in my bed. I haven't been able to stop looking at her. Asleep she looks more peaceful, like she's happy. I'm planning on keeping her that way for the rest of her life. Premature? Not from where I'm standing. The morning light catches the auburn in her hair, and I brush a strand away from her face like the lovestruck fool I am.

In the kitchen, I make coffee and sit at the table she's cluttered with half-written lyrics and an empty bag of peanut M&M's. Huck snores on his rug while Georgia Peach lectures at a squirrel outside the window.

I can't stop thinking about that guitar. About nineteen-year-old Dixie, so sure that one clean demo could change everything, willing to sacrifice something precious for a shot at her dream. *It feels mean, God, that You didn't let it work.* Not that she quit. Dixie is relentless that way. I love her refusal to quit.

I can't give her the recording contract she's dreamed of, but maybe I can find that guitar.

I open my laptop and type: Nashville pawn shops 2017.

Dozens of hits populate the screen. Hundreds. That's okay. I'll pick one and start there.

I grab a sticky note and jot down what I know: *Old Gibson. Missing knob. Duct tape pickguard. "Dixie + Granddad" carved on back. Pawned 2017-ish.*

It's a long shot. The guitar may be gone, broken, trashed. But maybe—just maybe—it's still out there, waiting.

I try the first phone number and wait through three rings.

"Bill's Buy & Pawn, what're you selling?"

"Not selling," I say. "I'm trying to find something. It's a long shot, but—"

I tell them the story. A girl with a dream and a guitar that was part of her before she ever stepped onstage. They can't help, but they give me the name of another shop that sells vintage instruments.

I write it down and call the next name on my list.

And the next.

Nineteen

Girl wrote a song

Dixie

Three more days of living with Jack Carter and I'm losing my damn mind. In the best possible way.

Like, who knew a preacher could make scrambled eggs look sexy? This morning I watched him crack shells one-handed, and I almost climbed him like a tree. The man has no idea what he's doing to me, which makes it worse. Better. Both.

I've been walking around his little rectory in a permanent state of "what the hell is happening to me" mixed with "please don't let this end" and a healthy dose of "I am so screwed." Not in the fun way. Well, definitely in the fun way, too, because Jack's a big believer in making up for lost sexy times.

I'm humming fragments of the song I've been working on since the fair. *Hallelujah for the mess we are, small-town sinners 'neath Southern stars...* The chorus is solid, but the bridge isn't right. Something about found family, about how broken people can still lift each other up. It's dancing just out of reach like a word on the tip of my tongue.

Jack is out doing his daily rounds, which means he's busy being disgustingly useful to everyone in a fifty-mile radius. He texts me updates throughout the morning like some kind of good-deed live blog. He delivered groceries to one of his seniors because her hip is acting up. Then he fixed a leaky sink for someone whose landlord is allergic to basic maintenance. By lunch, he's been roped into moving furniture for someone's college-bound daughter and now he's reading to an old guy at a nursing home. Each text ends with some variation of "Thinking about you" or "Can't wait to get home," which should be cheesy but instead make my stupid heart do flip-flops like a gymnast.

I'm taking a break from scribbling lyrics when my phone buzzes. River and Pine are swinging through Wickham Hollow on Friday night. Do I want to meet up for a drink?

My thumb hovers over the keypad. I guess they've got my location from my social media. It's no big deal. Should I ask Jack to come with—introduce him to my people, show him off like some kind of trophy boyfriend? The other part of me, the smarter part, knows that River and Pine are a lot. They're road-hardened, industry-cynical, and have about as much filter as a microphone with a broken pop screen. Jack doesn't need my Nashville chaos shoved in his face, complete with war stories about pay-to-play gigs and the kind of dive bars where the health inspector has given up and gone home.

Sure, I text back finally. One night of old life can't hurt, right?

When their truck pulls into Southern Comforts' parking lot, I'm waiting by the front door like some kind of eager puppy. River leans out the passenger-side window, waving a cowgirl hat and yelling at Pine to "Pull over right now, goddammit!" with loud enthusiasm. Classic River—subtle as a freight train and twice as loud.

River's a year or ten older than me, blonde, with a fresh blowout and flippy, curled ends. She sings with Pine and has pipes that could make angels weep—or at least make drunk guys in honky-tonks chuck their wallets at the stage. Of all the musicians I've met on the road, she's also the only one still with her original partner. Pine loves her to death, which is either really sweet or really codependent, depending on how you look at it.

Pine rolls his eyes as he climbs out. "You sure are in the middle of nowhere."

He's grown even more weathered since the last time I saw him, like someone left him out too long in the sun. Still broad-shouldered, still shoving his longish hair beneath a cowboy hat, but the beard's new. It doesn't quite hide the deepening lines around his mouth.

"We've played worse," River announces, hopping out of the truck. Familiar gear crams the bed. "Cumberland Country Live? Remember that shit show? They stuck us in the middle of a run-down arena with like twelve drunk guys in the audience. Plus, the rodeo had just been through and they hadn't bothered cleaning up the literal shit. As long as the beer's cold and the bathroom doesn't require a tetanus shot, this place is paradise."

She throws her arms around me and hugs it out.

Pine crunches around the truck and looks me over when River lets go. "So, this is where you broke down. It sure isn't Nashville. How long are you stuck here?"

I paste on my best fake smile. "Parts are on their way from Mexico."

I actually like these guys. We've spent weeks on the road together, doing door deals where we get by on a percentage of ticket sales. We talked about maybe co-writing or record-ing a track, but my voice and River's don't work so well to-gether. Plus, country radio would rather play the same three dudes on repeat than risk putting two women back-to-back.

River is already sizing up Southern Comforts. "You play here? Do they do pay-to-play or offer guarantees?"

"Strictly karaoke," I say.

She makes a face. River is the one who keeps her eye on the money. Pine just has his eye on his next drink and his next complaint about the industry.

"It's not like I got to pick where my van died." I lead them toward the door. "Sometimes life happens in the middle of nowhere."

"Wow." River stops dead in the doorway. "Welcome to the taxidermy palace."

She mouths a silent *yeehaw* and Pine snorts. Southern Comforts does look like someone looted a hunting lodge and decorated with the evidence.

"Those things are *expensive*," I say lightly. "They sell for serious money on eBay."

Slate, who is behind the bar looking like he'd rather be anywhere else, definitely hears us. His scowl is Grand Canyon levels deeper than usual as he glowers at Pine and River with all his crusty, grumpy heart. I may wink at him, just to mess with him.

"You know him?" River asks.

"Sure. He's the local ogre." I say it loud enough for Slate to hear and he dials the scowl intensity up from ten to infinity.

"Does he bite?"

I shrug. Honestly, I'm not sure if River's joking, and I also can't tell if I just hurt Slate's feelings. Which is weird, because since when do I care about hurting his feelings?

I don't have time to figure it out because River steamrolls ahead. "So, I hear you've got a man!"

"What?"

River beams like I just announced I'm pregnant with twins. "I wanna be a bridesmaid!"

"What?" I say again, because apparently my vocabulary's shrunk to one word.

Pine barks out a laugh and heads to the bar to order Jack

and Cokes. When River yells after him to bring back a pitcher as well, he lifts a hand and carries on.

River drags me toward a booth. A few regulars nod as we pass, and I nod back like we're all part of some weird small-town secret society.

"Dixie freaking Pearl!" River throws an arm around me. "Girl, 'Hot for Preacher' is blowing UP."

I've been watching the numbers climb all week, but my stomach still drops. "How blown up are we talking?"

"TikTok," Pine says, dumping glasses on our table. Coke sloshes everywhere. "You're viral. Like, actually viral. My sister's youth group is obsessed."

He looks way too pleased about this.

"Wait—fully viral?" My heart hiccups. Probably a heart attack. I knew my song was picking up steam, but I hadn't checked the numbers since yesterday. "How viral?"

"The song!" River is digging her phone out. "That one you posted on Instagram where you tell some guy to shove his proposal up his ass? Someone mashed it up with footage of this sexy priest from a Netflix show, labeled it 'Hot for Preacher,' and now it's everywhere. I thought you named it that!"

"I didn't." My palms are sweating. I'm definitely having a heart attack. "I didn't name it anything."

She's scrolling through her screen like a woman possessed. "You've got fan accounts now. Look—@PreacherManUpdates has fifteen thousand followers posting theories about who inspired it."

Pine leans over her shoulder. "Think that Google Earth screenshot of his church is legit?"

My stomach falls through the floor. Fan accounts? Google Earth? This is way beyond anything I've imagined or even my agent has talked about. "Show me."

The fan account has everything: screenshots of our town website, photos of the chapel, even a blurry picture of Jack at the hardware store looking like he has no idea he's about to become internet famous. The caption reads: "PREACHER MAN SPOTTED? Sources say this is the inspiration behind @dixiepearlmusic's viral hit ⊙⊙." No wonder River and Pine knew where to find me—the whole *world* knows.

"I should delete it," I say. "Take it all down."

"Are you insane?" Pine stares at me like I suggested burning money. "You've got a song in the top one hundred."

River tries to high-five me. "Congrats, Mama. It's your best song. Real, dirty, catchy as hell."

"Don't." The word comes out sharper than I mean it to. "Don't talk about him like that."

Pine shrugs. "Are you touring it? You should come with us. We've got Asheville tomorrow—they're paying half the door. Just say you're our merch girl."

"Crash in our hotel room," River adds. "Or find another preacher to put you up. Wait—" She's zooming in on something. "Tell me this isn't him. The church site has a 'meet the pastor' page."

She flips the phone around.

Jack smiles at me from the screen, all kind eyes and button-down shirt.

"Oh my *God*," Pine practically yelps. "He's hot in a 'bless me, Daddy' kind of way."

"Did you do him in the chapel? Was he a virgin?" River's voice gets higher with each word. "Did the town throw holy water on you? Like, you walked into the diner and someone slapped a scarlet letter on your boobs?"

They're cracking up, buzzed on drinks and the smell of low-level fame. Normally, I'd be right there with them, talking shit and laughing at the absurdity of it all. This is our language—music, mess, and making fun of everything. We've all dreamed of internet fame and winning at music life.

But—

Jack isn't a joke. He's the guy who makes me coffee and gives me chances. Who lends me a bed and anything else I need. Who sees me at my worst and somehow still likes the person he sees.

And I turned him into a song. Worse, I let the internet turn him into a meme.

"He's a good man," I say, and the words feel weird coming out of my mouth.

"Oh, honey." River raises a brow. "You caught feelings, didn't you?"

I shake my head. *Not really.* Sip my drink to stall.

"You sure?" Pine smirks. "Because you've got that look. The one songwriters get when they write something that's gonna bite them in the ass."

They howl with laughter.

And I laugh, too, because that's what I do.

But inside, I'm freaking out. Has Jack seen it? He said he wasn't going to look, but what if he did? Will he ever look at me the same way again?

Or worse—will he look at me at all?

I tell them I need to pee and escape before I say something I can't take back, leaving them to argue over the ancient jukebox.

Outside, the air's cool and the street is dead quiet. I pace behind the bar, gravel crunching under my boots, trying to remember how to breathe.

Fuck, I didn't mean for it to blow up like this.

I didn't call it "Hot for Preacher." I didn't hashtag it or turn it into a meme or echo some thirst-trap Netflix priest. That isn't the point.

I just needed to write something. Anything.

And now it's a punch line. A TikTok trend. A joke to go with cheap well drinks.

The back door opens and I flinch. But it's just Slate taking out a trash bag.

He frowns. "Okay?"

I nod my head. "Fine. Be right back."

I'm such a liar.

Twenty

Girl goes viral. Preacher finds out.

Jack

I stop in front of Southern Comforts and pat Huck on the head. "We're being discreet. You're here as my wingman, so don't let me do anything stupid. We're not stalking her, just making sure she's doing okay."

Huck bays enthusiastically. He's on board with this Friday night plan of mine.

"Are you ready? You take the lead, okay? No barking, no more baying, no stealing the ladies' handbags. Got it?"

Technically, animals aren't allowed inside the bar, but Huck gets a religious exemption.

"Here we go!" Huck is happy to go—I'm the one who needs a push. What am I even doing here? Dixie said it was business, catching up with people from the industry. She didn't ask me to come along, which should tell me everything I need to know.

A wave of sound hits me when I open the door and I scan

the room. Don't be obvious. Play it cool. Except now I'm standing here uninvited, and I feel like an idiot.

Slate stalks in the side door and disappears into the bathroom. In addition to the usual suspects, there's a man with a goatee beard and a blonde woman. Since I don't recognize them, they're probably Dixie's industry friends. The guy sports a music festival T-shirt and a cowboy hat, plus the tired, rundown look of someone who's driven too long without a break. The blonde hanging on his arm is pretty and bright, her long hair bouncing as she points at me.

"Heeeyyyyyyy!" she yells. "It's you! Preacher!"

Huck bays and bolts for their table. I chase after him.

They've got a phone propped up against a bowl of Deacon's stupid boiled peanuts, playing a video on loop. A bunch of folks are clustered around, watching.

Huck goes nuts at the sound of Dixie's voice coming from the phone. She's on his favorite-persons list, so he'll greet her with enthusiasm, even though he can't figure out how she's gotten stuck in that teeny-tiny box.

"Huck, we've talked about this. We don't jump on strangers."

The woman snickers. "Oh, *we* don't, do we?"

I wrestle Huck off the table and back down on the floor, but not before he's snagged the woman's purse. I'm torn between apologizing and setting things right, when I start paying attention to what Dixie's singing.

"Never gonna be preacher's girl…"

The blonde winks at me and turns up the volume. The phone screen shows a stock photo of a black sweater on rumpled sheets—I recognize that image from the bishop's call—and it's definitely Dixie's voice pouring out of the speakers. The words dance across the bottom in pink text. *TikTok*, my brain supplies. *She made a TikTok video about you. Or is that Instagram?* I have no idea. I've avoided looking it up, but here it is anyway.

The guy holds the phone out to me. Thick calluses cover the fingertips of his hand. "You're internet famous, my man!"

He wags the phone in the air like an offering. I can read the caption now, no problem—and I've definitely seen it before.

@dixiepearlmusic: when you accidentally hook up with a preacher man and have to own your poor life choices. Am I hot for preacher? #preacherman #nashvilletok #oops.

A stream of emojis follow: a church, some flames, an egg-plant.

Four people comment while I stare at the screen. Her post has ten thousand likes and far more comments than fit on the screen.

Fire emoji. Not me relating to "not one of those girls" energy <u>100</u>

Hot face. The way she said "never gonna be preacher's girl" but then...

Devil emoji. She really said "I'm my own girl" then wrote a whole-ass song about him.

Cowboy emoji. Girl just converted me.

Deacon turns with a grin. "Nice song, Jack."

"It's—" I have no idea how that sentence ends. I knew Dixie had written something—hell, the bishop called me about it and I *saw* this caption. But knowing she wrote a song and actually hearing it are two completely different things.

Deacon leans on the bar beside me. "Not you? That really what you want?"

I stare at our reflections in the mirror behind the bar. The party around the phone continues with no sign of Dixie. "You know what I am. I'm not made for that kind of attention."

Deacon shrugs. "Could be worse."

I don't know what to do.

Dammit.

"Those Dixie's friends?"

"Think so." Huck hops up on a barstool. Deacon groans but rubs his head affectionately.

Whether they are or aren't, they won't stay. They'll be gone tonight, tomorrow at the latest.

I give up on playing it cool. "Where's Dixie at?"

The blonde is checking out the karaoke stage now and flashing a thumbs-up at the guy singing.

"Out," Slate grunts. "In the back."

She and I, we've talked. Lot of hours, if I add them up, but they've been about little things, I guess. The details of our days. Nothing huge. Nothing really important. I remember touching every inch of her, and yet I still don't know her well enough to know what she needs right now.

We're two different parts that only fit together in bed.

And now I'm the subject of a viral thirst-trap ballad.

Deacon moves away when someone gestures for another drink. I don't make eye contact with anyone as I pull out my own phone to check for messages from Dixie. Nothing.

I text her anyhow: Are you okay?

There's no response.

On the TV screen, the Tennessee Volunteers are losing spectacularly to the Kentucky Wildcats. Someone turns over the ball to jeers from the audience. It won't make up the difference in their scores.

Deacon slides a Coke in front of me.

I look at him. "Who are those people?"

"Pine and River." He makes a face. "River and Pine? Don't give a fuck, really, but that's their band name. Dixie's played with them before. They decided to stop by and look her up."

The game ends and the players line up to shake hands and slap backs.

I guess I knew she wasn't staying.

They'll give her a ride. I know it.

"She's not gone yet," Deacon says.

She isn't, but she also hasn't introduced me. Or any of us.

"I think they're like sharks," he says thoughtfully. "The scavenging kind that comes 'round when you're cleaning off the boat and you've had a good day fishing. They come for what they can get, an easy meal."

Dixie knows people here. I've introduced her, made her part of my world. I didn't turn her into a Sunday sermon where I listed the ways she'd fallen down. I certainly didn't write one and invite her to sit through it.

"Dixie's not looking for an easy meal." She works hard. I'm very conscious of how much time she's spent coaching the choir. Rewriting parts. Talking up individual singers.

"That song's blowing up. People are noticing it. And without knowing how it's gonna end, I'll predict she's gonna get the kind of attention that can help a career."

"I hope she does," I say truthfully. "I think it would be good if everyone saw Dixie for the talent she is."

Deacon nods. "You think that, but I don't think River and Pine feel that way at all. They're here to see if they can ride along with her."

But the thing is, they *can* ride along. I can't. I have Bible study at six and a church roof held together with duct tape and prayers.

She belongs to bright lights and fast highways.

I belong to folding chairs and potlucks.

Someone from the group gathered around Pine's phone squeals. "Look, she's tagged the church in this one. Said y'all were raising money."

The *church accounts*? I'll get emails. Phone calls. Questions.

"She's trying to help," Deacon says.

I nod like a bobblehead. "Looks that way."

"In her own way."

He's right. You take all of someone, not just the easy parts. I know her, even after just a few weeks. She's loud and bright, says what she thinks. Maybe this is her way of trying to help with roof money. Or paying me back for letting her stay. Hell, I don't know.

I've been dealing with the roof all week. I lined up the contractor, but I'm still short more money than I want to think about. I pick up shingles every time I walk outside. But Dixie—she's the good part of all this mess. Living with her, talking with her, those moments when she laughs at something I've said. It's like sunshine after a long winter.

My phone buzzes. Bishop Caldwell. Perfect timing.

"Jack," she says when I answer, stepping outside for privacy. "I think it's time we had that conversation."

My stomach drops. "About the song."

"About the song. And the fact that my phone hasn't been silent since this morning." There's no amusement in her voice this time, just a wealth of concern. "Apparently, half the diocese has discovered TikTok."

"Bishop, I—"

"Coffee. Tomorrow morning. Nine o'clock."

It isn't a suggestion.

"Of course. I'll be there."

I hang up and stare at the night sky. The bishop wants answers I don't have and half the diocese is talking about a song I've never actually heard. But Dixie has those answers and it's time to find her.

Twenty-One

**Girl turns love life into content.
Preacher requests editorial control.**

Jack

I need to find Dixie.

I check the rectory first—empty except for Georgia Peach, who gives me a look that says *your girlfriend's drama is not my problem.* Then I walk up and down Main Street, peer back into Southern Comforts (where River and Pine are still holding court with their phone, replaying my viral humiliation for anyone who'll listen), and finally end up at Sweetgum Auto.

The van door is wide open, her guitar case visible inside, but no Dixie. I'm about to give up when a soft thump has me looking up.

She's flat on her back on the van roof, staring up at the cloudy night sky like it holds the answers to life's mysteries. I'd settle for an explanation for how she's turned me into a TikTok sensation. Or why, when Dixie Pearl needs to think, she apparently imitates a mountain goat.

"Rapunzel, Rapunzel," I call, "let down your hair."

She props herself up on her elbows and looks down. Even in the dim parking lot lighting, I can see her defensive walls fly up. "Wrong fairy tale, Preacher Man. I'm not trapped in a tower."

"No, but you're definitely running away from something."

"I'm not running. I'm stargazing." She flops back dramatically. "Very different activities. One involves cardio."

I walk around to the back of the van and the built-in ladder. "Mind if I join you in your astronomical observations?"

"Free country," she says, which is Dixie-speak for *climb aboard, but I'm going to be difficult about it.*

Getting onto the roof of a van isn't covered in seminary, but I manage without falling off or denting anything important. The metal feels cool through my jeans, and there's barely space enough for two, but Dixie scoots over some and I don't mind squeezing in.

I lie down beside her, close enough to feel the warmth radiating from her body, and look up. The clouds are thick enough that only a few stars peek through, but the moon casts everything in silver light.

"Nice view," I say.

"Mmm-hmm." She doesn't look at me. "I'm guessing you finally heard the whole song."

No point in beating around the bush. "Not quite, but River and Pine made sure the bar knew I was your 'preacher man.' They played it on repeat. I heard enough."

She makes a sucking sound. "That sounds awful."

"It was enlightening." I turn my head to study her profile. "I learned I make you hot. And also that you like your kisses to go."

Her cheeks pink up. "Those are accurate observations."

"Dixie." I wait until she looks back at me. "I knew you'd written about me. But having it played on repeat in front of a bar full of people while they stare at me like I'm some kind of viral joke? That's a hell of a way to find out what's actually in the song."

She frowns. "So? It's just a song. People write breakup songs all the time. Taylor Swift built an empire on it."

"We didn't break up. And last I checked, Taylor Swift doesn't usually blindside her exes with surprise singles."

She sits up, pulling her knees to her chest. "Look, I never thought anyone would actually listen for long. My songs usually get like two hundred plays, maybe five hundred if my aunt shares it with her book club and adds a weird GIF."

"But this one got more."

"This one got a thousand likes in the first hour." She scrubs her hands over her face. "I don't know what happened. The algorithm gods smiled on me, I guess. Or decided to ruin my life. Jury's still out."

I prop myself up on my elbow. "I know you said you'd posted something. But why would I ever think it would blow up like this? Why wouldn't you warn me? *Tell* me?"

"Because…" She's quiet for so long I start to think she might not answer. "Because I write songs when I don't know how to just say things. Feelings. It's like translating emotions into a language I actually speak."

"And what were you trying to say?"

"That I was confused. And scared. And maybe falling way too fast for a guy who prays over his breakfast and fixes broken things for fun." She shoots me a sideways look. "That I didn't know what to do with someone who's actually good."

I nudge her with my shoulder. "See? You could've told me exactly that. You just did."

"Could I? Because in my experience, when you tell people how you feel, they either run away or use it against you later." She picks at the hem of her jeans. "Songs are safer. If you don't like the message, it's just music."

I think about that. About how she grew up performing, always on display, never knowing if people liked her or just what she could do for them. About her dad treating her feelings like business propositions.

"For what it's worth," I promise her, "I don't run. And I've never used someone's feelings as ammunition."

"Yeah, well. You're weird that way."

We lie back down, shoulders touching, staring up at the clouds together. After a few minutes, she says, "Being a minister means everyone's watching, doesn't it?"

"Pretty much. I knew dating would be complicated, but I didn't expect to become a meme. And now my boss wants to have a conversation tomorrow."

"Are you in trouble? Because of the song?"

I think about it. Am I embarrassed that the entire town knows—or thinks they know—intimate details about my bedroom activities? That my bishop heard it? That some people may never look me in the eye again?

"No," I realize. "There's no trouble. I'm not embarrassed or worried—but I am hurt."

She grimaces. "On a scale of one to ten, how hurt would that be?"

"I don't mind being in your songs, Dixie. I mind feeling like a character in your story instead of... I don't know. A partner."

Her face crumples. "I fucked up."

"Yeah. You did."

"I'm sorry."

"I know."

We're quiet again. A plane blinks across the sky, red and white lights disappearing into the cloud cover.

"What if I want to write more?" she asks quietly. "About us?"

"Then let's write them together. Or at least let me know when you're turning our life into art."

"You want creative input on my songs?" The teasing note in her voice is better than the defensiveness.

"I want to know when my personal life is about to become public domain."

"Fair enough." She rolls onto her side to face me fully. "For the record, I'm scared shitless about this viral thing."

"Why?"

"Because I'm closer than I've ever been to everything I thought I wanted. Record labels are interested. My agent actually responds to my messages now. There's talk of tours and radio play and all the stuff I've been chasing for years." She picks at a rust spot on the van roof. "But I really didn't mean for it to come at your expense."

"What if it doesn't have to?" I reach out and cover her restless hand with mine. "What if we figure out how to do this together?"

"Together how? You gonna be my roadie? Follow me around the country in the church van?"

"I could learn to play tambourine."

That startles a laugh out of her. "You'd look ridiculous in leather pants."

"I'd look amazing in leather pants. I've got the legs for it."

"God, you do." Her grin transforms her face. "Okay, but seriously. How would that work? You've got a church. A calling. A chinchilla who depends on you. I'm assuming Huck would be happy to be your ride-or-die."

"And you've got a van and a guitar and more talent in your pinkie finger than most people have in their whole bodies." I thread our fingers together. "I don't have all the answers, Dixie. But I know I don't want to lose this. Whatever *this* is."

She studies our joined hands. "You know what's funny? I used to think you were like a Boy Scout. All rules and regulations and moral fiber."

"I am like a Boy Scout. I can tie seventeen different knots and I know how to start a fire with dental floss."

"But you're also…" She searches for the words. "You're not

trying to fix me. You're not trying to make me smaller or quieter or more convenient. You just let me be."

"Because you're perfect as you are."

She narrows her eyes. "I'm really not."

"Perfect for me, then."

"You can't just say things like that."

"Why not?"

"Because it makes me want to believe in things."

"What kind of things?"

"Stupid things. Like maybe the stars really did line up to break my van down in your town. Like maybe some cosmic DJ decided we needed to meet."

I smile up at the cloudy sky. "You still think the stars have more say than God?"

"I think maybe they're in cahoots." She curls into my side, resting her head on my chest. "What do you think? Still got that divine clipboard theory?"

"Maybe God's got better things to do than micromanage our love lives. Maybe He just sets up the right moments and lets us choose what to do with them."

"So what are we choosing?"

I wrap my arms around her, breathing in the scent of her shampoo. "I'm choosing to trust you. Even when you turn me into viral content without warning."

"And I'm choosing to trust you back. Even though you could probably bench-press my van."

"Probably?"

"Definitely. I've seen your shoulders." She tilts her head up to look at me. "So we're doing this? Whatever this is?"

"We're doing this."

"Even though I'm a disaster?"

"Especially because you're a disaster. Life was getting boring before you showed up."

She traces a pattern on my chest with her finger. Knowing her, it's probably the words to a song. "Jack?"

"Yeah?"

"The next song I write about you is going to be so much worse."

I groan. "Define *worse*."

"Oh, you know. More detailed. More specific. I might include sound effects."

"Dixie."

"What? I'm an artist. I need to express myself."

"Please don't express how I sound in bed to the entire internet."

"Too late. I already rhymed 'hallelujah' with 'what you do to my—'"

I silence her with a kiss, which is probably what she's been angling for all along.

"For someone who doesn't believe in astrology," she says much later, "you're pretty good at reading the signs."

"I'm learning."

Above us, the clouds shift, revealing a handful of stars. Dixie points up at them with the hand that isn't trapped between us.

"Make a wish."

"On what?"

"Those stars. That one looks like a guitar."

I squint in the direction she's pointing. It sure looks like a blob of light to me, but I'm not about to argue with a woman who thinks the universe has a sense of humor.

"What are you wishing for?" I ask.

"That's cheating. You have to make your own wish."

I look down at her—hair mussed, makeup smudged, wearing yesterday's clothes, and lying on top of a broken-down van in the middle of Nowhere, Tennessee. She's absolutely perfect.

"I already got mine," I say.

She rolls her eyes. "That's disgustingly sweet."

"You love it."

"I love—" She stops, the words hanging between us like a held breath.

"Yeah?"

"I love that you climbed up here to find me."

It isn't what she started to say, but it's something. A step.

"I'll always come find you," I promise.

"Even when I'm being difficult?"

"Especially then."

Twenty-Two

Preacher says: Please don't put that in a song

Jack

I arrive at Perked Up six minutes early for my meeting with the Right Reverend Dr. Morgan Ellery Caldwell, which makes me five minutes late by her standards. My bishop lives her life in a perpetual state of ahead-of-schedule that makes the rest of us look like we're moving through molasses. Sure enough, she's already at a corner table, two coffee mugs at parade rest in front of her. Between them sits what looks suspiciously like a printed copy of "Hot for Preacher," certain phrases highlighted in neon yellow.

Great. Nothing says "serious professional discussion" like your boss reading lyrics about how you made your girl hot.

"Jack." She glances up, her expression neutral behind some seriously stylish reading glasses. Unlike most bishops who dress like they're perpetually attending a funeral in 1963, Morgan favors tailored clerical shirts with dark jeans and her signature Doc Martens. The diocese gossip mill once debated an entire week whether her red ones were "proper church attire." She'd responded by wearing purple ones to the next synod.

"Bishop." I slide into the seat across from her, grateful she's chosen a spot where the morning coffee rush creates a buffer of ambient noise. No chance of being overheard discussing my viral song situation.

She taps the printed lyrics with one perfectly manicured nail. "Quite the literary masterpiece you've inspired here."

Heat crawls up my neck. "It's not exactly a hymn."

"Clearly." A smile tugs at the corner of her mouth. "Though I have to say, the theological framing is surprisingly nuanced for a country song."

I reach for a coffee, needing something to do with my hands. It's black and strong enough to strip paint. The Bishop doesn't believe in cream or sugar—or mercy, apparently.

"I'm assuming someone called you," I say.

"Mrs. Lancaster, Mrs. Peterson, Mr. Jenkins, and three anonymous voice mails that I suspect were all the same person disguising their voice." Bishop Morgan removes her glasses, setting them beside the paper. "They were quite detailed in their concerns."

"I can explain."

"Can you?" She raises an eyebrow. "Because I'm very interested in hearing how Wickham Hollow's vicar became the subject of a song that currently has—" she checks her phone "—over one hundred thousand streams since yesterday."

I open my mouth, close it, then try again. "Dixie's van broke down in town. I offered her the guest room at the rectory since we don't have a hotel. She's a musician, so she wrote a song."

"About wanting you to, and I quote, 'break all your rules with your calloused hands'?"

My coffee goes down wrong and I cough, heat crawling up my neck.

Bishop Morgan takes a careful sip of her own coffee. "Look,

Jack, I didn't call you here to scold you like you're a seminarian who missed curfew. You're an adult. You're allowed to have a personal life."

"But?"

"But you're also the spiritual leader of Wickham Hollow, and some members are concerned about what this—" she gestures to the lyrics "—suggests about your judgment."

I lean back, forcing myself to meet her gaze. "And what do you think it suggests?"

"That depends." She studies me over the rim of her mug. "Is this a passing infatuation with a stranded musician, or something more serious?"

The question hangs between us like a particularly awkward piñata. I consider deflecting, giving the safe answer—the one that will make this conversation easier and shorter. But Bishop Morgan values honesty above comfort, and frankly, she'd see through any BS faster than a window washer on espresso.

"I've never felt this way before," I admit. "About anyone."

Something in her expression softens. "Go, you."

"It doesn't matter, though, does it? She's Nashville-bound as soon as her van's fixed. She's got a career to build. And I have a church with a leaking roof and a congregation that's counting on me."

Bishop Morgan drums her fingers against her mug. "When did you last take a vacation, Jack? Three years ago? Four?"

That's not the question I'm expecting. "What does that have to do with—"

"The Church has survived two thousand years. It will survive you taking some personal time." She leans forward. "We don't need perfect ministers, Jack. We need authentic ones."

I shake my head, trying to process. "So you're not mad?"

"Mad that one of my ministers is human enough to fall in love? No." She taps the lyric sheet again. "Although I would prefer if future love songs were perhaps a touch less explicit about what you do with those 'calloused hands.'"

My face heats to approximately the temperature of the sun's surface.

"That said," she continues, "there are practicalities to consider. If this relationship continues, there will be talk. Some people will leave the church. Others will watch you like hawks for any perceived misstep. The vestry will have opinions. So. Many. Opinions."

"I know." Boy, do I know.

"But some will support you. Those who see that having a minister who understands love, loss, and difficult choices makes you more effective, not less." She hands me the lyrics. "These are yours. It's your choice what you do with them." As I take the paper, she adds, "Just promise me one thing, Jack."

"What's that?"

"Whatever you decide—about Dixie, about Wickham Hollow—make sure it's because it's what you truly want. Not because it's what you think you should want." She smiles then, genuine and warm. "The world has enough martyrs already. What it needs are people brave enough to be happy."

"I'll try to remember that."

"Good." Bishop Morgan checks her phone. "Now, I have to get back for a budget meeting that will make me question every life choice I've ever made. Any questions before I go?"

Just one, but I'm not sure I want the answer. "Did you listen to the song?"

She stands, shouldering her bag. "Three times. It's quite catchy." Then, with a wink that nearly stops my heart: "My favorite part was the bridge. Very evocative."

As I watch her leave, I feel lighter than I have in days. Whatever comes next with Dixie—whether she stays or goes, whether we have a future together or just this strange, beautiful moment—at least I know I have one unexpected ally in my corner.

And honestly? The lyrics aren't that bad.

Well, except for the one verse about my beard. That's definitely coming up at my next performance review.

Despite the bishop meeting going better than I expected,
I'm still processing it all when I get home. I'm halfway through
making lunch when Dixie pads into the kitchen, guitar in
hand and that particular grin on her face that usually spells
trouble. She hops up onto the counter beside the stove, bare
legs swinging, and settles the guitar across her lap.

Georgia Peach immediately appears on the windowsill
above the sink, chittering her disapproval at the musical in-
terruption.

"Want to hear what I wrote for your choir?" Dixie's already tuning a string.

I set down my knife and wipe my hands on the dish towel.
"You finished it?"

"Oh, I finished it alright." Her grin widens. "Fair warning—
it's no 'How Great Thou Art.'"

She strums the opening chords, and then her voice fills the
kitchen, warm and sure:

"I came here runnin' from a dream gone cold
With nothin' but heartache and stories untold
But these back-road angels took me as I am
Broken and lost with an empty-handed plan
Now Sunday morning coffee tastes like coming home
And I ain't lonely even when I'm all alone
'Cause home ain't a place you can find on a map
It's the folks who'll catch you when your world's 'bout to collapse."

I'm in trouble from the first line. She's sitting on my kitchen
counter, her bare legs swinging, and she's singing about coming here broken with an empty-handed plan. Well, hell. She
offered to write something for the choir, but this isn't just a
song—it's our whole damn story set to music. When she gets
to the part about finding home in people who'll catch you,
I have to grip the edge of the counter because something's

shifting in my chest that feels dangerously close to hope. She's looking right at me when she sings it, not performing but telling me something, and I realize this woman who's been planning her escape since day one just wrote a love letter to staying put. That's a good thing, right? Georgia Peach chirps her approval, the little traitor, and I'm standing here in my own kitchen completely undone by a country song. I should probably say something profound, but all I can think is that if she's writing songs about putting down roots, maybe I won't have to watch her drive away after all.

But as Dixie keeps singing, something shifts. I brace my forearms against the counter on either side of the stove, leaning back to listen.

"Deacon's pourin' whiskey with a knowing grin
While Slate just grumbles but he lets me in
Dee's got flowers bloomin' everywhere she goes
And Georgia Peach judges all my highs and lows
Found a family in the strangest places
Gruff old hearts and sun-kissed faces
Who knew home could wear overalls and boots
And a chinchilla with some attitude."

Georgia Peach climbs down to investigate, and I absently stroke her soft fur. Dixie isn't mocking us—she's celebrating us. Each verse paints a picture I recognize: Slate's gruff exterior hiding his soft heart, Dee's relentless optimism, the way we all show up for each other despite our flaws.

"Hallelujah for the mess we are
Small-town sinners 'neath Southern stars
We ain't angels but we've got big hearts…"

When she hits the bridge—the call and response about lifting each other up—I know for sure. She's written a love song. Not to me, but to all of us. To the community that's become her home.

She finishes with a flourish, letting the last chord ring out.

I open my eyes to find her watching me, guitar still cradled in her arms, Georgia Peach now sitting possessively on her thigh.

"So? Think they'll go for it?"

I set the guitar aside, careful not to knock it against the cabinet, then move in close. My hands find the counter on either side of her hips, and suddenly she's caged between my arms. I can smell that vanilla scent she always carries. "It's perfect. It's us."

"Even the sinner part?"

"Yeah." I brush a piece of hair away from her face, my rough fingers probably too calloused against her soft skin, but she doesn't pull away. "We are a mess."

Her grin goes crooked and she tries to play it off with a half-hearted shrug. "Well, you're not *that* much of a mess. Most of you, anyway."

"Just most of us?"

"Slate's still terrifying."

I kiss her then, one hand fisting in her hair, the other gripping her hip hard enough to bruise. Her mouth opens under mine immediately, and Christ, she tastes like the coffee she's been drinking and something that's purely her. When she makes that desperate sound in the back of her throat, the one that drives me crazy, and her nails dig into my chest through my shirt, I lose what's left of my control. Her legs wrap around my waist, pulling me against her, and I can feel how much she wants this through the thin fabric between us.

Georgia Peach hisses and bolts for the windowsill, but I barely register it. All I can focus on is the way Dixie's tongue slides against mine, the way her hips rock against me, seeking friction. Her hands are everywhere—tangling in my hair, scraping down my back, tugging at my shirt like she wants to tear it off.

"Jack," she breathes against my mouth, and hearing my name like that, all rough and wanting, makes something primitive snap inside me. I press her harder against the counter, my mouth moving to her neck, tasting the salt of her skin.

I bite gently at the spot where her neck meets her shoulder, and she arches against me with a gasp.

"Bedroom," I growl against her skin, but she shakes her head.

"Here," she pants, her hands already working at my belt. "Right here, right now."

For a second, I consider it. God knows I want to take her on every surface in this house. But she deserves better than a quick fuck against the kitchen counter, no matter how much we both want it.

"No." I pull back to look at her, taking in her swollen lips, the flush spreading down her chest. "When I have you, I'm taking my time."

Before she can argue, I slide my arms under her thighs and lift her off the counter. She wraps her legs around my waist instinctively, and the feel of her pressed against me makes me stumble slightly as I carry her toward the bedroom.

"Jack," she whispers, her mouth finding that spot just below my ear that makes my knees weak. "The talent show—"

"Later," I say firmly, kicking the bedroom door shut behind us. "The bishop, the song, all of it—later. Right now, there's just us."

I set her down beside the bed, my hands framing her face as I kiss her again, slower this time but no less intense. Everything else can wait. Right now, she's mine, and I'm going to worship every inch of her until the rest of the world disappears.

Her fingers find the hem of my shirt, and when she pulls it over my head, her eyes go dark with want. "Show me," she says, and I know exactly what she means.

I intend to.

Twenty-Three

Girl crashes. Preacher catches.

Dixie

I'm *not* getting sick. I don't have time for this shit.

Jack gave me a long look this morning when he handed over my coffee mug before he went out to save the world. He's not supposed to have to take care of me, too; the man's busy as fuck rescuing the rest of the world. The look in his eye when he says goodbye, though, says he's just postponing his questions until later. But rheumatoid arthritis is a fickle mistress, so some mornings I feel like I've been run over by a stampede of cows while other mornings make me think I could climb a few mountains. I hate not knowing which version of myself I'll wake up as.

Selfishly, I want to hold on to every normal moment I can with Jack. I'll be his hookup and his nemesis, his choir director and his lover—but the one thing I won't be is the sick-ass woman who needs taking care of.

The flare, however, doesn't give a fuck about my feelings. It comes right on in—first the stiffness in my fingers, then the low buzz of pressure behind my eyes, and finally a dull, familiar ache in my wrists. Something heavy's hanging off my bones, dragging me down.

My phone buzzes. Dad.

DAD: Sent you contracts. Check your email.

I type back with one thumb: Got them.

His response is both brutal and predictable. So why the delay in signing? That's not how pros handle business, Dixie. You've gotta move faster if you want to make it.

That's the supportive wisdom of a man who once told me a CMT feature wasn't a "real milestone" unless it led to network coverage and a record deal.

I'm not feeling great, I text. Gimme a minute.

I get two seconds from him.

You never feel great. That's the problem. The hustle doesn't wait for you to feel good.

He follows this with a sun emoji, a rocket ship, and flames. I guess he wants to light a fire under my ass.

My thumb hovers over the keyboard, trembling ever so slightly—might be from the RA or it might be due to the slow-boiling fury.

Wow. Thank you for the motivational poster. Should I tape it next to my heating pad?

Don't get snippy, he texts. I listened to that Hot for Preacher song you posted. It's good. Real good. So why are you wasting time in a backwoods town when you could be in Nashville making valuable connections?

I may not have mentioned the van breakdown and my lack

of cash and van parts. I should slip it in there now, but I can't
bring myself to do it.

DAD: You should be playing that song in every bar on Broad-
way. Getting noticed. Signing something real. Not hiding out
with farmers and Bible thumpers in the middle of nowhere.

That hurts. Not because it isn't exactly what I expected him
to say—but because it is. Word for damn word.

ME: You think I'm throwing myself away?

I think you're better than this. He adds two trophy icons.
You've got a window, Dixie. A real one. Don't waste it.
Maybe I'm not wasting it, I fire back. Maybe I'm just tired.
He doesn't get it.

DAD: Tired? Of what?

Of being measured. Of being told I'm behind. Of grinding
myself into the ground for someone else's dream. Of wondering if the only reason I ever make it anywhere is because of
him. Of not being enough when I try and too much when
I don't.
Instead of answering, I mute our conversation and press the
heels of my hands into my eyes.
In the next minute, I'm grabbing my notebook and a pen.
If he thought I was wasting my time, maybe I'll write a song
about it. Maybe I'll write a whole damn album about choosing something different.
"Touch me with those morals," I snarl at the ceiling. It's a
joke. Except… It kind of isn't. It's the name of a song.
And now there's a melody playing in my head, bluesy and

defiant, and the words feel like they've been waiting in my chest for weeks:

"You walked in wearin' flannel and grace,
With that Sunday school smile on your sinner's face.
Talked like a hymn but you looked like sin,
And Lord help me, I let you in.
Your 'No strings' sounded like a prayer,
But your hands on my hips didn't fight fair.
You've got conviction written in your bones—
But, baby, you touch me like a man who's been alone too long.
So, touch me with those morals, Preacher Man,
Break all your rules with your calloused hands.
You quote the Good Book, I rewrite the page,
Let's sin real soft and then misbehave.
You may think it's wrong, but it feels so right—
Holy hell, keep me warm tonight."

The words pour out faster than I can scrawl them:

"You bless your food, I bless the mess,
I wear my damage like a sequined dress.
You say I'm trouble and I don't deny it,
But I've seen the way you stay quiet.
You burn like guilt in a gospel song,
Tryna prove you're pure when the pull's this strong.
Your faith's a fire, mine's not even a spark—
So go on, light me up in the dark.
Yeah, touch me with those morals, Preacher Man,
Preach me into your redemption plan.
Read me your heart in that basement bar,
Confess in whispers across my guitar.
You say it's wrong, but we're past pretend—
Save your soul, then sin again."

Time for the bridge. I write it down and hum a few notes, leaning into its vulnerability:

"So, touch me with those morals, Preacher Man,
Kiss me like grace with a shaky hand.
Let me be your hallelujah mistake,
The kind you'd risk it all to make.
You say you can't—well, maybe you should.
A little bit of bad might do us both good.
So, touch me with those morals…
And I'll touch you like only a sinner could."

This isn't just about Jack—it's about wanting something I've never craved before. Security. Stability. Someone who'll run up against my sharp edges and choose to stay anyway. Someone worth risking everything for.

My phone buzzes again. This time it's Dee, asking if I want to help plant stuff in the town's planters. Six weeks ago, I'd have laughed at the idea of voluntary gardening. Now I'm feeling better and text back yes.

When I walk outside, I find Dee directing a small army of volunteers with the efficiency of a general and the enthusiasm of a golden retriever. She spots me approaching and waves a dirt-covered hand.

"Dixie! Perfect timing. We need someone to help with the hanging baskets."

I spend the next two hours elbow-deep in potting soil, listening to one of the choir ladies tell stories about her late husband's failed attempts at growing tomatoes, while Slate stoically shoves marigolds into a planter.

"You're getting good at this," Dee says, watching me tease apart the roots of a stubborn petunia. "Might make a gardener out of you yet."

"Don't get ahead of yourself," I snark back, but the truth is, I can see the appeal. There's something hopeful about planting things, about believing they'll grow and bloom and make the world just a little more beautiful.

"Speaking of getting ahead of ourselves," Dee continues, shooting me a sideways look, "how are things with our resident minister?"

I concentrate very hard on the flower in my hands. "What things?"

"Oh, please. The man looks at you like you hung the moon and personally arranged all the stars for his viewing pleasure. And you stare right back like you want to climb him like a tree but are too stubborn to admit it."

"I do not—"

"Honey, I have eyes. And so does everyone else in this town." Dee's grin is positively wicked. "The question is, what are you going to do about it?"

I open my mouth to give her my standard speech about being a free spirit who doesn't do commitment, but the words don't come.

"I wrote a song," I say instead.

"About him?"

"About what it might be like. If I stayed."

Dee's face softens. "And what would it be like?"

"Terrifying," I admit.

Twenty-Four

Girl down

Dixie

I have to cancel.

Again.

Jesus fucking Christ, why can't I do this?

The church is full of people who've come for our big dress rehearsal the night before the talent show. So many people. Crowds of them. Not showing up isn't an option, so here I am.

Slate looms at the back of the choir, looking like he wants to murder someone except when he has Dee in his line of sight. Then I'm pretty sure he wants to discuss her baked goods. In great, sexy detail. She can't sing for shit, but like I told Jack, my song doesn't require perfect pitch—it just needs heart. Toby's practicing his stomping pattern, while someone else whose name I've forgotten because I'm a bad, bad person is the self-appointed wardrobe mistress and handing out cowboy hats and bandannas to lean into the country vibe.

Unlike me, they're all working hard and singing their hearts out. They've shown up.

Exhaustion, my old nemesis, you win. Insta-cure for numbing exhaustion, I google. And also: menopause crushing fatigue in twenties?

It's only been five, maybe six months since my last flare. I'd driven to a music festival in South Carolina and then hadn't been able to drag myself out of the Motel 6 for three whole days. That particular booking coordinator will never work with me again. Sure, it had been an excused cancellation because I'd been legitimately sick, but I'd lost my fee (no singing means no cash) and it had cemented my flaky rep. The bookers and promoters my agent works with are understandably hesitant because I don't always show up.

Apparently, I can learn my lesson because here I am, standing in front of the Wickham Hollow Chapel Choir, clapping the beat with zero enthusiasm while twenty people belt out "Hallelujah for the mess we are!" with varying degrees of success. Mostly, I fantasize about lying down on that wooden pew over there and passing out.

I can't even throw the reins to Jack because he texted earlier that he'd be an hour late as he's at the hospital.

At least I'd remembered to check that he was okay, had all his limbs, and wasn't lying in an ER somewhere bleeding out.

He's fine.

Me? Not so much. My fingers have been transmuted into lead. My joints scream. A furnace burns in my forehead and a spike in my temple pulses in time with the organ. But I keep smiling (it may be more of a grimace), keep clapping, keep pretending this is all just peachy keen because what kind of leader bails the night before the big performance?

Someone somewhere says something. About the bridge? Don't care. Just keep singing.

"Are you okay?" Dee slants a cautious smile my way. I have a lot to apologize for after they win the talent show because I might have snapped at Dee. And the tenors. And, okay, the entire choir with the exception of Toby.

"I'm fine! Let's take it from the top."

Our performance is scheduled for six o'clock. That means I only have to finish this run-through, drive ninety minutes tomorrow to a rural fairground on the opposite side of the state, and lead my minions through an energetic rendition of "Hallelujah for the Mess We Are." Just hold it together for approximately twenty-three more hours. I can do it.

The music stops.

Or maybe it's me.

Yeah, the problem is definitely me.

"I'm good." My voice cracks halfway through the sentence. "Just need a sip of water."

I march toward my bag. Back pew. Not that far. My water bottle is in there, so I'll just sit for thirty seconds and hydrate.

I land hard in the front pew instead, legs buckling before I can cover and pretend they haven't.

Slate rumbles something.

"What?" I snap, opening my eyes. When did I shut them?

He's crouched in front of me, a crinkle of worry digging into his forehead as he holds out a glass bottle of something dank and green-looking. Poison. Garden fertilizer. Don't know, don't care. It's green. I hate green.

"Tell me it's alcoholic."

"Juice." He shoves it into my hand, then forcibly raises my hand to my mouth. I'm his puppet.

"Jesus. That's foul."

It actually isn't the worst thing I've ever drunk. Light, refreshing, tastes like apples and lawn mower clippings with a hint of mint. Slate guides it to my mouth like I'm a helpless, blind kitten. I'll have to kill him.

I put it on the list for Future Me to deal with.

"Maybe we should wrap?" That's Dee popping up at the end of the pew.

Please go away. I need to lie down. This wooden pew is better than a top-of-the-line Sealy Posturepedic.

"Give me five," I growl.

The world swims in and out. I must nod off because the next thing I know, I'm horizontal, the church has gone blissfully quiet, and the choir may have been struck mute. My body is a war zone, joints stiff as cinder blocks, and someone is talking way too loud nearby.

"...she didn't want to leave. Said she was fine."

Dee, my brain supplies.

The grunt is Slate's.

"She's not fine." Jack. Jack's voice, low and certain, very worried. "Dixie?"

He doesn't need to overreact. I just need a nap. *Sorry I fucked up your choir rehearsal.*

I try to share that thought with him, but what comes out isn't any kind of a word. Shit. I try again.

"What's up?" Jack crouches down beside me, all flannel and beard and those absurdly gentle eyes.

"Is rehearsal over?"

His mouth curves up in the smallest smile, but it doesn't reach his eyes. "Choir's gone. I stayed behind. You fell asleep sitting straight up. That's some talent."

"I didn't mean to."

"I know."

I try to push myself upright, to stand, to pretend I have this handled—but my joints are on strike and a fuzzy pattern messes up my vision.

"Nope." Jack's arms come around me. "This is me ignoring that you're a strong, independent woman for a second."

"Caveman Jack."

"Yeah. I do a pretty good barbarian, too."

He's warm and solid. Smells like cedar. Instead of protesting, I lean into him.

He carries me effortlessly, cradled against his chest like a damsel in distress from a really great romance novel. I hate how good it feels.

"Put me down." I make a token protest. *Please ignore me.* "I can walk."

"Nope again." He says something to Dee and Slate—who seems to be using actual words and even full sentences now—and I zone out.

The walk back to the rectory takes an eternity. My entire life has been reduced to Jack's arms around me, my head on Jack's chest. Trying not to fall asleep. I have stuff to do.

I must say that last one out loud, because he looks down at me and growls. Jack Carter *growls.* It's a red-letter, groundbreaking kind of night.

"You have one job," he says. "Taking care of yourself."

He sounds like he means it.

"Are you firing me as your choir director?"

"Jesus Christ."

"Because you should know that you have the performance of a lifetime tomorrow. I think you need me."

"Yeah, I do."

By the time we're inside, I'm shivering. Stupid RA. It makes me feel like I have the flu.

He sets me down on his bed and covers me with the ugliest handmade quilt I've ever seen. It's offensively bright orange and green, patterned with cartoon pumpkins and something that might be turnips.

"Dee brought it. Said it was comforting and autumnal."

"It's spring." I bet she puts her Christmas lights up in August, too.

"She's bringing herbal tea and chicken soup later. Consider yourself warned. You okay letting me look at your meds? You've got something for the pain, right?"

When I nod, he disappears into the bathroom where I keep a ridiculous pharmacy of bottles. After he returns, he has ibuprofen and my menthol rub. "This?"

"Yeah. But I already took some before rehearsal. Can't take more for a few hours."

He nods, sets the bottles down, and settles beside me. The silence stretches. It should feel awkward, but somehow it doesn't.

"I shouldn't have pushed it," I say finally.

"You wanted to do right by the choir."

Yeah. "I also wanted to prove I'm not weak."

Or lazy. Unmotivated. Self-indulgent.

Suck it up, my dad's voice says in my head.

"Needing help isn't weakness, Dixie."

"Says the man who tried to fix the roof himself during a thunderstorm."

"I had Deacon with me and that was different."

"Sure."

Jack leans forward, resting his elbows on his knees. "You've been in pain for days, haven't you?"

"Maybe."

"Why not say something?"

So many reasons. "It's not something I like talking about."

"You'd rather pass out in a pew than admit you need help?"

"I didn't pass out. I just powered down a little."

His laugh surprises us both. "Powered down?"

"Like a Roomba. Hit a wall and stopped moving. It was a nap, not cardiac arrest."

Jack rubs his face with one hand, half amused, half exasperated. "You're impossible."

"Thanks."

We lapse into silence again.

"Jack?"

"Yeah?"

"I'm not fine."

His eyes meet mine.

"I try to be." Let the record show I'm protesting. "I try real hard. I push and smile and flirt and lead choirs and make jokes, but sometimes my body doesn't get the memo. And I hate it. I hate feeling like I'm letting people down. Like I'm broken. Like the RA is winning and that means I'm losing. At life. At whatever."

"You're not broken." He sounds like he believes it, too.

"You don't know what it's like."

"No. But I know what it's like to feel like you have to carry everything alone. You don't have to prove anything to me, Dixie. I don't need you to be perfect. Just real."

"Real me isn't very glamorous."

"Good thing I've never been into glamour."

I let Dee's super-ugly quilt cocoon me and close my eyes. Jack doesn't move, but just in case—

"Stay?" I ask.

"I'm not going anywhere."

I sleep for what feels like hours. At some point, Jack tucks an army of hot water bottles into the bed with me. He reads to me from the orc romance I just downloaded onto my e-reader. And he stays. Solid. Steady.

The next time I wake up, the pain is better. Not gone, but it's more manageable. Jack is sitting beside me, reading something non-orc-related.

I'm sure he'll need time to recover from what he found on my Kindle.

"How long was I out?"

He sets his book down. "A couple of hours. You scared me."

"Sorry."

"Don't be. I just hate seeing you hurt."

"You know I can't do the show tomorrow, right? I should have given you some warning, but who wants to admit that they're a quitter? 'Oh, hey! I have to let you down!'"

"You're not letting anyone down," he says. "You carried this thing farther than most people would have. The choir's ready because of you."

"It's still quitting."

"It's not. It's knowing your limits."

I watch him for a moment. "You're kind of amazing, you know?"

He smiles—and there's that strip of pink on his cheeks that I love. "Don't let the beard fool you. I'm just a guy trying to do right."

"You definitely did right by me."

My eyes sting, but I refuse to cry because I hate it. "I've been alone with this for a long time."

"You're not alone anymore."

I don't know who moves first—I'm Team Tie—but suddenly he's holding me and I'm holding him right back.

"Thank you," I tell his shoulder. It's a really great shoulder.

"For what?"

"For staying."

He presses his lips to the top of my head. "Always."

Twenty-Five

Girl concedes defeat

Dixie

I wake up in a fog of heat and pain. Someone's run me over with the church bus and then reversed to make sure I got the message. My joints are on fire, my knees have jumped into the conflagration, and when I attempt a vertical position, a wave of nausea rolls through me so hard that I have to flop back against the pillow and breathe through it.

At least my thumbs work.

I text Dee: Hypothetically, if someone's hands decided to stage a rebellion, what's the going rate for a personal assistant? Asking for a friend.

And Deacon: I'm having a bad day and I need someone to open things for me and not be weird about it?

And then because it really can't wait, I give up and text Jack (who will be nearby, I know it): Fuck. FUCK. Okay fine, I can't do this alone today.

For the next few minutes, I try to block my dad's voice

out of my head. *Try harder,* his voice orders. *You can do it. Just try harder.*

I can't remember the last time I was this tired. I did a virtual appointment this morning with my Nashville doctor, but she was fresh out of miracle cures. She said she'd look into adjusting my biologics, but for right now all I can do is take ibuprofen and rest. My fifty-dollar co-pay buys me the gem: *You have to listen to your body, Dixie.*

And now my body's grumpier than fuck and my inability to get out of bed is embarrassing.

"C'mon, Pearl. Get it together."

I swing my legs over the side of the bed. Progress! The next step is simple: I plant my feet on the floor and push myself upright. I've been doing it since I was two, so I'm a pro. I'll just power through this.

Someone knocks on the door.

"Dix? Can I come in?"

Of course it's Jack. I wouldn't put it past him to have been sitting outside my door.

"Yeah," I grouse. "Ohhhh. You thought I texted for *help*? You must have misread that, but while you're here... Can you help me stand up and get dressed?"

Jack comes in with a travel mug in one hand and a deeply concerned look in his eyes. This is bad. He's dressed for going out in dark slacks and a crisp white shirt, sleeves rolled up to the elbows. His tie hangs loose around his neck. I want to drink him in, but even that's too much effort.

He crosses the room in three steps. "You don't look better."

Fortunately, I still have enough strength left to raise my right hand and flip him off. "You're such a charmer, Reverend."

"I'll be nicer when you're back in bed."

"You always are." I wink at him. Flirting feels safe. Flirting means not admitting the truth.

He doesn't wait for me to lie down because he's bossy. He

sets his travel cup on the dresser and then eases me back down himself. I don't know how he does it, but he scoops me up and he's my very own human elevator. It feels so good to be horizontal that I don't even bitch about him taking over like that.

Once he's got me arranged to his satisfaction, he crouches down beside to me, his hand smoothing my hair back from my face. "What can I do?"

"Well, you did promise to be nice to me once I was in bed."

"I think you need a rain check on that. And—"

I need to tell him that I'm fine, that I'm totally making it to the talent show. Easy-peasy. But his fingers are applying this delicious pressure to mysterious points on my skull and it feels so good that I decide to just lie here.

"Okay, you're not fine."

What? No! Why isn't he convinced?

"It's just a flare," I say. "It'll pass."

"Yeah," Jack says, his voice full of sympathy. "But not in the next twenty minutes. You have to stay home."

I rage internally as I imagine what everyone will say when I don't show up. Having my dad's voice stuck in my head is turning out to super inconvenient. *He* thinks I should suck it up and go.

"I don't want to leave y'all hanging. The choir needs someone to keep tempo and Dee's got stage fright, and—"

Jack's hand strokes over my hair. "Dixie, I came in here planning to tie you to the bed."

"Kinky," I whine. "Why are you teasing me like that?"

"Because you need to take care of yourself. You come first." His hand is cupping my cheek now. "You already did your part. You wrote a song. They learned it. You gave them confidence. You made them believe. Now it's time for them to show it."

"Is this the speech about the mama bird pushing the baby bird out of the nest? And how we're all supposed to yell FLYYYYYYY and not think about what happens if mama bird has really bad judgment or startles baby bird so badly that baby stumbles over its wings and then it's a splat fest?"

"No." He gives me a small smile. "Although I might steal that for a sermon."

"Copyright, Preacher Man." I reach up and smooth his beard down where it's sticking up some. Somehow my hand stays glued to his face.

I refuse to cry. I hate crying and crying in front of people is the worst. Tear ducts, you've been warned: no misbehaving.

"I have to be really honest and then you and I will talk about what happens next," Jack says and then waits until I nod. I'm a captive audience and we both know it. "I want to stay. God help me, Dix, I want to stay here with you. But this talent show is our best shot at raising enough money for the roof. If I thought me staying would take away your pain, I wouldn't move from this spot. But I can't fix this. What I can do is take what you taught them and get them on that stage. I can show up—for you. Even if you're not standing beside me, you'll be there."

My hand falls. Gravity has won. "Go. Kick butt."

"You're not gonna be alone. I asked Deacon to come sit with you."

What? No! I mean, sure, I sort of, not quite accidentally texted the man about an assist, but this feels suspiciously like babysitting. At the very least, it's an unequal exchange. Jack's getting sex out of this and sex is the great equalizer.

I frown. Force the words out. "Jack, absolutely not—"

He's unswayed by my glower. "You need someone here. Someone to nag you to drink water and keep an eye on your fever. I trust him."

"I must look real sexy right now."

He brushes the damp hair back from my forehead. I could get used to this. Just a little. "You always look sexy. Even when you look like you could murder someone for a heating pad."

"I want to go," I say. "I'm not a quitter."

"You'll be there. I'm FaceTiming you in. You think I'm going on that stage without you? Hell, no."

He kisses my forehead (my forehead!) and leaves before I can get any more sentimental. A few minutes later, Deacon shows up with a blue sports drink and a bag of frozen peas. When I tell him I'm not sure what the peas are for, he grumbles that I should google it. He also grumbles about being drafted into nurse duty but tucks Dee's ugly-ass blanket around me and glares until I've polished off half the sports drink. It's disgusting and when I tell him so, he argues that I must be feeling better and that he's the best nurse ever.

"Don't think I won't sit on you if you try to sneak out," he warns, flipping through the Netflix offerings on his tablet. Apparently, we girlfriends are having a movie night.

I make wide eyes at him. "Are you threatening assault? I'll have you up before the nursing board, Backwoods."

"Don't tempt me, Nashville."

He keeps one eye on me while pretending to care deeply about reruns of *Storage Wars*. I drift in and out, the ache in my joints dulling to a constant throb. When Jack's name lights up my phone, Deacon grunts and hands it over.

Three photos have come through in quick succession. After hours of driving deep into rural Tennessee, the fairground looks exactly like what you'd expect—a sprawling collection of metal buildings and wooden pavilions scattered across red Tennessee dirt, strings of lights twinkling between structures. There's a shot of the main barn with its doors thrown wide, through which I can see a stage flanked by hay bales and backed by a hand-painted banner for Raise the Roof. The third makes me smile despite everything: the choir van parked between two pickup trucks, with Slate lurking in the background. Not surprisingly, he looks like he's questioning the life choices that led him there.

Jack's text arrives a second later: Your venue, m'lady. Very fancy.

"Time to watch the train wreck," Deacon says as I scroll through the pictures.

"It'll be amazing."

"Yeah." He winks. "We could pray on it, you and me."

"From your mouth to God's ears," I say lightly. That line hasn't worked out for me, but I'm willing to be proved wrong.

When I hit Accept on Jack's call, his face fills the screen, backlit by stage lights. His beard is ruffled like he's been running a hand over it.

"Hey, gorgeous," he says.

"Hey yourself, showstopper."

He flips the camera around to show the packed theater. A lot of people have shown up. The choir's stage left, fidgeting and giggling. I spot Dee straightening someone's cowboy hat and Slate cracking his knuckles like they're about to fight, not sing. Down front, five judges sit at a long table with scorecards and water bottles, looking official and ever so slightly bored.

"Totally ready," I say.

"Thanks to you."

He adjusts the phone while we talk, maybe putting it on a tripod near the edge of the stage. It's hard to tell because the image tilts and I mostly get a shot of his beard followed by a flash of the ceiling and the lighting rig.

"Am I about to be your emotional support livestream?"

"Stay with me, okay?"

"Always."

The choir is up ten minutes later. I have a good view of them as they file out onto the stage in their matching cowboy hats and bandannas. They've gone full country with denim and boots, looking like they're ready for a barn dance rather than a church talent show.

The room quiets. Jack steps forward, clears his throat, and gives a brief, heartfelt intro about community and music and roofs that don't leak. It's a great speech. He even talks about why they chose this song—"it means a lot to our choir direc-

tor, who's absent tonight due to illness, but who's right here
in our hearts nonetheless"—and then… "Sometimes the best
families are the ones you choose."

Then they start.

"Hallelujah for the mess we are
Small-town sinners 'neath Southern stars
We ain't angels but we've got big hearts…"

It's my irreverent anthem about small-town misfits, turned
into a rollicking, gospel-infused barn burner with handclaps,
stomping boots, and a call–and–response section that no one
can resist.

"Hallelujah for the mess we are
Small-town sinners 'neath Southern stars
We ain't angels but we've got big hearts—
Hallelujah for the mess we are!"

The whole audience is on their feet, stomping along with
the choir's boots hitting the staging in perfect rhythm (and by
perfect, I really mean enthusiastic as hell). "Come on, y'all!"
Jack yells, and the crowd roars back: "Give it all!"

They aren't just watching the performance. They're part
of it.

I have to admit, it isn't perfect. Dee doesn't get a single
sound out. Slate's rap is downright terrifying.

They nail it.

By the end, I'm crying. It's so stupid. Deacon hands me a
tissue without a word as the applause thunders through the
phone, right up until the call cuts out. It's an hour before Jack
calls me back, although the group chat with the choir has
blown up in the meantime.

Dee: We did it!! We're on the podium!!!

Slate: This is not the Olympics. There's no medal ceremony.

Walter: They're gonna SHOW US THE MONEY

Dee: Very Christian

Walter: They're gonna SHOW US THE MONEY

Toby: Did you hear me? I was SO loud!

Walter: Shoot. How do I unsend a text message? Toby, get over here and show me.

Slate: Everyone heard you. You were great.

Walter: I do have a few notes for our next performance.

Slate: I'm never doing this again.

Dee: We've got to do it at least once more, but with Dixie. She's choir now. We love her.

Walter: Can we say that?

Slate: [[Sends black heart emoji]]

Slate also sends me a picture, although I think that might not be on purpose. It's an out-of-focus shot of Dee's hand and her shoulder.

"We placed third," Jack announces when I answer his call later. "Out of twenty-five acts. We got a check for fifteen grand."

"Third place?" I'm either going to joke about this or cry. "Fifteen grand's nice, Jack, but that's not an entire roof. We needed a win. Like, full-on miracle territory. You can't order a third of a roof. It's the whole roof or nothing."

"Okay," he says, as if it's no big deal.

"What?"

"Okay, it's a third—but that's a third further than we were this morning. Why can't this be a start of the solution and not a catastrophic, gloom-and-doom ending?"

"I failed you." It seems super clear to me. "I didn't get the win. Hell, I didn't even get to the *venue*."

He can't argue with me on that. It's the truth, as is the fact that he's still twenty-five thousand dollars short for a new roof.

If I suddenly discovered a magic lamp with a wish-granting genie, I'd totally wish him up a new roof right now. I'd give up a chance at a different dream if it would get him what he needed.

And if I could fast-forward time and skip ahead ten years or even twenty to some fantastic time when I'm a successful country music singer who sells out big venues and gets signing bonuses and charts every other week—I'd give him that roof. I'd put a big, pink bow on it and say *Merry Christmas, Jack. You deserve this! Love, Dixie.*

Wait. I mentally rewrite my gift tag. *With warm regards, Dixie!* Or maybe *Best, Dixie*? This isn't love. It can't be.

"Dixie Pearl," he says, for once oblivious to my inner turmoil. "You got us this far. You did this."

"No," I tell him. "We did this. You and me."

He smiles, soft and full of something I don't want to a name just yet.

After we end the call, I lie back against the pillows. The pain's still here, my fever hasn't broken, and my body feels like a skin sack full of wet cement. But inside, somewhere real deep down, I feel warm. Not just from Jack. From all of them. From the idea that maybe I don't have to be the one holding everything together all the time.

Maybe trusting someone isn't the same thing as giving up.

Maybe being vulnerable doesn't mean being weak.

Deacon nods at the tablet. "Want to see what other disasters are airing tonight?"

"Sure. But nothing with singing. I think I just got my fill."

He snorts. "You're the boss."

I'm not, though. Not here. Not tonight.

And for once, that feels okay.

Twenty-Six

Bronze medal. Gold-level group hug.

Jack

I should be happy.

Our choir sang their hearts out and got the audience on their feet.

We've celebrated with hugs, passed out high fives, and shed some joyful tears. Slate disappeared somewhere with Dee, who stood behind him the entire song. People come up and pass out compliments like Tic Tacs. Our song's fun. Fresh. Who doesn't want to be part of a mess that felt like family?

But we've come in third.

We needed to win first to fix the church roof without taking out a second mortgage or holding eight million bake sales.

Fifteen grand doesn't cut it.

I stand offstage in the wings, behind the black curtains that keep the audience from seeing how the magic happened. It's crowded as it's crammed with crap from the performances. Tape on the floor marks where the choirs stood. There's a folding chair, an errant bandanna from one of our costumes.

The wooden floor has a slightly sticky feel from years of dance recitals. The stagehands started cleanup a half hour ago, pulling cables and putting away mic stands. Most of the audience has filed out, and now there's just a handful of people left, gathering music and water bottles prior to heading out. My phone buzzes in my pocket.

DEACON: She's alive. Still cranky. Still sweaty. Still too good for you.

A second buzz. Proof of life.

I tap the tiny thumbnail. Dixie's curled up on the rectory couch under the world's ugliest quilt, all mismatched florals and crooked seams. Her hair's in a messy bun, eyes shut, one arm flopped over her head like a half-hearted protest against existing. Georgia Peach is asleep on her feet.

Another buzz.

DEACON: If she wakes up and catches me taking pictures, I'm telling her you asked for nudes.

I huff a laugh, although this is my fault. I asked Deacon to stay with her, so of course he's going to give me shit about my feelings. He'll rib me for her, even as he watches her back.

I save the picture to my photos. I don't have many of her and she looks like herself rather than the slick, pretty version on her website. I mean, she also looks tired. But still there. Still ours. *Mine.*

"Well. Look at you, hiding from the spotlight," a familiar voice says behind me.

"Not hiding," I say. "Just thinking."

I slip my phone back in my pocket and turn around. There's no reason to be nervous. I've been nothing but open with my bishop, and she, in turn, has been nothing but supportive and understanding. Also, I've just helped raise fifteen thousand dollars. I don't think she could have seen the picture of Dixie on my phone, and even if she did, I'm a single man who's entitled to a life.

She—and her Doc Martens—steps into my peripheral view. "Congratulations. That was a heck of a show."

"Thanks." I wait.

"A new roof, right?"

"Part of one."

"Still," she says. "That's a big win."

"We didn't win. Not really."

She shakes her head. "You earned fifteen thousand dollars and the community's goodwill. That's not nothing."

"No. But it's not enough." I'm not sure where this conversation is going, but I need to get back to Wickham Hollow and Dixie—despite the three hours of driving ahead of me, I can't wait to see her. "We're still twenty-five thousand short. And I promised I'd fix the roof."

"You also promised not to spontaneously combust under pressure. How's that going?"

Yeah. Not so well.

When I don't answer, she plows ahead. "And Dixie? How's she doing?"

"She'd tell you she's fine. But I'd say she's not feeling good today. She couldn't make it and she's super mad about that."

That's the truth without oversharing Dixie's personal business. I know she's mad at herself and frustrated that she wasn't on that stage tonight.

The Bishop lets out a low laugh. "So. You and the country music star are still an item."

"Yes, ma'am. Although I'd rather everyone moved on and stopped talking about us."

"So, you're serious?"

"I'd like to be."

"But she doesn't feel the same way?"

"I hope she does."

"Do you love her?"

"Yes, but with all due respect, ma'am, this isn't church business. It's *my* business."

She nods and takes a step back, scrubbing a hand over her forehead. I'm sure my nerves and discomfort are obvious. "You're right."

"I am?" I half expect her to quiz me on my income and my estate next.

"You are. It's between the two of you. It's your relationship, not ours. It's just that, to be frank, I have eyes and ears. And a diocese full of gossips with high-speed internet." She looks at me for a long moment. "Let's talk pastoral boundaries, media management, and—if you want—personal courage."

I remind myself that grinding my teeth isn't helpful. "It's complicated."

"So's real life. If you want to be with her, be with her—and then we'll figure out how to balance that with your job."

"We're two different people, from two different worlds." I hate voicing that fear out loud, but I do think it needs to be said.

"You can't ride two horses with one behind. Plus, she's a fundraising asset." She pauses, and I wait for her to continue. "And sure, she's pretty loud. On her way to being famous. Not your usual preacher's wife. She's all those things, but that's on her and I'm worried about you. You know I admire your heart. But you don't owe the world a rescue mission. Ask yourself—are you in this because she needs help? Or because you need her?"

"Did I see someone hurting and think—I could ease that? At first, yeah. That's what I do. That's who I am. But I know she doesn't need me to fix her. She wouldn't let me even if she did—and she doesn't."

"Okay," my bishop starts. "That's—"

Wait. I realize I'm not done, so I talk over her. I can apologize later. "She'd say that she's *just fine* as she is. I'd say she's *just right*. I don't want to save her or change her. But I want to be with her, if she'll let me. Some folks aren't going to understand. I know that. You know that."

"Of course they won't. They've spent their whole lives defining love as something neat and quiet and appropriate. You think I haven't made unpopular choices? Try being a woman in a collar for five minutes."

That makes me snort.

She softens. "Jack, you are steady to a fault. You live by principles. You think before you speak. That's what makes you a good minister. But sometimes, the right choice doesn't come gift-wrapped with approval."

"I don't want to mess this up."

"Then don't. If you love her, don't hide her. And don't hide from what you want. Your church is strong because you are. You don't have to play small to make people comfortable." She pats my arm. "If you survive the gossip mill, I'll officiate."

That escalated fast. I know I want Dixie in my life, my whole life even, but *is* it too soon? A lot of people would say it is. But we haven't done anything by the book, have we? Maybe we could skip a few chapters and go straight to the happily-ever-after. When did this happen? How did I go from providing roadside assistance to thinking about forever? I don't know, but I have and right now I feel like I'm in the wrong place. I should be with Dixie, not miles away when she's sick.

I shake my head. "Thank you. I need to get back home."

"I hope the drive back to Wickham Hollow gives you time to think about what we discussed." She winks. "I've got a sermon about unconventional unions that I've been dying to use. Don't deprive me."

I grin and she walks off to buttonhole the director of the first-place choir. I'm heading for my truck when my phone buzzes again.

DEACON: She woke up. Asked how you did up there. I told her you sang lead. She muttered "Jesus Christ" and passed out again.

This time I smile for real. The photo's of Deacon, in full grump-mode, holding up a handwritten sign scrawled in thick black Sharpie: "I'M NOT YOUR MAN'SITTER."

I put my phone away, get in the truck, and hit the road. I'll drive a little too fast for the next three hours to get home that much quicker, ready to ask Dixie a few questions.

Twenty-Seven

Girl falls hard for preacher

Dixie

Falling for the preacher isn't part of the plan, but two weeks after the talent show, when azaleas riot in pink and white along every porch in Wickham Hollow, here I am. Living in the rectory. Eating Jack's cooking. Writing songs in his guest room while contractors hammer away at the church roof that our prize money finally made possible. Or, more accurately, 37 percent possible—Jack's had to settle for repairs.

At least I feel better. Not perfect—my hands still ache and I get tired fast—but I've stopped eating ibuprofen like candy. I'm writing again. Singing in the kitchen again. Laughing. I blame Jack.

Jack, who fixes the wobbly porch step without saying a word about it. Jack, who's a conveyor belt of hot water bottles and who silently reads a book next to me while I nap. Jack, who demands I take up space in his life because he's sure I belong there.

I don't, of course. Not really. But I want to. God help me, I want to.

Lately, things between Jack and me are cozy. Not just the occasional knee bump on the couch or the hand brush in the kitchen kind of cozy, but the real, tangled-up kind. Somewhere between me stealing his flannel shirts and him learning how I like my tea, we've started sharing a bed. Not just for sex—though we've been doing plenty of that—but for the scary stuff. Now it's me crawling under the covers when my joints ache or when I'm lonely but don't want to admit it out loud. He never makes a big deal out of it. Just curls his big body around mine, warm and solid, his hand on my hip or tucked under my shirt at the small of my back like he's been sleeping next to me forever. Like we're normal.

Which is why I've written a song.

Not a serious one. Not a burn-down-the-charts power ballad or one I'll send to my agent. Just a fun ditty I strum out on Jack's front porch with Huck at my feet and Georgia Peach sulking in the window. She's such a little murder bean!

What's it called? I'm so glad you asked! "Asking Out My Man."

Okay, yeah. Bold-as-hell title. But I'm ready to stop playing it safe and pretending I don't care. If he doesn't feel the same way, whatever. I'll make a joke out of it, go back to acting like I'm not stupidly, ridiculously gone for a man who says shit like "let's fix it together" and means both the leaky church roof and my disaster of a life.

I wait until we're elbow-deep in dishwater to spring it on him. Also noted: When I finally make it big—*when*, not if—I'm buying my man a damn dishwasher.

"You doing anything Thursday night?" I hand him a plate to dry.

He looks up from the dish towel. "Thursday?"

Yes, Jack. The fourth day of the week for those of us who don't start our workweek on Sunday.

"Karaoke night. Southern Comforts."

To be fair (which I'm not interested in being), Deacon and Slate are willing to karaoke any night Southern Comforts is open. I can hit Jack with my new lyrics anytime.

He gives me that look—equal parts curiosity and fond exasperation. It's so damn cute. "You're performing?"

"I wrote a new song. Thought you might want to hear it."

God, I like him. Like, I totally want to jump on him right now, wrestle him to the floor, and demand he make space for me in his life. You know, more than he already has. I'm a greedy bitch.

Jack folds the towel into thirds. "You inviting me to karaoke night?"

I nod vigorously. *Let there be no doubt, Jack!* "Technically, I'm inviting you to be serenaded."

He pauses. He smells a rat. "Should I be nervous?"

He's rubbing a hand down his beard, so he's already nervous. I've gotten to know his tells over the last few weeks, and he's uncomfortable. That makes two of us.

"Also," he adds, trying to look casual, "shouldn't you be posting cryptic song lyrics on Instagram first? Build the suspense? Get your—what is it now, half a million?—followers wondering what Dixie Pearl's up to next?"

I make a face. "God, don't remind me. They're all waiting for 'Hot for Preacher: The Sequel.'"

"So—" he grins "—it seems like you're breaking your own social media protocol here. Giving me an exclusive preview instead of teasing it online first."

"Don't let it go to your head, Preacher Man. Maybe I just want to see your face when you hear what happens next before the rest of the internet does."

"What the hell are you up to?" Deacon hands me a Diet Coke. We're standing in front of his crappy, makeshift stage in Southern Comforts.

I wink at him. "Tonight is my world premiere of a brand-new song. You should thank me. I accept Venmo and French fries."

"Nah." He gives me that deadpan look. "You're not just singing. You're fixin' to cause trouble."

Technically I'm not singing right now, either. I'm talking. Pointing that out, however, is likely to get my ass tossed out the door.

He's got a decent-sized crowd tonight—bigger than usual for a Thursday, probably because word's gotten around that the girl from the viral preacher song is doing something new. The faces are friendly, however, which is a relief.

"Think I should cancel karaoke night."

"You can't do that," I pout.

"Why's that?"

"I invited Jack. My brand-new song is for him."

Deacon's eyes narrow, and I almost laugh. "You wrote a ton of songs *about* him."

"Yeah, but this one's a present. FOR," I emphasize. "It's *for* him, Deacon. So shut up and let me sing, yeah?"

He curses, but then Jack walks in and he just starts groaning instead. I pat him on the shoulder. He'll get over it.

Jack's dressed for the occasion in a black button-down shirt that makes his shoulders look extra wide and his jaw extra carved. He's wearing dark jeans and cowboy boots.

He nods to Slate, who's posted up at the bar, judging everyone in silence like a particularly grumpy gargoyle.

When Jack sees me, he smiles. Not the polite preacher smile he flashes around at church. The real one. The one that makes me want to write a thousand more songs just to see it again.

Deacon insists I have to wait my turn ("You're lucky I don't make you go fucking *last*, Pearl, because you're gonna show everyone up for the amateurs they are") so it's a while before I get to go up onstage. I spend the time cozied up to Jack at the bar. He's ordered the hot honey chicken sliders and a plate of buttermilk biscuit nachos, and I've generously agreed to help him out with those. A girl's gotta eat, after all.

"I'm buying next time," I tell him.

He laughs. "Of course you are. I'll bring my appetite."

I'll have to save up because Jack's appetite is as giant as the rest of him.

When it's finally my turn (*Jesus, Deacon, what took so long?*) I take the stage and make Deacon haul up a chair for me to sit in. Then I make him scoot it around a bit because I'm feeling bitchy about the wait. He gives me major stink eye but does it anyway.

When I sit down, my hands are only slightly shaky as I adjust the mic and my guitar. "So, this is a little song I wrote."

That gets a reaction from my audience.

"Wait, is she allowed to do an original?"

"Doesn't she have to pick off the list?"

"Hope it's not one of those slow, mopey ones."

I ignore them.

"This one's for a guy I know. He's been feeding me, sheltering me, fixing broken things around the house, and putting up with my bullshit for weeks. Which, let's be honest, is a *lot* of bullshit. So, I thought I'd thank him the only way I know how. Through public embarrassment."

A few people laugh. Jack crosses his arms and smiles. I start to play.

"He brings me coffee, black as sin,
Fixed my van and the life I fell in.
He's a preacher man with a heart of gold,
And I'm just a mess with a suitcase full of songs.

But he makes me feel like maybe I could stay,
So here I am, singing it anyway—

Would it be weird if I asked out my man?
Even though I'm crashing in a secondhand van?
Is it tacky to say, 'I want more than this'?
'Cause I'm pretty sure I'd give up Nashville for his kiss."

The crowd whoops. I don't look at Jack until the last chord fades. When I do, he's still standing at the bar, still smiling, but now with that soft, stunned look on his face. Like I just sucker punched him with feelings. *Now go get your man!*

I hop down from the stage and make my way through all the Wickham Hollowites who want to give me unsolicited feedback on my performance. Jack meets me halfway.

"So," I say.

"So," he echoes.

"That wasn't a joke." Subtlety has never been my strong suit.

"I figured."

We stand there for a second. Close enough that I can feel the heat coming off his body, close enough to smell that stupidly good soap he uses. I look up at him. "Are you gonna say something preacher-y or are you gonna kiss me?"

He laughs. "Neither. Yet."

I blink. "Yet?"

"I'm gonna take you on a proper date first."

"You mean this isn't it?"

"This is karaoke night. You asked me out in front of half the town. I think you've earned pie."

"Alright, but there's no pie in Wickham Hollow at nine o'clock at night."

He laughs. Then he tugs me out the door and down the street. I don't really care where we're going. Our fingers are laced together and we're officially on our first date. A *date*.

I'd wanted him to like my song. I'd wanted him to feel like the center of attention. *My* attention. Seen. I hadn't thought about what came after, though.

"Here," he says, tugging me around the corner to the back

of Dee and Tilly's bakery. Behind the building is an unexpectedly elaborate display of hostas in terra-cotta pots, each
one covered with a glass cloche like they're precious botani-
cal specimens. Dozens of varieties create a miniature greenhouse effect along the back wall, their leaves impossibly lush
and full for March in Tennessee. Ferns in matching pots frame
the whole setup, creating what looks like a secret garden that
belongs in a Victorian conservatory and not behind a small-
town bakery.

Tilly's gone completely plant-crazy back here. But I'm having trouble focusing on her green-thumb insanity because I'd
rather look at Jack. His back view is incredible. His jeans hug
his ass and his shirt rides up, showing a strip of dark boxer
briefs and skin when he bends over to mess with some kind
of metal box attached to the building. And pulls out—

"Pie!"

Turns out Dee has one of those honor-system pie safes out
back for after-hours emergencies. My girl is brilliant.

We split a slice of coconut cream sitting on her back patio
and talk about nothing important—music and pets and childhood stories we haven't told each other yet.

When we're walking back, he holds my hand. Just reaches
out and laces his fingers through mine like it's the most natural thing in the world. I watch our joined hands while he tells
me about his day. When we get to the rectory, I pause at the
bottom of the steps.

"So," I say. "About that song."

"I liked it."

"I meant what I said."

"I know."

I don't need him to call me a liar, but that's not exactly the
answer I was hoping for.

"You gonna do something about it?"

He steps closer. "I want to be that man for you, Dixie."

I wait all of a second. My heart *pounds*.

"Are you asking me to be your girlfriend?"

He nods. "Yeah."

"Exclusively? No more hot church groupies?"

His mouth twitches. "I'm pretty sure they're a figment of your amazing imagination but agreed."

I grin. "Good."

Then he kisses me.

And I know—really know—that maybe this could work.

I don't belong here, but I kind of want to.

And if that's not terrifying, I don't know what is.

Twenty-Eight

Daddy drama

Dixie

"Look at this one." Jack angles his tablet toward me. On the screen, a solemn golden retriever is wearing a crocheted broccoli hat. "Think Huck would tolerate haberdashery?"

I snort. "Huck would pose for the camera. It's Georgia Peach who would kill us in our sleep."

"She's already plotting," Jack agrees, nodding toward the window where our resident murder bean glares at us from the top of the dresser. "I swear she understands English."

"Of course she does. She's cataloging our transgressions for her revenge list." I'm sprawled against Jack's side, watching water droplets from his recent shower sneak down his very distracting torso. "She's probably got a whole spreadsheet."

Jack moves on to the next video—a basset hound in what looks like a corn-on-the-cob costume. "We could start small. Maybe just a bow tie."

"Don't you dare. I'm not sleeping with one eye open because you gave her fashion accessories."

My phone buzzes against the nightstand. Deacon's name flashes on the screen.

Jack nudges me. "You should take that."

"It's probably about the van." I don't want to know. "And I'm too comfortable for bad news."

But Jack has already handed me the phone, as he's annoyingly responsible about things like returning calls promptly.

"Hey, Deacon." I eye the corn-dog costume with suspicion.

"Van's ready," he says without preamble. "Runs like a dream now."

Someone has cut the elevator cables in my torso. *No!* If the van works, I can hit the road. Return to Nashville. Stop complicating Jack's life with a live-in girlfriend he's only known for weeks.

"Are you sure?" It's smart to double-check. Maybe he's a crap mechanic.

"Took her for a spin this morning. She's purring like a kitten."

I can't help grinning despite my panic. "She's never purred in her life, so that's impressive."

"New fuel pump. Fresh oil. Cleaned out some wildlife behind the glove box."

"What?" I'm 99.99 percent certain he's joking.

"Nothing you need to worry about now. She's parked outside when you're ready."

Jack's gone still beside me, his hand frozen on my shoulder.

"Thanks, Deacon. Seriously," I manage.

"Don't make me regret it," he mutters before hanging up.

I stare at the mournful basset hound in its corn costume. *I feel you, dog.*

"So," I try. "The van's fixed."

Jack leans back against the headboard, managing to look like a lumberjack underwear model even while processing life-altering news. He wraps his arm around me more securely. "Do you want to hit the road?"

You're stuck with me, Preacher Man. "Do you think I should go?"

"We've done everything backward." His voice is carefully neutral. "Moving my girlfriend in before we'd even been on a date was pretty crazy."

I twist to look at him properly. His eyes are warm as chocolate lava cake, which is reassuring.

"Totally impulsive! Plus, she's got a job that involves travel. When are you going to see her if you don't move her in?" I press my face into the cedar-scented hollow of his shoulder. This is way better than cute animal videos.

Jack switches off the tablet and kills the lights. I immediately starfish all over him like I do, and he adjusts so I don't slide off the bed.

"You realize we'd never see each other if you weren't living here, right?" he says into the darkness.

"Oh really? Absolutely never?"

"Nope. We'd waste so much time scheduling things. Texting. Driving. Trying to figure out which place to hang out at. It'd be inefficient."

"Tragic," I agree solemnly. "All that wasted gas money."

Jack hums his agreement. "This is just fiscally responsible. Splitting utilities? That's good stewardship."

"We're basically cohabiting geniuses."

"Pure logic," he says, and I can feel his smile against my neck.

We settle into comfortable silence, but he's still thinking.

"I thought about sabotaging your van, you know," he admits. "So, you'd have to stay."

"Me, too."

"Deacon would have killed us."

"Totally worth it, though."

"Yeah," he says.

I listen to the steady rhythm of his heart beating beneath my cheek. I've imagined red carpets and recording contracts. Playing bigger venues. Actually earning a living from my music. Those things won't happen if I stay here, but right now—right now I'm unexpectedly happy. Not quitting. Just readjusting.

Totally worth it.

So here's the deal with today's Dirty Girls meeting—and before y'all start getting ideas, let me explain why there are actually *guys* at what's usually a ladies-only plants-obsessing situation.

We're officially set up on Dee's front porch, which, by the way, looks like it fell out of a *Southern Living* magazine and landed smack-dab on Main Street. After Slate hauls three bags of dirt up the steps (because apparently his grumpy ass is super useful for manual labor), he just sits down and doesn't leave. Boom. He's an honorary lady. No worries—we pot around him, pressing ridiculously tiny snapdragon seeds into the dirt. Feels like kindergarten, except instead of finger painting, we're gossiping about every soul in Wickham Hollow while sprawled on Dee's perfect porch furniture.

Then Jack shows up (because Slate's paved the way for gentlemen everywhere), and the ladies perk up like they've been waiting for this moment all day. He does that thing where he leans against the wall—you know, that whole I'm-off-duty-but-remember-I'm-your-preacher pose. Arms crossed, shoulders relaxed, body slouched just enough to look casual. No one's kicking him out, either—he's too pretty. So yeah, that's why there are guys at Dirty Girls club today. Sometimes the good ones just show up and make everything better.

The corners of his mouth turn up behind his beard when he brushes a kiss over my cheek. "Hey," he says to me. Which is basically a goddamned Shakespearean sonnet right there.

"Hey yourself." And there I am, channeling my inner bard like some kind of literary genius.

Cut the chorus of enthusiastic hellos, one grunt from Slate (because emotions are hard), and a bunch of finger waves. The older lady on the far end of the porch actually claps her hands together like she's watching her favorite soap opera couple finally get their act together.

I plop down on Dee's ottoman—seriously, the roundest piece of furniture known to mankind. Jack has to move what looks like half of Pottery Barn's pillow collection before he can sit down and pull me into his side. And damned if I don't just melt into all that warmth and that delicious cedar scent that follows him around.

The ladies are doing that thing where they exchange looks and satisfied smiles. Yeah, there's some side-eye happening, but it's the *good* kind—the kind that says they've been rooting for us this whole time and are pretty pleased with their matchmaking skills.

I want to climb him like a tree. Kiss him back with tongue. He's told me I don't have to hold back in public, but I've tried to keep things G-rated (okay, maybe PG), because screwing around in the workplace isn't really my thing, and honestly? All of Wickham Hollow feels like Jack's workplace. Looking at him right now, I'm seriously regretting that commitment. Feels like way too long since I've properly kissed him.

"Well, look at you two!" Dee beams, already reaching for her phone. "Quick! Let me get a picture for my Insta!"

I give her a little salute with my middle finger behind my back.

Jack covers my saluting fingers with his own and tugs them back between us. The man knows me way too well.

When I say, "Scold me later, Preacher Man," Slate actually snorts.

Jealous I mouth at him. He shakes his head, but we both know the truth.

I've never had this kind of easy, everyday relationship before. I'm leaning in to kiss him back when we hear the rumble of a truck coming up the street. Everyone turns to look, and

Jesus—it's this electric-blue monstrosity with oversize tires and a custom mesh grille with LED light bars.

"Hot damn," someone says.

Tilly squints up the street, having taken off her glasses. "Can't plant what I can't see," she mutters, more to herself than to anyone else. "What is that?"

The truck slows to a crawl and I get a bad feeling.

Slate decides he has to answer the question literally. "Lifted F-450 with chrome running boards and custom rims."

"No." Dee shakes her head. "You're missing the point. That's a famous-person car."

"Do you think it's Luke Combs or one of those Osborne brothers? I can't decide which is prettier."

"Luke *Combs*? Does he drive a truck?"

When the truck slows in front of Dee's house, I get a good look at the license plate. My stomach drops like a stone. RHINESTR.

Oh, hell no.

I've parked behind that ridiculous vanity plate more times than I can count—in studio lots, outside honky-tonk bars, in the driveway of every house I ever lived in growing up. You can't miss that frame. The top reads, in bold, engraved script: "Nashville Called—Again" and the bottom announces "I Let It Go Platinum, Baby." The whole thing is bracketed in tiny, silver guitars and Swarovski-studded cowboy hats. It doesn't just say "I'm a country legend" (my dad's usual brand of exaggeration). It screams, "I have backstage access and I drink my Jack Daniels through a gold-plated straw."

Jack's arm tightens around me as my whole body goes rigid. This isn't happening. Not here. Not now. Not in front of Dee, who texts me plant updates at midnight. Not in front of Slate, who actually grunted *good morning* at me yesterday— practically a declaration of eternal friendship from him.

My dad's in town. *This* town. My I'm-a-big-deal father who believes small towns are where dreams go to die.

"Prepare to be starstruck," I warn the group.

"GARTH BROOKS?"

That question's gonna answer itself.

The driver's side door pops open and my dad swings down. His truck is lifted so high that he has to navigate a four-foot drop.

It might be April, but he wears his trademark white shirt with the pearl snap buttons tucked into blue jeans and a massive brass belt buckle. The seams on the front are picked out in gold thread. The man's a walking poster for bling, because the gold thread is just the start. He's got fringe. Embroidered flowers. Metallic studs. More is always better in Dad's world. His suspiciously dark hair is swept back from his face and you just know he's thinking: *Alright, Mr. DeMille, I'm ready for my close-up.*

He pauses on the sidewalk, looking up at us.

"Not Garth," one of the ladies says. She sounds disappointed.

"Billy Rae?"

He grins when he spots me, arms outstretched for a red-carpet reunion. "Darlin'! I missed you."

That's my cue.

"Hope you told the Maldives." I stand up slowly. Jack's arm falls away from me, which makes me mad. Dad's already ruining my afternoon and he's just arrived. "Wouldn't want them feeling unappreciated."

"You got a moment for your old man? If you folks will excuse us?" He gives a thousand-watt smile to the group assembled on the porch.

They mostly smile back. I mean, Slate glowers, while Dee looks as if she's about to hand him some snapdragon seeds. People are too friendly here for their own good (with the exception of Slate).

"Walk with me," I say. "We can talk over at the rectory."

"The rectory?" Dad looks amused. "Is that for real? The guy in your song?"

I'll take difficult questions for a thousand bucks, Alex! I don't look at Jack, who doesn't follow me down the steps.

I start walking toward the rectory, leaving Dad's vehicular monstrosity behind us for folks to gawk at, mostly because I don't know what to say. Which isn't a problem as Dad holds up the conversation all on his own.

By the time we reach the rectory and I sit us down on the steps by the church side door, he's launched into The Pitch. The studio is locked down. Backup vocals scheduled. Just needs me to "slide on in" and knock out a few verses for the Christmas album.

"I'm not doing it," I tell him, not for the first time.

He doesn't hear me. Or chooses not to. He keeps going, talking about family legacy, about how my voice will "elevate the whole damn thing."

"I said no," I repeat, louder this time.

Yeah, you heard me.

I take a breath before he can start talking again. "I'm not always fine, Daddy. I know that's what you want me to be. Tough-as-nails, keep-truckin'-through-it Dixie. But I'm tired. I'm hurting. I've been broke and broken down and stuck in a small town and living in a preacher's spare room."

His eyebrows rise at that one.

"But I've got things happening. *My* things. I've got songs going viral. I've got—hell, maybe I've got a future. And whether I do or I don't, it's gonna be mine. Not yours."

He shakes his head. "I just thought that maybe when you sign with that label, you'd keep an eye out for a spot for your old man. I ain't saying I'm outta juice yet. I just—I want in. Somewhere."

He isn't just trying to pull me into *his* world. He's scared I won't let him into *mine*.

I pull out my phone. "You want a project? Watch this." I

queue up the video of the choir's third-prize-winning performance.

My daddy stares at the screen. Then he laughs, hard. "They're awful."

"They're also kind of amazing," I point out. "They're *trying* and you can't buy that kind of raw joy in a studio. They don't care about sounding perfect because they're having fun."

Dad's still chuckling, shaking his head like he's watching the world's funniest blooper reel. "Honey, that poor woman in the front row sounds like she's gargling gravel. And the kiddo on the end isn't even in the same key as the rest of them."

"That *poor woman* has been in the choir for thirty years," I snap. "And Toby's ten years old and shy as hell, but he shows up and he tries. Which is more than I can say for some people."

The dig lands. Dad's smile falters for just a second before he recovers.

"Now, sugar, don't get all defensive. I'm just saying—"

"You're just saying what you always say. That anything that isn't Nashville perfect isn't worth doing. That small towns are where dreams go to die. That I'm wasting my time with people who aren't gonna make me famous."

I'm on my feet now, pacing because sitting still feels impossible. "But you know what? These people? They're not trying to use me. They're not asking me to be something I'm not. They just… They like me. For me. Crazy concept, right?"

Dad's face softens, and for a second he looks like the man who used to braid my hair before school instead of the walking country music cliché he's become. "Dixie, baby, I know you think I don't—"

"Nope." I hold up a hand. "You hold that thought because you came here looking to save your career. To ask me to be your backup singer on some Christmas album nobody's gonna remember next year. But I'm done being your get-out-of-jail-free card, Dad. I'm done being the thing you use to prove you're still relevant when your own stuff stops working. And

I'm done playing it safe, hiding behind your name instead of making my own."

Dad's quiet for a long moment, and when he speaks again, his voice has lost that performative quality it usually has. "You really like it here, don't you?"

"Yeah," I say. "I really do. Although to be fair, I'm also really broke and at first it was the best of a bad set of options. So what if you didn't do the same tired album? What if you rewrote something, made it fresh? Used real people like the choir instead of studio singers? You could do a whole Southern gospel send-up—like you did with 'Jingle Bell Dash.'"

His eyes light up the way they did every Christmas Eve growing up when he'd rewrite a carol just to make us all laugh. "You think they'd go for that?"

"They'd love it. You just have to meet 'em where they are."

I hand him my notebook—full of scribbles and half songs. He flips through until one catches his eye.

"Oh, now *this*," he says, tapping the page, "this right here is gold."

He clears his throat and begins to sing, low and slow:

"God rest ye merry, gentlemen, but don't you take your ease,
The missus has a list so long, it's bringin' grown men to their knees.
You'll brave the mall, the gift-wrap stall, the store with seventeen cheeses—

O tidings of Black Friday panic and deals so barely legal!"

He looks up at me. "You wrote this?"

"You get full credit for inspiring the cheese."

He cackles. "Darlin', that's a hook if I ever heard one."

He sets the notebook down and pulls out his phone—the newest model, with a rhinestone-studded case that screams "midlife crisis but make it country."

"I'm not stupid. I'm transferring you some cash." He doesn't look at me. "Let's unstick you from this town and get you out of the spare room. You should have told me."

I groan. "No."

"It's already happening," he replies. "I just need help with this damn Venmo-CashApp-Zelle-whatever-the-hell thingy. I tried to send money to your Aunt Rita last week and accidentally paid a man named Dante in Kansas City."

"I am seeing the preacher," I blurt out.

"Dixie—"

"He's not the punch line to a joke—"

"Dixie."

"I really like him."

"Point is—" he stabs at his screen "—I'm not taking no for an answer. Consider it a producer's advance. Or a tax refund. Hell, call it Christmas money if that makes you feel better. You pick."

I look at him—really look at him—and see past the tan and the charm and the ridiculous shirt that cost more than most people's rent. He's not trying to control me.

This time, he's just trying to take care of me the only way he knows how.

Which, let's be honest, has always been throwing money at problems and hoping they go away.

I hold out my phone. "I could use your help with this. Can you read it?"

He sure can. In fact, he reads it twice.

"Well, show me the money," he says finally. "We're gonna have two stars in the family."

So here's the thing. A producer for a record label just called my agent. They want to sign me and I'll have studio time and production support, a PR team and tour support. It's a two-album deal, with what they're calling a "small" financial advance. Their definition of *small* and mine are worlds apart—I could live on that money for a year or more.

"Congratulations," Dad says, downloading the contract on his phone because of course he is. "You want me to take a look at this for you?"

I laugh, because there's no stopping him. "Yeah. Obviously,

my agent's going through it, but I'd like to know if you have suggestions."

I hear the door behind us open and close while Dad's brainstorming a list of questions to hit my agent with. They're actually good questions, which is annoying because I want to stay mad at him.

Jack's standing behind us. "Are you okay?"

Not a chance. I can't deal with this right now. He's dressed for a memorial service I'd forgotten all about—dark suit, crisp white shirt, black tie—and it somehow manages to make him look both hot as hell and completely untouchable. He's 110 percent minister and 0 percent my Jack.

"A genuine minister?" Dad asks. He sounds amused.

Well, yeah?

Jack keeps his gaze on me. "You can go in the house, you know. If you want some privacy."

"No problem." Dad *winks* at Jack. Actually winks. "We're about to get Dixie out of your hair."

Jack holds out his hand. "Jack Carter."

Dad bounces to his feet. He's shorter than Jack by a ridiculous degree and looks like a peacock preening its tail feathers. "Hank Pearl."

They exchange some pleasantries and then Jack smiles at me. It's not his usual smile. It's tighter, less happy. "I've got a memorial service. I'll be done in about two hours."

Dad laughs. "This is your boyfriend, the preacher? I know you said he existed, but I really thought you'd made him up."

Jack looks at me, calm as ever, but I can see he's not happy. I've been so busy thinking that I can't fit into his life here in Wickham Hollow that I never thought about it the other way around. Does he fit into my Nashville life? We're pieces from two different puzzles and there's no forcing us together in a way that genuinely works.

"Jack's my boyfriend."

Dad barks out a laugh. "Guess it's good y'all already answered the wedding question." And then, when we both look at him blankly, he sings, "'She's not one of those girls who says yes to a preaching man.'"

He's freaking quoting the opening line to my very first song about Jack, the one I wrote when I didn't know him at all. The one where he was a dream, and maybe a good one.

"Dating a preacher!" My dad's way too amused by this. "Did she tell you she got a deal?"

The corners of Jack's mouth pull down.

"It literally just happened and it's not definite," I say quickly. "I haven't signed anything."

Dad laughs. "You've been chasing this record label for years. I'd say the signature is just a formality, wouldn't you?"

"Congratulations." Jack brushes a kiss on my cheek and then turns to go back inside. From the robes and the number of cars now flooding the parking lot, the memorial service will be starting soon. "I look forward to hearing it."

"Dixie, tell me you're not thinking about staying here," Dad says.

Jack freezes.

Yeah. He heard that.

But he recovers quick and goes inside. The door bangs shut behind him.

"You should capitalize on this preacher thing," Dad says. "Get him in some photos, maybe a music video. Strike while the iron's hot."

Not happening.

I yank my phone out of his hand and run into the church. "Jack!"

He's headed for his office. I speed up and tug on his sleeve. "Listen to me!"

I know from looking at his face that he's hurt.

"You turned everything we did into a song? You're about to put out an album about us? Everything we did was just some kind of creative writing exercise for you?"

"It wasn't like that."

He gives me a look. He's not buying what I'm selling.

"It was just business," I try. "Not personal."

"Yeah." He holds up a hand. "It was very personal, Dixie. I'm your boyfriend and I want to support you, but you're not letting me matter. I'm just a punch line."

"I didn't know Hank—my dad—was going to just show up here."

He lets me change the subject, but he's still not happy.

"Why wouldn't he? You come and go all the time. You won't make plans or talk about a future—and clearly you haven't made room for me in yours."

"Jack—"

"You didn't tell your dad about us."

"He didn't need to know—"

"Because you didn't think it *mattered*." I hate the hurt on Jack's face. "Tell me this, Dixie. Are you embarrassed by me?"

I stare at him.

It's not that.

"Because I'm not embarrassed by you," he continues. "I'm proud of you. You're an amazing person with an incredible talent, and I'll support you however you do or do not want to use that talent. I love you."

He tosses those three words out there.

Boom.

Just oh, and yeah—*I love you*.

I don't know what to say and we both know it.

He kisses me on the cheek and walks away.

Twenty-Nine

Preacher scrolls. Reads the comments.
Regrets everything.

Jack

I couldn't concentrate on the service. I take off my vestments as soon as I can and shut myself in my office. Then I get out my phone, ignoring my messages, and for the first time I really look at Dixie's social media.

She's posted 846 times and has 450,000 followers.

Dixie Pearl.

Musician

Country singer

MEET MY PREACHER MAN.

A finger emoji points to her Linktree. I skip that. Some things I still don't want to know.

She only has three Instagram Highlights, the stories that she's chosen to keep on her profile permanently. Music. Life in a Small Town. Tour.

Mostly, it's just post after post of Dixie singing. They're clips, pieces and not the whole song, but they all have captions.

Wrote this country love song about a preacher. Oops. Y'all think I should release it or repent first?

Not a love song. Just a song about someone who feels like coming home... Okay maybe it's a love song. Should I release it?

Just a little hymn I wrote at 2:00 a.m. in someone else's bed. Send this song to someone who makes you feel the same way. Not me catching feelings for a preacher like it's a Hallmark movie. Here's the theme song. Let me know if I should put it on the soundtrack.

She must have laughed herself sick when I told her I wanted our life together to have a soundtrack because she's already written one. She certainly did it better than I ever could: the curiosity, the awe, the excitement and the rush of feelings and the *certainty* that this is something special. And now we've reached the end of the movie, the part where THE END flashes up on the screen and the credits start rolling.

It isn't like I didn't see it coming.

A voice like Dixie's? It was only a matter of time before someone in Nashville pulled their head out of their backside to make her an offer. Still, hearing it out loud hits harder than I expect.

She didn't come to the memorial service. I'd have seen her, even in the back where she likes to sit. That's the pew for the sinning backsliders, she claims, the ones who aren't Jesus's besties. I've had to bite my lip to hold back the preacher part of me who wants to promise her that there's plenty of love to go around and she's welcome in every pew. I can be too intense when faith comes up. I have it, and yeah, I want everyone else to have it, too. It's a gift and gifts are for sharing.

I skip the doughnuts and coffee that are in full swing over in the hall. Instead, I slip back into our house and listen. She must've been a cicada in a former life because she's almost never silent. She can buzz for hours and, man, is she loud. Sure enough, I hear humming coming from the back bedroom she's "using for its closet space."

She's packing. My heart sinks. I almost turn around so I can pretend for just a little while longer that I don't know for sure she's leaving.

"Hey," she says, real casual. "They want me to come back to Nashville this week. Cut a demo. Talk touring schedules. Sign for real."

And just like that my belief in Maybe We Could Work dies. It's an ugly, quick death.

"That's good. That's… That's great, Dixie."

She gives me a smile like it costs her something.

This is all so wrong.

Still, I say the right things. *Proud of you. You earned it. You deserve this.* Then I go outside and split a half dozen logs I don't need to split. The muscles in my shoulders burn, but they're the sacrifice to keep my hands busy.

I'm out there for ages and I'm almost out of wood when I hear her daddy's voice cutting through the open bedroom window. She must have put his call on speaker, probably because she's still packing. He isn't happy.

I put the ax down so I can hear better, hating myself for it.

"Tell your preacher boyfriend I said hallelujah and goodbye," he says.

Knowing Dixie, I'm betting that the muffled sounds she makes are mostly curses.

"…no, Dad, he's not some hillbilly preacher with a savior complex."

More cursing. Something slams.

I don't catch what Hank says, but he isn't happy. Is, in fact, unhappy enough that he's called her from the road just hours after talking to her here.

"He's not— Dad, that's not fair."

"…fixer-upper preacher weighing you down when you're finally getting traction."

Yeah, that part's plenty clear.

"He's been good to me."

A pause.

"…they all are at first. But how's that gonna work when he's there in small-town Tennessee and you're on the road?"

"It's not that simple. I want—"

"…not made for that life. You're a stage girlie, all the way through. Don't toss all your work aside."

"So now I've worked to get where I am?…No! You don't get to talk about him like that."

The next pause is so long that I think they've finished. It's not a win, but maybe I can count it as a draw—or at least not as a loss. She did stick up for me.

I'm still in love with her and I'll never be over her.

It turns out Hank isn't finished. He's not letting this be.

"There's no future for you with a man like that. I'm trying to keep you focused. You want this record deal or not?"

She does. We both know that.

"…I already feel like I've ruined something here."

I shouldn't be listening. I go back to stacking wood and remind myself that I was never going to be her Nashville life. Just a detour on the way to somewhere bigger. A speed bump on her way to Nashville. Of course, I'm letting her go because I'm not going to be the person who takes her dream from her.

I stand there until her voice goes quiet and then I pick up another log.

Set it on the stump.

Raise the ax and split it clean through.

Come to me, all you who are weary…

The verse settles into my chest like it always does.

…and I will give you rest.

I don't know if she believes in anything close to rest, but I'll

give it to her if I can—carry everything she'll let me pick up.
But I won't ask her to stay. Some things you let go of, even
when you love them.

We eat dinner together like nothing happened.

It's her turn to cook, so we have Cup Noodles and banana
bread, with cupcakes from a box mix for dessert. Dee's teaching her to bake. It's a work in progress. We don't talk much.
Just what Georgia Peach got up to, the wedding I'm doing
Saturday, the bridge Dixie's been messing with for weeks.

"You okay?" she asks when we finish eating.

"I'm fine."

I start cleaning up, stacking dishes in the sink. Then I feel
her behind me.

When I turn, she steps into me.

Her hands flatten against my chest, then slide up—over my
collarbone, around the back of my neck. I wrap my fingers
around her wrists before she pulls away.

"Jack," she says. "I don't want to feel like this."

"Like what?"

"Like if I leave, I'm walking away from something that
matters."

I should say something steady. Something comforting. I
don't.

I kiss her.

First it's just my lips brushing hers, and then it's more. Every
nerve in my body fires up. She makes a sound in the back of
her throat—half gasp, half growl—and presses against me like
she's thinking to crawl inside my skin. *Me, too, baby. Me, too.*

"One more time, Dixie."

"Yeah. Okay. Good idea."

Her hands grab my butt and yank me closer.

I walk her backward. We're all over each other. Her legs
slot between mine, her hands push through my hair, the nails
biting enough to make me grunt. It's like high school or the

back seat of a car. Any minute now there'll be a knock on the door or the windows will steam up and we'll have to stop.

The moment we come together, everything ignites. One second, we're talking, the next I'm wrecked.

Touching her feels so good. The curve of her waist under my hands, the hot silk of her skin, those freckles that start under her jaw and trail across her shoulder. One breath of her and I'm gone.

I pull her tighter against me. Half a sentence spills out. *One more time*. And then *let's*—

"Oh, yeah. Let's." She pushes up on her tiptoes to reach my mouth. There are other words, rough sounds, nothing we should say out loud. Unlike the other times I've held her, I know this is the last time.

I shove my hand deep into her hair.

Stay.

I toe off my boots. She yanks her shirt over her head.

This Dixie is just mine. Her hungry eyes and impatient fingers. The sexy, sarcastic songwriter turns into a sweet, hot woman wrapped around me.

This isn't casual. She's *mine*. And she's beautiful, all soft curves and wicked dimples.

She pulls my shirt over my head, her fingers skating down my chest. I spin her, pin her back to the wall, and kiss the side of her neck while her hips arch into mine. She's gasping, needy, and I'm half out of my mind wanting her.

I need more from her. I don't care if she's made up and dressed up, I always want her. No matter how close I get, it's not enough.

Maybe this is why people hook up so often. This need to connect, to get lost in someone else. I've never felt it before.

I've always liked sex. It feels good, but more than that it makes me feel close to my partner. That's the best part. I had a girlfriend before Dixie and I cared for her. But we grew apart and split, and I carried on fine. I can't imagine losing this. Losing Dixie.

"Bedroom," I grunt.

She shakes her head. "Right here. No more talking."

She kicks her jeans off. Her bra goes next, then she hooks her fingers in her panties and teases them down. When she gets naked, my brain goes offline. I kissed her in the kitchen because we only have so much time. I'm not wasting one second of what we have left. I need to memorize each inch of her, like I could forget.

Since she ordered me not to talk, I end our not-conversation by slinging her over my shoulder and carrying her toward the bedroom.

"Jack! What are you doing?" I can hear the smile in her voice, though. "You're not listening to me!"

She smacks my butt and I nip her back.

"You said no talking."

"And you listened?"

I always listen to you.

When I set her on the edge of our bed, her hair's tumbled around her face, cheeks flushed. She's the prettiest thing I've ever seen.

"Jack," she chants. "Jack, Jack, Jack."

Show, don't tell. Right?

I drop to my knees in front of her, kissing every inch of skin I can reach. It's not often I let myself take, but she's calling my name. *Here I am.* Her breath catches when I run my hands up her thighs and push her knees apart.

"Are you tired?" I press a kiss against her inner thigh.

Sometimes we do things differently if her RA is acting up. Sometimes, that means sleeping, even when she protests that she's totally *up for all the action and that's just mean, Jack.* Sometimes, it means she lets me take care of her.

Her sultry "Are you offering to do all the work?" indicates she's feeling good tonight. She shoves up on her elbows. "What's your plan, Jack?"

"I thought I'd start here—" I brush a kiss over her hip bone. "And then I'd move here." I trace the crease of her hip with mouth. "And I definitely need to spend time *here*." I move lower.

"Jack…"

"Yeah?"

"You have the best plans," she moans. "Carry on."

I do.

After, I follow her down onto the mattress and cage her with my arms. Get right between her legs and line myself up with her entrance. She's wet and warm and I'm all over her.

Laughing, she holds her arms up. "Come here, you."

I trace her with my fingers and she arches up with a gasp. *I love you so much.* "I won't last long."

She smiles. Then she watches me roll on a condom and after that everything is hard and deep, slick and fierce. I sink into her, find her with my fingers so she can keep up. My other hand tightens on her hip, pins her down.

Dixie comes fast and hard, taking what she needs.

That's all I need. Having her take.

I come so hard and for so long that it's almost too much, the pleasure sparking through me, a tightness that goes on and on.

"Wow." She flops back on the pillows, throws an arm over her face. "You sure know how to say goodbye."

Because of course she's making light of this. Breathless and dazed, smelling like our sex.

I think, *I love you.*

And that's not enough.

Dixie

I should be basking in post-sex bliss, but instead I'm try-ing not to let Jack see me wince. Shit. Too late. He's already up, moving with that quiet efficiency of his to grab the hot water bottle from the bathroom.

He tucks it against my lower back. "Better?"

"Getting there." I roll over to face him, studying his profile in the lamplight. "Can I ask you something that might piss you off?"

His mouth quirks. "Shoot."

"Why do you live your life according to some ancient book? All those rules, all that—" I gesture vaguely. "What if you're wrong? What if there's nothing up there and you're missing out on everything down here because some invisible someone else is dictating what you do?"

"You want to know what really got me into ministry?" He shifts, propping himself up on his elbow so he can trace circles on my hip bone with his thumb. "It wasn't the Bible verses or the theology classes. It was watching my mom try to hold our family together when we lived in that van. She'd sing to my sister every night—hymns, mostly, because they were the only songs she knew all the words to. And I'd think, what kind of God lets a good woman sleep in a parking lot with her kids? What kind of love lets that happen?" His fingers stop moving for a beat. "I was angry for years."

"What changed?"

"I met this chaplain in the Marines. Guy named Rodriguez. Found me after I'd gotten into my third fight in two weeks and my commanding officer was ready to kick me out." Jack's smile is rueful. "He didn't quote scripture at me or tell me God had a plan. He just said, 'You're carrying around a lot of broken glass, son. You can keep cutting yourself with it, or you can learn to make something beautiful.'"

I reach up, run my fingers through the dark softness of his beard, following the line of his jaw beneath. "And?"

"He showed me that faith isn't about following rules to avoid punishment. It's about believing broken things can heal. That people who've been thrown away still matter. That someone like me—angry, messed up, living out of a van—could be worthy of love." His eyes meet mine. "And maybe even worthy of helping other people find that same thing."

Something tight in my chest loosens. "So it's not about the book."

"The book helps. But it's about showing up when someone's world falls apart and saying, 'You're not alone. You're not too broken to be loved.'" He brushes a strand of hair from my face. "Kind of like what you do with your music, actually. You write songs for people who feel lost. I just use different words."

"You're not what I expected." I straddle his hips, feeling better. "When I first saw you, I thought you had to be another guy with a savior complex."

His hands find my thighs. "And now?"

"Now I think you might need some saving."

I lean down and kiss him—not soft or sweet, but hungry. Demanding. My teeth catch his bottom lip and he groans into my mouth.

"Dixie—"

"My turn to take care of you," I say, already making plans. "And, Preacher Man? I'm very thorough."

I don't want to think about Nashville. About the record deal waiting for me or how I'll be leaving all this behind. Leaving *him* behind. I shove those thoughts down deep. Whatever comes next, I have right now.

Jack sprawls beneath me like some kind of pagan god—all broad shoulders and dark hair scattered across his chest, muscles that come from real work rather than a gym. His legs are long and powerful, taking up most of the bed, and that thick beard makes him look wild despite the careful way he carries himself in public. This is Jack unleashed, and he's mine. At least for tonight.

I cup his face in my hands and kiss him hard, all tongue and teeth and desperate need. He kisses me back just as fierce, but when I start working my way down his chest—pressing my lips to the hollow of his throat, the hard plane of his collarbone, the spot where his heartbeat hammers against his ribs—his breathing goes ragged.

"Dixie." My name comes out rough, broken. "What are you—"

His laugh turns into a sharp intake of breath. By the time I reach his hip, his hands are fisted in the sheets.

"Jesus Christ," he breathes.

"Wrong name." I look up at him through my lashes. "Try again."

His guttural groan fills the room when I reach my destination, his hands tangling in my hair. Not pulling, just holding on like I'm his anchor in a storm.

"Look at me," I whisper, meeting his eyes as I take him into my mouth.

The sound he makes—half curse, half prayer—sends heat shooting straight through me. He tastes like salt and heat, something purely *Jack*, and I breathe him in deep, letting myself get drunk on it. On him.

"Christ, Dixie, you're—" His words are cut off in another groan as I work him with my tongue. "So fucking good, baby. So perfect."

I trail my nails down his sides, feeling him shudder beneath my touch. Cup him in my palm while my mouth does things that make his hips jerk helplessly. I want to lose myself in this—in the weight of him on my tongue, his breath coming in sharp bursts, the gorgeous broken sounds spilling from his lips.

"You're gonna kill me," he rasps, voice wrecked. "Gonna be the death of me, and I don't care."

I pull back just long enough to grin up at him. "Good thing you believe in resurrection, Preacher Man."

His laugh is breathless, desperate. "You're terrible."

"You love it."

"I love—" He cuts himself off, but his eyes say everything his mouth won't.

His hands tighten in my hair then, and something shifts. The careful control he always wears like armor finally cracks, and he moves, taking what I'm offering with a desperation that makes my heart race. This is what I've wanted—to give him permission to let go, to be wild, to stop being so god-damned careful all the time.

My mouth stretches wide around him, jaw aching, and the sounds we make aren't pretty—gasps and groans, the wet slide of skin. But God, it's beautiful. He falls apart beneath my touch, this voice cracking on my name.

Jack

Seven hours later, she drives out of my life.
I watch the taillights fade. I'll be fine.
I have to be.

Thirty

Big city, small comfort

Dixie

I've made the right decision.

That's what I tell myself while waiting for wardrobe fittings and glancing at my phone like an idiot.

But I can't shake the feeling that somewhere along the way, I've left the best part of myself behind.

Maybe I'm coming down with something. A flare. Bubonic plague. Scabies. Don't know, don't care.

I'm tired all the time, even though I don't sleep in the van or spare rooms anymore. A musician who's just been booked on a cruise gig has sublet her East Nashville apartment to me for five months. The neighborhood is artsy and hip, full of quirky shops, coffee places, and bars. My days are pretty much the same: get up, squeeze in writing time, and then head into the studio to lay down rough versions of my songs to test arrangements.

I spend time with a sound engineer and the vocal coach the record label has hired for me. Meet with the PR and marketing teams where everyone argues. Should I lean into the small-town-preacher's-lover vibe? Hone my scrappy origin story? Own the RA?

Later, I'm told, there will be photo shoots for press kits and album art, but right now I have wardrobe fittings, styling sessions, and constant opinions about my "look." I think about texting Slate when the makeup artist shares a nugget like: "Fans love authenticity—but also contour." He'd die.

I have a social media posting schedule and more meetings with my new manager, Rachel, to go over release timelines, PR, and next steps. Discussions about touring, radio promotion, and which single to push first ("Hot for Preacher," everyone says). I can't remember how I did things in Wickham Hollow. I wrote an album there. I went viral. But now it feels like some perfect dream I can't get back to, no matter how hard I try. I can't go back, not even in my dreams.

Dad lobs question-jabs at me about dating a bona fide preacher but gives up when I don't respond. I'm too tired to fight with him.

Today I have an industry event at the sleek, upscale hotel connected to the Country Music Hall of Fame. A valet in a dark jacket opens my door. Rachel sent a luxury car to pick me up, as this is a no-vans kind of place.

"Thanks." I get out and sort of stop. Am I in the way? Yeah, probably. Do I care? Probably not. My attitude's totally ready for superstardom. "Wow. Shiny, huh? You know, you should hand out sunglasses."

The valet shuts the door. "Ma'am."

Jesus Christ, I can hear him thinking. *I don't get paid enough*.

Or maybe he's heard everything already.

I'm right, though. The bright Tennessee sunshine bounces off every polished surface and reflective window of the hotel's glass-and-steel exterior. It's basically a massive tower. Would they let me shoot a music video here where I'm an imprisoned country music princess and they hire a flannel-shirt-wearing hero to climb up the walls to rescue me? I mentally flip the script. Stick hero dude in the tower and do the climbing myself.

"I ain't lettin' down my hair,
I'm pullin on my boots,
I brought a rope and a light and a stubborn truth.
You're the one up in that tower,
Thinkin' love ain't got no power—
But, darlin', fairy tales ain't through,
This time I'm the one
Climbin' to you."

"Dixie!" From the snap in my manager's voice, she's said my name more than once.

She points to the glass doors below the porte cochere. *Yeah, yeah. I'm going.*

The Omni is one huge-ass hotel. Glass and stone and people who smell like they bathe in expensive soap. You either belong here—or you don't. There's no in-between. A valet opens the door before I can touch the handle. Another one's already got my guitar case and is wheeling my gear around like it's some fancy room service cart instead of the half-busted road rig I've had since high school.

Rachel's beside me, talking a mile a minute. Probably getting ready to drag me by my hair if I freeze up.

"Showcase at eleven fifteen. You're opening. Three songs. Play something upbeat first—I'm thinking 'Walk Me Home and Kiss Me Good Night.' Then play something with heart. Not too much edge, but enough to make them remember you."

Super. Word salad for breakfast. My favorite.

I nod. "Got it."

The lobby's all echoes and marble floors. There's some kind of weird art installation on the wall that probably means something deep and meaningful. Everyone looks polished. Calm. Like they were born wearing suits and holding lattes. I can't tell if they're hotel guests, music executives, or backup dancers, but they've all got the same expression: bored and successful.

Rachel keeps going.

"Lunch with that SiriusXM guy after. Smile like you want to marry his playlist and have its babies. Then suite 1421 at three for the influencer thing. Keep it stripped down, acoustic. Maybe 'Hot for Preacher' if it feels right."

I stop near a pillar and shift my weight. My boots feel too loud on the marble. "Is the embroidered top okay?"

Rachel blinks at me. "Better than flannel."

A beat later, she adds, "And no fringe. I'll text you the itinerary."

I nod again. Apparently that's my only setting today.

There's a woman across the lobby with a platinum blowout and snakeskin boots. She doesn't look at me. Neither does the guy beside her wearing a VIP badge and a sullen expression.

My phone buzzes like an angry paper wasp in my back pocket. I fish it out, thinking it's the promised itinerary.

JACK: You didn't have to do that.

JACK: But you did.

JACK: Thank you. The roof's going to hold up this time.

Another buzz.

JACK: I hope you're holding up, too.

He's sent a picture of Georgia Peach glaring from her perch on a stack of Jack's books.

JACK: She hasn't acknowledged the roof money, but she did claim the higher ground.

I didn't tell him I was wiring the money. Just sent it. Twenty-five grand. If this music thing's about to go somewhere big, the least I can do is fix the roof before it falls on his head.

I don't write back. I don't have the words yet. But I keep the message open, thumb pressed against the screen like I'm holding his hand through it.

The elevator dings. Rachel's already in it, holding the door with her arm. Surprise: She's still talking. What would happen if you put her and Slate in the same room? Would they cancel each other out? If his fascination with Dee ever dies, maybe I should fix them up.

"Hot for Preacher" is on the set list, but stuck in the middle. They want something more radio-friendly at the end. Something "sticky." I have no idea what that means, but I nod anyway.

I step in beside Rachel. My reflection catches in the mirrored wall. Hair curled. Eyes tired. Lip gloss I didn't pick. I don't look bad. Just not entirely like me.

Rachel starts rattling off timing cues and sound check logistics. I listen for about thirty seconds, then cut in.

"Hey," I say. "Wait up a minute."

She stops mid-sentence. "Yes?"

"Let me end with 'Hot for Preacher.' I want to close on something that really sounds like me."

Rachel nods. "Sure. That one's testing well."

I give her a half smile. "Good. I hope I do, too."

The doors slide shut.

Texting Dee is 100 percent accidental.

I'm taking pictures of my fancy hotel room. It's free—the record label's put me up here so I'll be fresh for this week's industry bullshit. It's a bucket list kind of room and I need to remember it. I feel more like washed-up diva than Dixie Pearl. I'm tired and just off.

The problem isn't that I can't imagine Jack here. Hell, my imagination's already seen him sprawled on the bed, stepping out of the shower, pointing out the stars twinkling over Nashville. He'd remember the night we met, when I said I believed in astrology, because Jack doesn't forget shit like that. He's wrecked me for anyone else. I don't want to move on.

But I have.

I just got back from the label dinner, still in my makeup and heels I can't feel my toes in. This hotel room looks like it belongs to someone with a lifestyle and matching luggage, not a girl who's held her granddaddy's guitar case together with electrical tape.

I miss that guitar.

I miss Jack.

I meant to go back to Wickham Hollow for a weekend. Then the label booked promo. Then I didn't text. Then it got easier not to go.

I don't do things for myself anymore. Don't reach out to the people I left behind in Wickham Hollow. I've left one or two of his last messages unread. Not on purpose, just... I don't know what to say.

And then he stopped texting every day.

We didn't have a big fight. There wasn't some dramatic goodbye. Just space—and silence—that stretched out too long without permission. He didn't ask me to stay, but I didn't ask him to come with me.

I miss him.

I've written dozens of songs about heartbreak and loneliness and putting on my walking boots to start over. Start *big*. Longer, richer, deeper songs. Because I don't care if I'm wearing my heart on my sleeve. Don't care if the record label tells me they aren't commercial. Don't even care if they chart or make the album cut. Ironically, the less I care, the more people love my music. They can't get enough of it. So I make money and I'm starting to get recognized, becoming a star.

And I feel so empty, it doesn't mean jack shit, because Jack isn't here with me.

I love my Preacher Man. I sure blew that pit stop in Wickham Hollow. I should've spent it convincing him to take a chance on life with me, and instead I turned him into a soundtrack. Now I'll hear him every day for the rest of my life and it'll never be as good as the real thing. Never be as good as Jack.

I take a photo of the bathroom. The towels are folded like origami and there's a rainfall shower I don't know how to turn on.

ME: Guess I'm fancy now. Should I steal the toiletries for you?

I follow my text to Dee with a second picture—the view from the window. City lights. A pretty skyline.

ME: They gave me a robe, too. I'm packing it for you.

Dee doesn't text back right away. That's fine. I don't even know what I'm trying to say. Maybe I'm just trying to prove I'm okay. Or pretend I am.

My phone buzzes five minutes later.

DEE: Wow! You are SO hosting the next Dirty Gals meeting, lady!

She texts me a picture of a succulent in a pot. It's got tall, narrow leaves, the edges lined with tiny baby plantlets.

DEE: My Mother of Thousands! Look at her, gestating baby plants! She's having trilliontuplets, though, so she's confined to her pot lest she take over the world.

ME: Holy clone wars!

If I ever go back to Wickham Hollow, the plants will have taken over.

DEE: You fine, fine, fine?

Am I? My fingers hover for a long time before I type. Then erased. Then type again.

ME: I don't know.

When she calls me thirty seconds later, I answer on the second ring. Jack would be proud of me.

"Hey," I say, voice scratchy. *Because of all the singing! Not because I'm sad!*

"Yes, to stealing the toiletries," Dee says. "But I'm more interested in what's wrong with you."

I let out a half laugh. "They've got tiny lavender soap shaped like a leaf. How is that not impressive?"

"It is. Very upscale. Almost distracts from the sound of you unraveling."

I shift the phone against my ear. "I'm not unraveling." *Much.*

"You texted me pictures of soap."

"I'm tired."

"And overwhelmed," she prompts.

I close my eyes. "Well, yeah."

Dee says nothing for a moment. From the rustling, she must be walking around her kitchen or maybe she's in the greenhouse. Somewhere real. Somewhere that smells like dirt and mint, rather than a promotional candle called "Nashville Nights."

"You're charting," she says gently. "And they're putting you up at fancy hotels."

"Yep."

"You've got photo shoots and interviews and catered sushi."

"I didn't eat the sushi," I say. "It looked like regret rolled in seaweed."

Dee laughs. "Do you want this kind of success?"

"I thought I did."

"But now?"

I exhale. "I don't know what I want. Other than everything."

There's a pause, but not the kind that makes you feel alone. Just the kind where someone's actually listening.

"You're allowed to want everything," Dee says. "And you're allowed to be unsure. When I was four, I wanted to be an astronaut."

That makes me smile. "Yeah?"

"Yeah. I had glow-in-the-dark stars on my ceiling and a lunchbox with Saturn on it. Then sixteen-year-old me discovered that physics had it in for her."

"What'd you do?"

"I cried in my guidance counselor's office. And then I picked something else. Still look up at the stars sometimes, though. Just without the pressure to land there."

I send her a shot of the stars over Nashville. The picture's blurry, but she likes it anyhow.

"I feel like if I pick this—really pick a singing career—I'm shutting the door on everything else."

Jack is my everything else. He's my everything.

"You're not," she says. "Think of it as walking through a room. It's just one room. You can always double back."

"I don't know how to do both. How to be——"

Jack's. Mine. Here and there at the same time. I'm tired of being pulled in so many directions.

"You don't have to," Dee says. "Not forever. Just hold what you need for today. The rest can wait."

"Okay?"

"Wow! Really? That worked?"

She makes me laugh. "You're the best."

"You should probably be specific," she says. "Really, really specific."

We wrap up our conversation with promises to stay in touch. She thinks she can come up to Nashville for a girls' weekend soon, and I promise to show her around town.

I'm totally robbing the housekeeping cart and mailing her my soap loot. She's an amazing friend.

You don't have to hold both. Just hold what you need for today. I pad into the bathroom that's the size of a dozen vans. Maybe a hundred. If I don't figure this out, I'll regret it. I run the water and sit on the side of the tub staring out the window.

When the water level's perilously close to the rim, I add half the bottle of fancy bubble stuff from the counter. It foams like crazy and smells like herbs.

By the time I've peeled off the day—dress, earrings, makeup—and sink into the water, the bubbles are chest-high. The heat makes my skin prickle. I rest my head against the edge and close my eyes.

For the first time all day, no one needs anything from me.

I don't have to pretend I know what I'm doing.

I sit there until the water cools and then I reach for my phone. Open the camera and flip it to front-facing. I'm pink-cheeked and foggy-eyed, surrounded by a sea of suds. Not glamorous. Not a photo shoot. Just me, in a hotel bathtub, with my hair going crazy.

I take the picture.

Then I stare at it.

Then I send it to Jack. No caption. Just the photo.

And then, after a second thought, I do add a message:

ME: There's room for one more.

I watch the little "delivered" notification appear, then power the phone off. I don't want to read what he writes back—not tonight, maybe not tomorrow. Because sending it isn't about starting a conversation. It's about not pretending I don't miss him, about saying: I remember. I still feel it. Even here.

Thirty-One

Go get your girl!

Jack

There's room for one more.

I read Dixie's text until the words are burned into my brain. Read it again. Then once more, like that will change what it means.

It feels like an olive branch. Or maybe I'm just telling myself what I want to hear.

She has bubbles up to her chin in that picture, shoulders bare, wearing that half smile of hers—the one that says she's flirting but trying not to care if I flirt back. She looks soft. Tired, too, like she's pretending real hard that she doesn't miss what we had. I stare at that photo longer than any grown man should, trying to decide if I'm reading it right.

For the first time in longer than I can remember, I don't know what to do next. I can't fix this. Can't rush in and make it better, much as I want to.

The front door slams hard enough to rattle the windows.

Deacon strides into my kitchen without so much as a knock, which annoys the hell out of me. I flip the phone over. Last thing I need is him seeing what I've been staring at.

He drops a large box on my table with enough force to make my coffee slosh right over the rim of my mug, then falls into a chair like the world's been riding his shoulders all day. "Special delivery."

I know what it is from the return address. Dixie's guitar. The one her granddaddy gave her.

I'd been looking forward to handing it to her, seeing her face light up when she had it back. Now I can't picture anything. Can't get excited about it. Hell, maybe I'll just mail it to her agent and call it done.

I open the box because sitting there staring at it isn't doing anybody any good. Plus, Deacon's hauled it over here. Least I can do is look.

The case inside is beat to hell—old leather, faded sticker peeling off the back, a busted latch. It doesn't look like much, but I know better. I lift it out careful-like. Dixie played this guitar. I can picture her as a kid, smaller but still scrappy, and full of dreams. Her fingers must have barely stretched across the frets. She never lets go of anything, this woman. She holds on with both hands and all her heart. I love that about her— the way she fights for what she wants, the sarcastic smile she wears like armor, the drive that never quits.

And God help me, even as fast as everything's happened between us, I want to spend the rest of my life learning all the things I don't know about her yet.

"Welcome," Deacon says, like he's prompting a toddler. "Thank you would be nice."

I ignore him. The strings seem loose. The wood's worn smooth where someone—a small girl with big dreams—played it down to nothing.

"Damn," I mutter.

"You gonna sit there and stare at it all or night, or are you gonna go get your girl?"

I look down at the guitar again.

Ten minutes later, I'm online, scrolling through venue schedules until I find what I'm looking for: Dixie Pearl—TONIGHT—3rd & Lindsley.

There are twelve tickets left and I buy every last one.

The church van stays with Slate because there's no parking left. 3rd & Lindsley has a small lot and it's packed tight. When we pull up, Slate points toward the door and grunts something. I take it to mean *Go on ahead, save me a spot*. He pockets the ticket I hand him as I climb out.

This isn't exactly church business, but I've invited most of the choir along. They haven't asked too many questions—the chance to hear Dixie sing is reason enough to pile into the van on short notice. Soon as they all get out, they look to me like I have the answers. I'm the mama duck to their baby ducklings in this scenario. I've been pastoring Wickham Hollow Chapel long enough that they trust me to know where we're going. Enough to drive several hours to Nashville, anyway. I hand out tickets and lead them inside.

3rd & Lindsley has that warehouse feel—high ceilings and an industrial vibe. It's more of an oversize dive bar rather than a theater with rows of seats, with tables scattered around the main-floor level and a balcony wrapping the upper level. Since I bought what was left of the tickets, we aren't sitting together. The room is packed with people. I get everyone settled and then leave Deacon holding down a two-top right in front of the stage.

I have maybe fifteen minutes before the show begins, so I start looking for the backstage entrance. It's a small, curtained-off side door that must lead to a green room and a loading area. A staff member in a black T-shirt and headset stands in front of the curtains, steering people away.

"You with the band?" He eyes the guitar case in my hands.

"Delivery." I hold it up. "This is Dixie's."

Sure, buddy, his look says.

"That right?"

"Yeah." I open it so he can see it's not packed full of taxidermized animals or dead flowers "She might want this tonight."

I should've said I was the Amazon delivery guy.

He takes it anyway. "You need me to sign for it?"

I shake my head. "No, just make sure she gets it, please."

The guy is already on his headset, paging someone to come collect it. Mission accomplished, I go back to my table.

Deacon's got beers waiting. He's staring at his phone but pushes a bottle toward me. Then he raises the phone and takes a picture.

"What's that for?"

"Memory book," he says. "You'll want to remember tonight."

"The show? Should be great."

"Not the music, jackass." He gives me a look. "I'm talking about the Jack Carter drama. The preacher-in-love show. The—"

I cut him off. There'll be more where that came from anyway.

"I want a really fancy one—an actual, physical book. No cheap digital crap."

"Already ordered it," Deacon says with grin. "Hot-pink scrapbook that says THE STORY OF US! Should be here by the time you two get back from wherever you're gonna chase her to."

I hope so.

The lights dim and the crowd gets quiet.

And I sit there with my heart hammering, waiting to watch the woman I love walk out on that stage and light the whole place up.

Dixie

"The minute you step foot out there, you're a star," my agent tells me as I stand up. "A spot on a huge tour just opened up and it's yours."

I smile, nodding my happiness because I'm supposed to be deliriously happy. High-five her and tell her what an awesome job she's done representing my mopey ass, but I can't be bothered because I left my heart in Wickham Hollow, dammit.

My agent natters on about how I'll hit the road ASAP, record, and do a billion professional things that will turn me into a legit country music star. I smile some more. My jaw's about to crack.

If I could go back in time, I'd pick life with Jack over life on the road. Holy shit, what's happened to me?

My manager pats my arm. "Overwhelming, isn't it?"

"What if it doesn't pan out? What if my songs don't hit?" I already know that "Hot for Preacher" has charted and the play time that "Touch Me with Those Morals" has been getting virtually guarantees I'll see my name on there twice.

"You've got this." She pats my arm again.

She may say something else, but the green room's wall-to-wall chaos. It's dimmer than an airline cabin at midnight. Water bottles, trays of snacks, and a stray fifth of bourbon litter the tabletops and gear cases line the wall where someone Sharpied BREAK A LEG. It's super loud, with people talking and yelling, tuning guitars and laughing. Someone's drummer bangs out a beat on the table and the dull roar of the crowd bleeds through the walls. The stage manager hovers in the doorway—it's time to go.

"Ms. Pearl?" Someone in a black T-shirt and headset—a staffer—holds out a guitar case to me. PEARL is scratched into the top in uneven block letters. I take it automatically while my manager huffs next to me. My guitar is onstage. It's in her notes, so this is a screwup.

I open the case.

Heads will roll, blah blah blah, conversations will be had. Except—

It's not my guitar at all. It's the one my granddaddy taught me to play on, the one I haven't seen since I pawned it eight years ago because I had to raise money for my demo track. If my life was a movie, I'd have shot to stardom right then and there and yet I didn't.

The edges around the sound hole are worn but still ringed in rosettes. Stylish, or so my granddaddy claimed. We both loved roses, their bright colors and overwhelming scents. He'd cut them from the bush in the front yard to bring to Grandma.

Someone shoved a note inside the sound hole. What kind of amateur-hour bullshit is this? That's literally the worst possible place—it'll scratch the interior wood and fuck with my sound. Do people not understand how instruments work?

The stage manager's barking *Five minutes, people!* as I fish the paper out, trying not to curse at whoever thought this was a good idea. But I already know who it is before I unfold the thing. There's only one person who knows about this guitar and would pull some misguided, wonderful romantic gesture like this.

Jack. Of course it's Jack.

That man understands exactly how much this meant to me—we talked about it, I told him about selling it and how I had a few, very occasional regrets. Like every damn day. So naturally, he went and did the impossible and tracked it down for me.

His handwriting is still the same disaster it's always been. For a man who takes his sweet time with everything else, he writes like he's being chased by wolves. All scrawled together, letters crashing into each other like they can't wait to get to the end of the sentence.

You said this guitar helped you find your voice. I hope it re-minds you how strong you are—and how much you mean to me. Love, Jack.

Yes, Jack. Yes, it does. I want to go find him right now even though the look in my manager's face declares, *The only place you're going right now is onstage.* But I've never met a rule I didn't break, so I settle (for now) for tuning my new old guitar. It's not badly out of tune at all. Then I text Jack while my manager has a cow.

ME: Are you here?

JACK: Front and center.

ME: What if I get performance anxiety ;)

JACK: You'll be fine. I know what you can do.

ME: OK, real question. Did you just send me my actual guitar?? The one I pawned?

JACK:...

ME: omg

ME: IS THAT A YES?

JACK: It's a "maybe I know a guy."

And that guy might've known someone who repairs vin-tage instruments.
And who owed him a favor.
And who overnighted it.

ME: And you're here.

JACK: Thought I should hear the song that's been stuck in my head for weeks. Live.

ME: I was fine before you. You know that, right?

JACK: Yeah. But now you've got backup if you want it.

Texting with him is the absolute worst idea I've had all week, which is saying something considering my manager vetoed my plan to dye my hair purple and to get a nose ring. Now I'm remembering exactly how good we were together and wanting a fucking time machine instead of a vintage guitar. I want to go back and replay those weeks in Wickham Hollow frame by frame, slow-motion style.

But there's no time for my quarter-life crisis breakdown because the stage manager's doing that frantic wrap-it-up gesture and hustling me out of the green room. I'm mentally composing and deleting about fifty different responses to Jack's note while someone touches up my makeup and checks my headset. They're fussing with this ridiculous white dress—strapless with a feathered hem that makes me look like a sexy swan, which is either amazing or horrifying depending on your perspective. Does Jack like avians?

The second I step through the curtain gap, the stage explodes in light. I can't see shit except people-shaped blobs sitting at table-shaped shadows.

Jack's out there somewhere. I know it.

I don't spot him until I'm three songs deep, sitting at a table with Deacon. And that's when my brain decides to completely abandon ship. *Bye, logic! Hello, feelings! Let's make some terrible decisions!*

Because what if I just stopped?

What if I didn't get on that tour bus?

What if I quit running around like a caffeinated hamster and just fucking *stopped*?

I've spent my entire life chasing this dream the way Dad taught me to—accepting his shit, doing everything his way, letting him critique every choice I make. Maybe he wants what's best for me, but maybe he doesn't actually know what that looks like. Maybe I could get in my van right now, drive back to Wickham Hollow, bang on the rectory door, and throw myself at Jack like some kind of romance-novel heroine.

I don't want to live on buses and in hotels, counting miles like rosary beads.

I don't want to always be thinking about the next song, the next album, the next milestone, never stopping to actually be in the moment I'm living.

I don't want to work ninety-hour weeks writing songs because even though I love songwriting, it can't be my entire fucking universe. I want *more*.

Jack is my *more*.

And yeah, he's hot as hell and looks like he could chop firewood for a naked-lumberjack calendar, but he's more than that. More than just kind or strong. More than patient or even holy (which I'm working on, God, I'm working on). He's definitely more than the fantasy I wrote songs about.

I've spent my whole life chasing stages and running from anything that looks like settling down. But looking at Jack right now, I finally get it. He's not asking me to stop moving—he's just offering me somewhere to land. A place to catch my breath. A harbor for when the road gets too damn loud.

I'm done saying NO to everything I actually want—so it's YES time, baby.

I launch into the opening of "Hot for Preacher." *Are you ready for this, Jack? Because you know what comes next.*

Jack's been right all along—I don't have to do this alone.

I'm not quitting or giving up or even being weak. I'm just choosing to trust him, same way he trusted me.

> *"She's not one of those girls*
> *Who says yes to a preaching man*
> *Walks down the church aisle*
> *Wears white on her big day."*

I jump off the stage like I'm escaping a burning building, completely ignoring the panicked looks from my backup singers and the crew. They're probably thinking I've lost my damn mind, and honestly? They're not wrong. But I'm finally doing something right for once.

I don't stop walking until I'm in front of Jack.

He looks like shit. There are bags under his eyes and his beard's all messed up like he's run his hands through it all night. But when he smiles at me, he's still my Jack. Still the man who makes me feel like I could conquer the world or burn it down, whichever seems more fun.

I didn't even ask him to come with me. God, I'm an idiot. He probably would have. Jack gets what matters—the people you love, your chosen family. And somehow, impossibly, he made me part of his. He put his ministry on the line, his whole family legacy, everything he believes, because he cares about me. Because I matter to him.

And I walked away.

I let him think all I wanted was my career, that there was no room in my life for him. That he was some small-town embarrassment who'd hold me back. I never planned to stay—I was always going to leave and I turned him into a punch line in my own story.

But he's not a joke. He's my hero. My man.

Jack.

As I dive into the last verse, I change some of the words. Screw the original—this is our song now.

"She's a once-upon-a-time girl
Thought she had to keep on running
Always just out of reach
But maybe she was always the preacher's girl
Scared to be that open girl
Yeah, yeah, yeah.
But he never tried to tame her
Just stood steady by her side
Now she's done running
So, baby—
be mine."

"Can I sit down?" I'm breathless, like I just ran a marathon instead of walking twenty feet.

He might say no. I might be too fucking late. I know that, but I'm all about taking chances today.

He pushes his chair back from the table and opens his arms.

I launch myself at them like a missile. I'm so happy to be back where I belong that I almost forget I'm still wearing a mic. But I've got one more thing to say, and everyone in this place needs to hear it.

"I love you, Jack Carter." I wrap my arms around him like I'm never letting go again. "Thank you for showing up."

"I'll always come for you," he says, and God, his voice.

"And I'm sorry for—"

He reaches down, flicks the off switch on my belt pack, and pulls the headset off. It disappears somewhere in the direction of the table. Smart man. This moment is ours.

My hands are shaking from something more than just adrenaline as I put my arms around his neck.

"I should've told you. I sang about you before I ever had the balls to tell you how I felt," I say. "I turned you into a hook and a hashtag before I could admit you mattered to me. I thought if I made it into a song, it wouldn't hurt as much when you didn't want me back. And then when you did want me—I still couldn't say it."

He pulls back just enough to look at me, those steady brown eyes warm and patient as always. "So, say it now."

"Jack Carter." I cup his face in my hands, feeling the soft scratch of his beard against my palms. "I'm hot for preacher. And I love you. I'm sorry it took me so damn long to figure it out. I want us to be together. I want the chance to do this every day for the rest of my life."

Jack looks at me like he always has—like he sees every messy, broken, beautiful part of me and still believes I'm worth keeping anyway.

He brushes his thumb across my cheek.

"I love you, too, Dixie Pearl."

Simple. Sure. Like a promise and a prayer wrapped up in four words.

And then he kisses me.

Not like before, when we were hungry and desperate, trying to outrun our feelings. This kiss is slow. Deliberate. Deep. Like we're building something new right here, with our mouths and our hearts and all the words we finally have the courage to say.

Somewhere through the haze of it, I remember we have an audience. And they're going absolutely insane.

Clapping. Cheering. Probably filming this whole thing for TikTok.

I feel Jack smile against my lips.

I break the kiss and press my forehead to his, laughing because of course this is how my story ends—making out with a preacher under stage lights while a roomful of strangers lose their collective shit.

"I think that's a yes," I whisper.

Jack grins. "Amen."

★ ★ ★ ★ ★

LET'S TALK

Romance

For exclusive extracts, competitions and special offers, find us online:

f MillsandBoon

X @MillsandBoon

⊙ @MillsandBoonUK

♪ @MillsandBoonUK

Get in touch on 01413 063 232

MILLS & BOON

THE HEART OF ROMANCE

A ROMANCE FOR EVERY READER

MODERN

Prepare to be swept off your feet by sophisticated, sexy and seductive heroes, in some of the world's most glamourous and romantic locations, where power and passion collide.

HISTORICAL

Escape with historical heroes from time gone by. Whether your passion is for wicked Regency Rakes, muscled Vikings or rugged Highlanders, awaken the romance of the past.

MEDICAL

Set your pulse racing with dedicated, delectable doctors in the high-pressure world of medicine, where emotions run high and passion, comfort and love are the best medicine.

Love Always

Celebrate true love with tender stories of heartfelt romance, from the rush of falling in love to the joy a new baby can bring, and a focus on the emotional heart of a relationship.

HEROES

The excitement of a gripping thriller, with intense romance at its heart. Resourceful, true-to-life women and strong, fearless men face danger and desire - a killer combination!

From showing up to glowing up, these characters are on the path to leading their best lives and finding romance along the way – with plenty of sizzling spice!

To see which titles are coming soon, please visit

millsandboon.co.uk/nextmonth